A shape crashed out of the ing, something was wr drunk. He lurched and weaveu au....

"You okay, son?" Kenneth called out.

The man didn't answer. He was wearing the blue uniform of a police officer, only it was covered in dirt and leaves as though he'd been rolling on the ground. As the man came closer, Kenneth recognized his face, although it was streaked with dirt, and more leaves were stuck in the tangles of his hair.

"Officer Patterson?" Kenneth said. "Adam, are you all right?"

Adam's eyes were wide but his mouth was wider, stretching into a toothy grin. He laughed, and the sound of it made Kenneth step back. Something was definitely wrong with Adam, and Kenneth didn't feel safe. He took another step back and tripped on a twig, sending him off balance. Kenneth fell to the paved path, the hip and arm that he landed on both flaring with sharp pain. Adam loomed over him. His pupils were so dilated his eyes looked like black pools. He brought his hand up to his mouth and blew across his palm, and a dark cloud of something that felt like powder struck Kenneth's face.

He coughed and choked as the powder went into his nose, mouth, and throat. His skin itched and burned where it touched him.

"What—what was that?" he rasped. His eyes watered. His throat was tight and dry. He could barely get the words out between hacking coughs. "What did you do to me?"

Adam stood over him, the delirious grin still on his face.

Frightened and confused, Kenneth watched as more dark figures emerged from the trees.

A Macabre Ink Production — Macabre Ink is an imprint of Crossroad Press.

Copyright © 2021 by Nicholas Kaufmann
ISBN 978-1-63789-941-0
For information address Crossroad Press at 141 Brayden Dr., Hertford, NC 27944
www.crossroadpress.com

First Edition

THE HUNGRY EARTH

NICHOLAS KAUFMANN

For my dear friend Dallas Mayr, who left us too soon.
New York City isn't the same without you.

"Mushrooms were the roses in the garden of that unseen world, because the real mushroom plant was underground. The parts you could see—what most people called a mushroom—was just a brief apparition. A cloud flower."

—Margaret Atwood, *The Year of the Flood*

"If those dried-up little scraps of fungus taught me anything, it is that there are other stranger forms of consciousness available to us, and, whatever they mean, their very existence, to quote William James, 'forbids[s] a premature closing of our accounts with reality.'"

— Michael Pollan, *How to Change Your Mind*

1

It was going on eleven o'clock at night when the flesh slipped off Kat Bishop's arm as easily as an elbow-length opera glove. Lying on her stomach on her bed and drawing in her favorite sketchbook, the one with the purple velour cover, she'd been having trouble concentrating ever since she got back from the park. She blamed it on her heart still racing after her date with Tasha. The secrecy of it only made it more exciting. She'd waited until nine-thirty, when her parents went to bed, before sneaking out of her converted-attic bedroom. The summer night air was humid as she climbed down the rickety trellis on the rear of the house. She biked the quarter mile to Dradin Park. Tasha was waiting on the park bench just outside the gate to the community garden. They'd chosen this spot because it struck them both as romantic and because they knew no one else would be there so late. They weren't worried about being alone in the park at night. There wasn't much crime in the city of Sakima, New York. The online police blotter was generally empty except for the occasional report of shoplifting or angry residents dumping trash on their neighbors' lawns. No, Kat's only real concern was her parents finding out. They'd always been supportive of her—of her desire to be an artist, of wanting to go to college out of state—but she heard the remarks they made when there were same-sex wedding notices in the newspaper and knew this was something they would never stand for. If they found out, she would be grounded for life.

She and Tasha had gotten to know each other when they were assigned to be lab partners in Chemistry class right at the end of the school year. Kat had only ever dated boys before, but she felt drawn to Tasha right away, with her short hair, pierced eyebrow, and ring through her nose. Tasha looked jailhouse tough, but underneath she was sweet and sentimental. She texted Kat poems she wrote herself.

On the park bench that night, she and Tasha had kissed with all the passion and intensity that came with something new and secret. Tasha braved sliding a hand under Kat's t-shirt for the first time, and it was like a jolt of electricity ran through her. She let Tasha keep her hand there, but she decided she wasn't ready to go any further than that. Not yet, but maybe soon.

Later, climbing back into her bedroom through the window, still high from the experience and Tasha's promise to see her again tomorrow, Kat felt so energized that she'd immediately thrown open her sketchbook and started drawing, pausing only to answer Tasha's text of *Did u get home ok?* with *No, I'm dead,* which summoned a flurry of laughing emojis. Kat returned her attention to the sketchbook and drew the butterfly tattoo that was on Tasha's right calf. Tasha didn't like it, she said the tattoo artist had messed it up by drawing one wing way bigger than the other, but to Kat it was the most beautiful thing she'd ever seen. The color of its wings started a deep, rich blue at the butterfly's body, then faded outward into an elegant lavender.

Kat let out a bark of euphoric laughter and found it impossible to stop. And why *should* she stop? She was happy! Everything was so perfect, the colors of her bedroom brighter than she'd ever seen. The closet door swelled as though it were breathing, and Kat found this so funny she laughed until tears poured from her eyes.

That was when the flesh slipped off her arm. "Off like a prom dress," as her dad liked to say, which she'd always found annoying but now only made her laugh harder. The bones underneath were made of jewels, glittering red, yellow, and green like a pirate's treasure in a children's book. They were so beautiful, the most beautiful things she'd ever seen. She flexed her sparkling fingers in fascination and felt her jewel-bones creak.

What's happening to me? she wondered.

She thought back to her date with Tasha. While they were making out, she'd felt something strange, like tiny, stinging pinpricks on her arms and neck. It stopped as quickly as it started, so she hadn't paid it much mind, figuring it was mosquitos. Some remote part of her brain tried to tell her the little stings hadn't felt like normal bug bites, but the thought was lost to the glorious feeling that swept over her. Somehow, she could feel things beyond herself. She could feel *everything*. It was an almost religious experience, this sudden, undeniable connection she felt to Tasha, to her family, to everyone and everything. Everything was connected—Kat, nature, God—and those connections were like cosmic strings, cords that stretched from Kat to the rest of creation.

She scribbled in her sketchbook, trying to capture the feeling on paper, her fleshless arm now miraculously encased in flesh once more. Around her, the air was alive with a flight of butterflies, their flapping, unevenly-sized wings a royal blue and imperial lavender. They filled Kat's bedroom like a swarm, like a flood, like a sense of excitement so overpowering you think you're going to burst. If she stayed perfectly quiet, she could hear her own heart beating in time with their wings, a clock ticking in time with the universe itself. The pulse of the cosmos, like the kicking of a bass drum. The heartbeat of God, like thunder in the mountains.

She jumped off the bed to chase after the butterflies. She ran across the room and saw, incredibly, another Kat, another version of herself running toward her. Was it future Kat? Kat from some alternate dimension? Was this other Kat straight or gay? What was *she*? Kat opened her arms to embrace the other Kat. A moment too late, some part of her brain realized it was her reflection in the bedroom window, but by then she couldn't slow down. Her knees hit the ledge below the window and her body pitched forward. Her head hit the glass first, the hard bone of her skull smashing through it, and still she kept moving forward. The daggerlike shards slashed her clothes and sliced small red nicks over every bit of exposed skin. And then Kat was flying, soaring with the butterflies, the wind through her hair.

She was one with the divine.

One with God.

One with something in the park that called to her, beautiful and important.

More than anything she wanted to answer that call, but the ground rose to meet her, and after a blinding, momentary flash of white-hot pain, seventeen-year-old Kat Bishop didn't want anything anymore.

2

The protest was already in full swing when Dr. Laura Powell arrived at the Sakima town hall. A couple dozen people stood in a cluster on the grass outside, chanting, "Hey hey, ho ho, Bluecoal has got to go," and waving signs that read SAVE THE PARK, SAY NO TO BLUECOAL! and HANDS OFF OUR COMMUNITY GARDEN! Laura admired their fortitude. It was another mid-August scorcher in the Hudson Valley. There was no shade where they were standing, and though Laura had only just stepped out of the air-conditioning of her car, the hot sun already had her sweating under her blouse.

She knew most of the protesters. There were only thirty-five hundred people in Sakima, and even if she hadn't lived here all her life, it wouldn't take long to know most of them. Laura was one of only two general practitioners in town, which meant a lot of them were her patients as well. Laura spotted her elderly neighbor Melanie Elster among the protesters, and her mood darkened. Twice now, Melanie had left handwritten, passive-aggressive notes in Laura's mailbox, both times pointing out that Laura's shrubs were an inch taller than the homeowners' association's approved height. Melanie glared at her as she walked past the protest, probably mentally drafting her next missive. Laura pretended not to see her and joined the crowd filing into the town hall.

This isn't going to go well, Laura thought.

The mayor and city council had sold Dradin Park, fifty acres of green space in the heart of Sakima, to Bluecoal, a bigtime developer from downstate. There'd been no public referendum. The land had been sold out from under them. After weeks of protests, petitions, and letter-writing campaigns, the mayor had invited the vice president of Bluecoal to come and try to convince everyone that the luxury condos they planned to build would benefit the community. He would be lucky to leave in one piece.

It wasn't just that the land had been sold without their permission that infuriated everyone, it was the loss of the community garden within the park. Sakima had been hit hard by the recent recession. The population dropped by half as people left to look for work elsewhere, or because they could no longer afford their homes. For those who remained, the community garden was what kept them going. It brought the whole town together during a difficult time. It gave residents something to do other than stare at the empty listings on job sites. It provided fresh produce for families in need. Even after the economy recovered, the community garden continued to hold a special place for the people of Sakima.

Now a faceless, corporate real estate firm from Manhattan wanted to pave over it for their luxury condos. Everyone was up in arms, which was why Laura was surprised so many people had turned out this morning to hear what Bluecoal's vice president had to say. The lobby was packed. It looked like everyone who wasn't at work today was here.

Piles of colorful Bluecoal brochures had been stacked on a table just inside the door, but they remained untouched. She noticed a stooped, gray man in his late seventies lingering near them. Kenneth Dalpe. Laura was glad to see him out of his house. He'd been in a deep depression since the loss of Isabella, his wife of more than fifty years, and rarely left his home.

"Hi, Kenneth," she said, approaching him. "It's been a while. How are you?"

"Enjoying the air-conditioning," he said with a thin smile. "It's another hot one this morning. I don't remember summers being this hot back in my day."

She smiled pleasantly. If he didn't want to talk about himself, they didn't have to. "It's good to see you. Are you coming inside? I could use someone to sit with."

"All right." He leaned in close and spoke confidentially, his breath smelling of coffee. "As long as I can sit on the aisle so I can make my escape if need be. I don't have much patience for bullshit. Never did."

"It's a deal," Laura said. "I'll probably make my escape right behind you."

They followed the crowd through the big interior doors to the auditorium inside and managed to find two seats on the aisle near the back. The stage at the front of the room was bare except for the United States flag on one side, the State of New York's blue Excelsior flag on the other, a podium with a light and microphone, and a SMART Board on a stand beside it.

Oh God, there's going to be a PowerPoint presentation!

She already regretted her decision to come.

Paul and Lisa Miller, who lived a few blocks over from Laura, took their seats in the row in front of her, along with their fifteen-year-old son Jeff. After exchanging pleasantries with Paul and Lisa, she noticed the violin case Jeff had stowed under his chair.

"I'm glad to see you're still playing, Jeff," she said. "I think it's great that you stuck with it."

Jeff glanced at her, then quickly looked down at his shoes. He'd been a shy, awkward kid for as long as she'd known him.

"I have a lesson right after this, so I had to bring it with me," he mumbled.

Laura nodded. "I'd love to hear you play sometime."

That was more than Jeff could handle. He flushed a dark red, stared at the floor, and didn't seem to know what to do with his hands. Jeff's mother grinned at her.

"You can hear him play soon enough at his recital next month," she said. "Isn't that right, Jeff?"

Jeff mumbled an answer that wasn't meant to be heard.

"What was that, young man?" his mother said. "What did I tell you about speaking up so people could hear you?"

Jeff's shoulders slumped, trying to make himself small enough to be invisible.

On the stage, Sakima's mayor, Thomas Harvey, walked up behind the podium. The crowd's chatter died down, and there was a thin smattering of polite applause. Laura leaned back in her chair, glad for an end to the conversation. She didn't want to embarrass the boy any more than he already was.

"Good people of Sakima, thank you for coming out today," Mayor Harvey said. His rumpled gray suit barely fit over his rotund belly. He unbuttoned it nervously, and stroked his bushy mustache. Another nervous tic. He knew he was outnumbered. "I know a lot of you aren't happy with the deal to develop Dradin Park. I've received your phone calls, your emails, and your letters, and I want you to know that I hear your concerns. To that end, I've asked Sean Hilton, the vice president of Bluecoal Development, to come and talk to you about our plans for Dradin Park and to answer any questions or concerns you might have. Now, without further ado, please join me in welcoming Sean Hilton, who was kind enough to come all the way up from New York City for this."

Mayor Harvey backed away from the podium, clapping. A man in his fifties stepped out of the wings in a well-pressed blue suit and red tie. If he expected applause, he didn't get it from anyone but the mayor, who quickly stopped, climbed down from the stage, and took his seat in the auditorium. The man on stage opened his mouth to speak, but just as he did someone in the audience let out a long, loud boo. Laura shifted in her seat to see who it was, but all she saw were craning heads like her own searching out the culprit. Nervous laughter rippled through the crowd. The man cleared his throat and began again.

"Good morning. My name is Sean Hilton, and I'm the vice president of Bluecoal," he said. "I'd like to start by thanking Mayor Harvey for inviting me to your lovely city today, and by thanking you, the citizens of Sakima, for lending me your time. I hope I'll be able to answer any questions you might have about the development we've planned. You know, I was excited to learn that Sakima is the Lenape Indian word for leader, because now, like this great city's name, you have a chance to be a leader in the Hudson Valley when it comes to luxury developments."

Laura rolled her eyes. For the next fifteen minutes, Sean Hilton spoke in a clear, well-practiced voice about how the development would be the best thing to ever happen to Sakima. It was nothing she hadn't heard before. He talked about how their city could be proud of the development's small carbon footprint, how it would be sustainable and LEED-certified with plans that had already been given a gold rating by the U.S. Green Building Council. He pointed out that Dradin Park used to be a landfill before it was capped in the 1980s and turned into a park, which he called the perfect illustration of how not all change was bad. He brought up the city's shrinking tax revenue, which had dropped considerably after so many people left during the recession, and promised that an influx of new residents with disposable income would increase that revenue, which meant better roads, better schools, and even the refurbishment the old Jack M. Haringa Bridge that connected Sakima to Kingston on the other side of the Hudson River.

Clearly, he'd done his research. People in Sakima had been petitioning for years to give the old, rusting bridge an overhaul, Laura included. Even so, Sean Hilton's words washed fruitlessly over her, and judging by the expressions of the people around her, they weren't any more moved than she was. No one had changed their mind. No one wanted to lose the community garden.

"I know part of the reason there's resistance to our proposal is because it's a *luxury* development. You're worried it will be out of your reach economically," he continued. "After all, why would you want us to build new housing in your beautiful city if you can't afford to live there? Well, the good news is that we're committed to reserving a portion of the units as affordable housing. That means—"

"Bullshit!" someone called from the audience.

It was the same voice that had booed earlier. Sean Hilton stopped talking. A low murmur rippled through the auditorium as people looked to see who'd interrupted him. This time, the culprit made it easy for them by standing up. He was a tall, skinny man in his sixties with a horseshoe of white hair on an otherwise bald head, a thin rat-tail braid in the back. He wore a garishly patterned Hawaiian shirt and aviator sunglasses.

Oh God, Laura thought. *It's Victor.*

Victor Cunningham was an old Gulf War vet who lived in the woods on the outskirts of town. Frankly, she was surprised him here. He mostly kept to himself and only appeared in town when he needed groceries or hardware. The last time she'd seen him was months ago, when she'd spotted him yelling about fascism and imperialism at the soldiers manning an Army recruitment table in City Square.

"Sit down, Victor," Mayor Harvey called from his seat.

"Like hell I will. I've heard enough from this braying jackass," Victor said. "The only reason Bluecoal promised to include affordable units was to sweeten the deal so our harebrained mayor would sign on the dotted line. Isn't that right, Hilton? You must think we're real easy to fool, don't you? Developers like you always promise affordable housing, but you *never* deliver on it."

A few voices in the crowd booed, then more joined in. Sean Hilton grinned, thinking they were booing Victor for interrupting, but the grin faded fast once he realized they were booing him.

He swallowed nervously. "If you'll just let me finish..."

Victor had no intention of letting him finish. He turned to the audience and spoke directly to them. "The last thing this town needs is to give up our community garden so these radioactive turds can build a sprawling playground for their rich friends looking for second homes by the Hudson. But we the people have a voice! Tell your friends! Tell your neighbors! Tell the mayor and the city council! If they kicked Amazon out of Long Island City, we can kick these pigfuckers out of Sakima! Who's with me?"

A cheer roared through the room. Laura joined in, caught up in the moment. Victor extended both his middle fingers toward the stage, and Sean Hilton stormed off into the wings. The cheers continued for a good thirty seconds after that. Victor faced the audience and bowed to a smattering of applause.

Laura leaned over to Kenneth. "That went about as well I thought it would."

The old widower chuckled. "I can't say I'm sorry I came. I wouldn't have wanted to miss that."

Laura left through the lobby, weaving through an excited crowd that was talkative and still laughing. Not surprisingly, Mayor Harvey was nowhere to be seen. Probably, he was backstage commiserating with Sean Hilton.

She spotted Ralph Gorney, Sakima's police chief, entering the packed lobby like a salmon swimming upstream in his tan uniform shirt and dark pants. The brass badge on his chest glinted in the light from the fixtures overhead. For a moment she wondered if Mayor Harvey or Sean Hilton had called the police on Victor for making a scene, but as soon as Ralph saw her, he waved her down. Laura sighed. If Ralph was looking for her, it couldn't be good.

"Sorry, Laura, are you busy?" he asked when he reached her. His dark brown skin was beaded with sweat from the heat, all the way down his cheeks and into his well-trimmed beard. He was in his late thirties and good-looking, but over the past couple of years the weight of the world had crept onto his face, etching deep lines around his eyes and mouth.

"What is it?" she asked, although she could guess. The number of suspicious deaths in Sakima could be counted on one hand every year, sometimes half a hand. The police department had neither the budget nor the need to keep a medical examiner on staff. On the odd occasion when they needed one, they reached out to Laura.

Ralph looked around as the crowd jostled past them. "Can we talk about this outside?"

He led her out of the town hall and through the parking lot to his police cruiser. The lot was full, and he'd been forced to park in one of the farthest spots from the door. No wonder he was soaked with sweat by the time he got to her.

"I need you to come down and perform on autopsy," he said. "This is a tough one. She was young, just a high school kid. You hate to see it."

Laura nodded. "I'll cancel my patients this afternoon and meet you at the station."

Ralph opened the door of his cruiser but paused before getting in. "Just a heads up, it might be a suicide. I thought you should know after what happened with your mother."

"Thanks," Laura said. "How'd she do it?"

"Jumped out her bedroom window," he said.

3

Overlooking the dappled banks of the Hudson and just a few streets over from MacLeod Avenue, Sakima's downtown area full of shops and restaurants, stood four city blocks collectively known as City Square, the seat of city government and the location of most of its public buildings. City Hall stood in the center of it all, a huge, domed building with granite pillars and vaulted windows. Around it were the courthouse, the public library, a handful of office buildings, and the central police station, a large, two-story brick building that ran almost the length of an entire block.

Laura parked her car in the police lot and hung a placard off her rearview that announced she was there on official business. Exiting her car, she cut through the row of blue-and-white squad cars that were parked in front of the entrance, the hot sun reflecting off the light bars on their roofs. Inside the station, Laura was hit with a welcome blast of air-conditioning. The lobby was divided by a gated, waist-high wooden barrier that separated the public waiting area from the rest of the station.

"Morning, Dahlia," Laura said to the young female officer seated at the front desk.

"Morning, Laura," Dahlia Mintz replied, buzzing her through the gate. She tucked a strand of black hair behind her ear. "Ralph is waiting for you in the morgue. Oh, and Adam left a note for you. Hold on."

She dug a folded piece of paper out of a drawer and handed it to Laura. Laura unfolded it. It had been torn from a standard-issue spiralbound field interview notebook, and across it was written in Adam's big, blocky handwriting:

MY PLACE TONIGHT?

It was clear from Dahlia's knowing smirk that she'd already read the note. Laura had been dating Officer Adam Patterson for two months now, and she still wasn't sure how she felt about him. They didn't have much in common. Conversations were forced. Sometimes it seemed like he was more interested in drinking beer and watching a ballgame on TV than talking with her, and yet he'd chased after her a long time for that first date. It was hard not to be flattered by that kind of attention, but after two months the flattery was wearing off, and so far, nothing deeper had taken its place.

That wasn't the only thing keeping her from fully committing. Sometimes she saw something in Adam's eyes she didn't like. A spark of anger, a hint of something violent. Once, she saw him go off on an older woman in the supermarket when their carts accidentally collided. The moment had stuck with her, worrying her mind. If he could yell at a complete stranger like that, would he ever do the same to her?

She folded the note again and put it in her pocket. "Thanks, Dahlia."

Laura went through an interior door into the back of the station. A long hallway stretched the length of the building, smelling of burnt coffee. She skirted around the stairs that led to the second floor, where the evidence room, uniform storage, and locker rooms were. She walked past Ralph's private office, a door marked holding, and another marked records, until she same to an unmarked door with an electronic pad on the wall next to it. She tapped a key fob on the pad, which unlocked the door, and she stepped into the part of the building affectionately known as the Science Wing, which housed the morgue and the forensics lab. As the door closed behind her, the scent of coffee was replaced by the odor of ammonia.

When she got to the morgue, Ralph was waiting for her just as Dahlia said. A black, zipped-up body bag lay on the stainless-steel autopsy table, its dark, oily folds absorbing the light from the LED tubes overhead. Six belt handles hung off the sides of the heavy vinyl acetate bag like the stunted legs of an insect.

"Is this her?" Laura asked.

Ralph nodded. "Her parents called 911 shortly after eleven

last night. She was dead when the EMTs got there. They kept her on ice until now." He nodded toward morgue refrigerator on the other side of the room, its eight cabinet doors like blank faces staring back at them.

Laura washed her hands, put on a pair of nitrile gloves, and approached the autopsy table. The bag was still cold from the refrigerator, radiating chilled air. She broke the police seal and pulled the heavy nylon zipper down just enough to reveal the head, neck, and t-shirt-clad shoulders of a teenage Caucasian girl with dark hair cut in a bob.

"Her name was Kat Bishop," Ralph said.

"I know." Laura recognized just about everyone who wound up on her table. It was inevitable in a city the size of Sakima. Each death was a tragedy, but this one felt worse. Kat Bishop was only seventeen years old. "She was one of my patients. I did her annual physical just a few months ago."

Kat's neck was bent and discolored. After going out the window, she'd landed on it hard. A broken neck would likely reveal itself as the cause of death, although she couldn't rule out blood loss. Dozens of slashes marked her head, face, and neck, thin red signatures etched in her flesh by sharp glass. Splotches of dried blood discolored her skin and clothes. Ragged holes in her t-shirt revealed more cuts underneath.

"You said she jumped out a window, Ralph. You didn't mention the window was still closed."

"My first thought was suicide, but her parents don't buy it," he said. "They say she was happy and social. She'd just started dating someone. She had plans for college. She took a shift working the high school's community garden plots over the summer for extra credit. But mostly, they're convinced it wasn't a suicide because she didn't leave a note."

"It's unusual for people to kill themselves without leaving a note," Laura said. "It's even more unusual for them to jump out a window without opening it first. You said she was dating someone. Has anyone questioned the boyfriend? Or girlfriend. I don't want to make assumptions."

"I asked the Bishops the same thing, even put it the same way you did. They seemed offended that I would suggest their daughter wasn't dating a boy, but they don't know who it was. Kat wouldn't tell them." He sighed. "Their theory is that Kat was on drugs, and what happened last night was because of that."

Laura studied Kat's face again. She looked peaceful despite the multitude of cuts and abrasions. When Laura had done her physical, Kat was healthy and in good shape. The girl had chatting excitedly about her hopes to attend the Rhode Island School of Design after graduation next year. She hadn't sounded depressed at all. There'd been no sign of drug use, either. But that was months ago, and a lot could change in that time, especially for someone her age. She'd started dating somebody no one knew about, somebody who might have given her drugs, or slipped them to her without her knowing.

"Have you ruled out homicide?" she asked. "Was anyone there who might have thrown her through that window?"

"Her parents were home but asleep. The sound of the window breaking woke them up. They said they didn't see anyone else in the house. That's what made me think suicide at first." He ran a nervous hand over his close-cropped hair. "There's one more thing, Laura. The Bishops are close with Mayor Harvey, and he's as shaken up as they are. Under any other circumstances, I wouldn't waste your time asking for a full tox screen and autopsy on a case like this, but with the mayor on my back..." He shrugged. "You know how it is."

She nodded. "Got it. I'll let you know what I find."

"Much appreciated," he said. "The sooner the better, okay?"

As soon as Ralph left, Laura went to the supply closet to retrieve the personal protective equipment she'd need for the autopsy: hair cap, surgical mask, safety goggles, scrubs, and a fluid-resistant surgical gown to wear over them. She changed in the small adjoining bathroom off the side of the morgue, squeezing between the sink and the shower stall. Back in the morgue, she lowered the blinds over the observation window that looked in from the hallway. It was standard procedure whenever an autopsy was performed, a signal to everyone in the building to stay out if they didn't want to see something they couldn't unsee. Laura also liked to think of it as giving the deceased one last bit of privacy. She could think of no procedure more personal or intimate than an autopsy.

She pulled the body bag's zipper down the rest of the way. The standard size of a body bag was seven and a half feet long, and at only five-foot-two the poor girl looked lost in its dark, cavernous interior. Laura pushed the bag's heavy vinyl sides away and photographed the body. An external examination revealed several small shards of glass still embedded in her clothes and skin, a handful of splinters from the window's wooden frame, and fresh dirt and blades of grass stuck in the treads of her sneakers. Laura removed all of it with tweezers and bagged it.

She cut the clothing and underwear off Kat's body and put them in another bag, then gently slid the body bag out from underneath the corpse. Because the bags could only be used once to ensure there was no cross-contamination of evidence from one body to another, she dropped it in the medical waste bin. Laura examined Kat's naked corpse on the table. There were fewer cuts on her torso and groin, where her t-shirt and shorts had done their best to protect her. Laura marked the location of each cut, front and back, on the generic female-shaped outline on the exam form. There were so many she had to go slowly to make sure she documented them all.

She couldn't imagine what it must have felt like to go through the window. The burning pain as countless glass shards tore at her skin. The fear as she plummeted helplessly to the ground. At least her broken neck indicated her death was quick.

What happened, Kat? What sent you through that window?

Laura filled out the rest of the form quickly: race, sex, hair color and length, eye color, age, and whether she had any identifying features like tattoos (none), scars (she was positively covered in them, but none were preexisting), or birthmarks (a small mole on her left breast).

The tox screen Ralph ordered required blood to be drawn, something that wasn't always easy with a dead body. The heart had stopped pumping, which meant the blood stopped moving through the circulatory system and settled wherever gravity caught it—in this case Kat's back, which had turned purple with postmortem lividity. Drawing from the blood vessels there wouldn't collect enough for a proper battery of tests. Laura's best bet was to take it from the heart itself. She found the correct spot between the ribs on the left side of Kat's chest and pushed the long needle of a 20 ml syringe into her heart. She pulled back the plunger. The barrel filled with a light-colored plasma first because the blood cells had already started to separate, but it was followed shortly by a thick, dark red liquid. After transferring the blood into four 5 ml fluoride oxalate vials with septum caps, she used a second syringe to pierce the bladder through the pelvic cavity and collect 5 ml of urine, which she transferred to another vial.

After stripping off her nitrile gloves and tossing them in the bin, Laura brought the vials down the hall to the forensics lab. She knocked gently on the door, then entered. Inside, the lab was filled with electronic equipment of various shapes and sizes, all arranged around a long central workspace. Sofia Hernandez, the department's forensic tech, looked up from loading a vial into the centrifuge.

"Hey, Laura." Sofia wore a white lab coat and protective goggles over her stylish, black-rimmed glasses. Her thick, dark hair was piled under a nylon hairnet. She was five years younger than Laura, with perfect, smooth bronze skin, but there was something about her eyes that seemed older, wearier. "I hear you've got a new customer."

It was the same joke Sofia made whenever Laura was called in to perform an autopsy. It had bothered her at first. She thought it was disrespectful to the deceased, but since she'd gotten to know Sofia better, she understood the woman's dark sense of humor was her way of coping with the often bleak nature of their job.

"A girl from the high school," Laura said, pulling down her surgical mask. "Much too young to be on my table."

"Shit." Sofia shook her head. "That's awful."

Laura handed her the vials. "Ralph wants a tox screen. Top priority."

Sofia put all five vials into the holes of a polypropylene plastic vial rack. "Hey, while I've got you, I wanted to thank you again for last weekend. That was a big help. I don't know what I would have done without you."

"It was no big deal," Laura said.

On Saturday, she'd gone with Sofia to get the last of her belongings from her ex-boyfriend Chuck's house. Laura didn't know all the details, only that Chuck and Sofia had lived together for less than a year and Chuck had hit her during an argument. Sofia wisely broke up with him before it could happen again. Chuck had refused to be elsewhere when Sofia wanted to get her things, so she asked Laura to come with her for moral support. While Sofia gathered her belongings, Chuck stood glaring at Laura, his bald head glistening with angry sweat and his arms crossed, his biceps bulging. Laura glared back at him—he looked so much like Mr. Clean that she had to force herself not to laugh—and didn't budge an inch until Sofia was ready to go.

"Is Chuck giving you any trouble?" Laura asked.

"Nah," Sofia said. "I had a hang-up on my voicemail last night that might have been him, but that's the extent of it."

"Let me know if there's anything else I can do," Laura said. "If your sister throws you out of her guest room and you need a place to crash..."

"Thanks," Sofia said. "I owe you one."

Laura shrugged. "Like I said, it's nothing. Just let me know as soon as you've got the test results, okay?"

Sofia gave a mock salute. "I'm on it."

Back in the morgue, Laura put on a new pair of gloves, pulled her mask up, and got to work on the autopsy. She placed a rubber body block under the corpse's back, which caused the body's chest to protrude forward while the arms and neck fell back, a position that made it easier to cut the chest open. Using a scalpel, she sliced a deep, Y-shaped incision into the torso, curving around the bottom of the breasts, meeting at the breastbone, and extended down to the pubic bone. She peeled back the skin and trimmed the red fibrous muscle and yellow fatty tissue away from the ribcage.

What the hell?

Stuck to the bones of Kat Bishop's ribcage and the organs underneath was a network of strange white filaments. More of it was attached to the muscle and tissue Laura had peeled back.

Some of the filaments were so thin they were almost invisible, while others were nearly as thick as electrical cords. They filled the body cavity like a chaotic, asymmetrical spider's web.

Laura slid the thin blade of the scalpel under one of the thicker filaments, lifting it gently away from the surface of a lung. The filament was long and branching, connected to so many other filaments that she couldn't be sure where any of it began or ended. She cut a small piece of it free and put it on a stainless-steel specimen tray, so small it looked like a single hair lying in a sink basin. She carried it carefully over to a microscope with a large LED screen mounted on top. Using tweezers, she wet-mounted the filament on a glass slide and transferred the slide to the microscope's specimen stage. She bent to look through the eyepieces. Once she adjusted it to the proper magnification, she stood back and examined the filament on the LED screen.

There were cells, which identified the filaments as organic rather than artificial. The protective cell walls were made from what looked to her like chains of modified glucose. Their formation reminded her of chitin, the large, structural polysaccharide most often found in insect exoskeletons and cartilaginous fishes. The only problem was that chitin didn't belong in a human body.

Could it be something else, something molecularly similar to chitin? Laura bit her nails, a nervous tic she'd never been able to shake. She needed a second opinion.

She called Sofia in, and a few minutes later the forensic tech was beside her, squinting at the LED screen.

"Sorry, I have no idea what it is," Sofia said. She turned back to look at Kat's opened body on the table. "What is that stuff? It looks like those stringy, polyester cobwebs in Halloween decorations."

"Except this is organic," Laura said. She poked at it with a scalpel. "It looks almost like vegetable matter, or a mold of some kind, but I've never seen anything like it."

"Booker might know," Sofia said. "You should ask him."

"Booker?" Laura asked, surprised. "I haven't spoken to him in years. What made you think of him?"

"You didn't hear?" Sofia asked. "He's back in town. He got a job as a science teacher at the high school."

The news stunned her. If Booker was back in Sakima, why hadn't he called her? She could guess the answer.

"He doesn't want to hear from me," she said. "Why would he?"

"Because he's a professional, and so are you," Sofia said. "It's just for work, and if anyone knows what this is, it's Booker. This is right in his wheelhouse."

Laura had to admit it made sense. Booker was a scientist with a PhD in botany. Probably, he *would* know what this was. But it'd been four years since they last spoke. Four years since she'd even laid eyes on him. If it was anyone else, she'd make the call in a heartbeat. But Booker?

"You know I'm right, Laura," Sofia said, leaving the morgue. "If you want to know what this is, Booker's your man."

Laura took another look at the filaments inside Kat Bishop's body cavity. There was no denying it. She needed an expert. She pulled out her cell phone and scrolled through her contacts until she found Booker's name, relieved she hadn't deleted his information. She tried not to think about why it was still in her phone four years later.

She also tried not to think about why it hurt her so much that he hadn't told her he was back in Sakima.

Booker's your man.

Not anymore, she thought.

She tapped Booker's contact, hoping it was still the right number, and listened to the rhythmic buzz on the line while she waited for him to pick up. She chewed her bottom lip, then her fingernail. This was a mistake. She should hang up. She—

"Hello?"

Hearing Booker's voice on the phone was a shock. It brought everything rushing back. Memories flashed through her mind like slides: cooking meals together in her kitchen, cuddling on the couch in front of a movie, picnicking at Storm King Arts Center, renting a sailboat on the Hudson for one of the most perfect days of her life.

But then life had gotten in the way, as it always did for her.

"Booker?" She tried to sound nonchalant, like calling him

was no big deal. But he'd slipped quietly back into town like a thief and she had no idea how he would respond to hearing from her. "It's Laura. Laura Powell."

"Laura?" He sounded surprised to hear from her, but not upset. That was a good sign. "I thought I recognized this number. How are you?"

His phone had shown her number, not her name. He hadn't kept her contact information the way she had. How long had he waited before deleting her? A year? A month? A day?

Laura closed her eyes. *I shouldn't have called him. I shouldn't have opened this can of worms.*

"I'm fine, thanks," she said. "I'm sorry to bother you. Um, Sofia told me you were back in town."

"I just got back last week," he said. "I meant to call you as soon as I settled in, but I didn't have your number anymore."

He sounded embarrassed. Good. Still, it made her wonder if he was lying. Maybe he hadn't planned to call her because he'd moved on with his life and didn't want to look back.

Why did it matter to her so much? She'd moved on with her life too, hadn't she? Her private practice had grown to the point where she'd moved to a larger clinic space. She'd moved out of her rental apartment and bought a house. She was dating Adam. What Booker did or didn't do shouldn't matter anymore. And yet...

She shook it off and cleared her throat. "The reason I'm calling is because I need your help with something. Do you have time to come down to the police station?"

"Yeah, sure," he said. "It's good to hear your voice again. It's been too long."

She blushed, her heart pumping hot, fresh blood to her skin. "Same."

"So what's this about?"

She looked at the corpse of Kat Bishop on the autopsy table. "I found something in the course of an autopsy that I couldn't identify, and I didn't know who else to ask. If you have the time, I could really use your help. Can you come?"

She felt like she was holding her breath. *Stay professional,* she reminded herself.

"I can be there in twenty minutes," he said.

"Thank you, I really appreciate it," she said. "Just tell them at the front desk that I asked you to come back to the morgue."

"Okay," he said. "And Laura? It really is good to hear from you."

True to his word, twenty minutes later Booker Coates stood in the morgue doorway, having been escorted through the building by Dahlia. To Laura, it was like no time had passed at all since she last saw him. He looked exactly the same. Tall, with a shaved head and broad shoulders, he was handsome in a way that reminded her of the actor Mike Colter. The only thing that was new was the short goatee adorning the smooth, dark brown skin of his face.

"I like it," Laura said, stoking her own chin.

"Thanks." Booker touched his goatee and smiled sheepishly. "I grew it last year."

He didn't come any closer. He was waiting for her to give him a cue on how to proceed. Laura wanted to hug him, but that didn't seem appropriate. Neither did shaking his hand, considering everything they'd shared, so they stood looking at each other awkwardly for what felt like an eternity. She couldn't help wondering what his life was like now. Was he seeing someone? Was he married? Did he have kids? Her gaze dropped to his left hand, searching for a wedding ring, but she stopped herself. She'd called him here for a reason. She needed to keep it professional.

"So, you wanted me to look at something?" Booker asked.

"Right, thanks again for coming," she said.

She had him put on a surgical mask and nitrile gloves, then brought him over to the autopsy table. She'd placed a sterile evidence sheet over the body so it wouldn't be the first thing Booker saw when he came in. Dead bodies, especially bodies that had been cut open for an autopsy, were not something you sprang on people.

She took a top corner of the sheet in her hand. "Are you ready?"

Booker took a deep breath and nodded. "Go ahead."

Laura pulled the sheet down, silently apologizing to Kat for exposing her so completely to a stranger. A man, no less. She doubted it actually mattered to the girl. Laura didn't believe in ghosts or spirits or an afterlife. She figured when you died it was like going to sleep and never waking up, resting in peaceful, silent darkness forever. Even so, she found it hard to turn off her empathy, even for the dead.

"Jesus," Booker muttered. Above his surgical mask, the expression in his eyes was one of sadness, not the disgust or fright people usually had at seeing a body in this state. "What happened to her?"

"She either fell or jumped out a window," Laura said. "Her parents think drugs might have been involved, so they asked for a full tox screen and autopsy. Come closer, I want you to see why I brought you here."

Booker approached the table, and Laura showed him the web of white filaments that filled the girl's chest cavity. His eyes went wide.

"What on Earth?" he said.

"They're all over the organs, muscles, and bones," Laura explained. "I haven't completed the autopsy yet, but I wouldn't be surprised if I found them all through her body. The problem is, I have no idea what they are. I've performed more autopsies than I can count, and I've never seen anything like this before."

Booker knit his brow and stared at the filaments. Even now, all these years later, she still knew him well enough to recognize when the wheels were turning behind his eyes. They stood so close that she smelled the familiar scent of his aftershave and felt the heat coming off his skin.

"I take you it already examined a sample?" he asked.

"It's over here." She brought him to the microscope and pointed to the LED screen. "The filaments are definitely organic in nature. They have a cell structure. At first I thought the cell walls were chitin—"

"They are." Booker's eyes narrowed as he studied the screen, and then he walked back to look at the body again.

"How is that possible?" Laura said, following him over.

"Chitin isn't native to the human body. There should have been an immune response."

"It must have used an immunosuppressant to override her defenses," Booker said. "Ciclosporin, maybe, or gliotoxin."

She looked at him over Kat's body. "You know what it is?"

He nodded grimly. "Each of these filaments is called a hypha. Together, they join to form a mycelium."

"I'm not following. What's a mycelium?"

"A fungus," he said. "When most people think of a fungus, they think of a mushroom, but that's just the fungus's fruiting body, a structure to produce and distribute its spores. The real fungus is the mycelium, a large, sprawling network of hyphae underground. That's why there was chitin in the sample. Chitin appears in the cell walls of fungi."

Laura stared at the white filaments threaded throughout the girl's body cavity. "How did it get inside her?"

Booker shook his head. "I have no idea."

She ran through a list of possible fungal infections in her head. Aspergillosis? No, that was confined to the lungs. Candidiasis? No, that tended to live in the mouth, throat, gut, or vagina, and rarely caused serious problems. Fungal meningitis? No, that was localized in the brain and spinal cord. This fungus wasn't localized, it was *everywhere*.

"Will you do me a favor?" Booker asked. "Will you let me know what else you find out?"

"I will," she said. "I really appreciate your help, Booker. I wouldn't have bothered you if it weren't important."

"It was no bother." He stripped off his gloves and mask and threw them in the bin. "I'm glad I could help."

To her surprise, he hugged her goodbye. She leaned into him, remembering the comfortable feel of his body against her. Even his breathing was familiar. It was like no time had passed at all.

He pulled away, much too soon. "It was good to see you again. I'm glad you called, even if the circumstances were a little...unusual."

"I'll call you as soon as I know anything," Laura said.

"Thanks." Booker turned, paused, then turned back to her. "I'm glad you're doing well."

"You too," she said. "And I really do like the goatee. It suits you."

He smiled, waved, and left the morgue. She listened to his footsteps recede down the hallway and wondered why, if she'd moved on with her life, it felt like her heart was breaking all over again.

4

"Her parents were right," Laura said. "There were drugs in Kat Bishop's system."

She sat across the desk from Ralph in his private office. Behind her, the door was closed so their conversation would be confidential. The deep lines that etched Ralph's face seemed to deepen at the news. Laura handed Sofia's tox screen report to him. He read it quickly.

"Positive for psilocybin?" he read. "The fuck is that?"

Ralph couldn't swear at home, especially with the new baby, so he made sure to get it all out in the office.

"It's a psychedelic drug compound produced by over two hundred species of fungi," Laura said.

Ralph looked up at her from the report. "Magic mushrooms?"

She nodded. "I didn't know much about it, so I did some quick research online. Turns out it's the same drug Timothy Leary experimented with back in the Sixties with the Harvard Psilocybin Project. He thought psychedelics could have positive effects on human behavior, particularly in the realm of psychotherapy. He even gave it to inmates at the Concord Prison to see if it would reduce the recidivism rate."

"He thought it could change someone's personality?"

"With a high enough dose," she said. "It was never proven. The project was shut down after two years, before they could determine if it had positive effects or negative ones."

Ralph let out a heavy sigh. "So where'd Kat Bishop get magic mushrooms?"

"I couldn't tell you for sure," she said. "I figure there are three possibilities."

"Hit me," he said, leaning forward again.

"The first is she bought the mushrooms from someone. A drug dealer."

"Shit. That's all we need." Ralph scratched his beard. "If someone's selling magic mushrooms to schoolkids, they're probably selling harder stuff, too. Coke. Heroin. LSD. Tell me the other possibilities before I get seriously depressed."

"The second is Kat grew the mushrooms herself," Laura said. "It's not hard to grow them at home. You can find kits online."

Ralph nodded and tapped his chin with the back end of a pen. "It's possible, but I have a hard time believing the Bishops wouldn't know what was happening in their own home. What else?"

"The third possibility is that she was dosed without knowing it."

"What do you mean?"

"A mushroom in a salad, or on a pizza or a burger," she said. "The thing is, psilocybin mushrooms look different from your average button mushrooms or portobellos. You can't mistake them. They have longer stems and smaller caps. If one found its way into Kat Bishop's food, it wasn't by accident."

Ralph put the tox screen report down on the desk. "Like slipping a knockout drug into her drink."

"Yes, except psilocybin wouldn't make her unconscious, just...altered. Hallucinating."

"Whoever gave her those mushrooms might as well have sent her crashing through the window himself," Ralph said. "I'd like to get my hands on him. I'll have someone dig deeper into who she was dating, that's usually the best place to start. What else have you got for me?"

"I performed a full autopsy like you asked," she said. "Aside from the cuts and bruises on her skin, she was as healthy as any other seventeen-year-old. But when I opened her up, I found something I can't quite explain."

His eyes narrowed. "What do you mean?"

"She had a fungus growing inside her," Laura said. "I haven't identified what kind yet, but it's—it's everywhere, Ralph. It's all through her body like a cancer. I've never seen anything like it."

"Could that come from ingesting the mushrooms?" he asked.

"I don't know," she said. "To be honest, I didn't even know it was a fungus at first. I had to call in Booker to identify what I was looking at."

"Booker?" He raised his eyebrows in surprise. Ralph knew their history. He'd taken her out for a beer after the breakup and let her cry on his shoulder a bit. "What's he doing back in town?"

"He's teaching science at the high school in the fall," she said. "Apparently, he sneaked back last week without telling anyone. I wouldn't have known if Sofia hadn't run into him."

"How was it seeing him again?"

"It was awkward, but not as bad as I thought it would be after four years." She stopped there. She wasn't ready to talk about it yet. She was still sorting through her own feelings about it. "Anyway, the important thing is that Booker knew it was a fungus, but he's just as stumped as I am about how it got inside her. You should see it, Ralph. It's attached to her muscles, her organs, even her bones. It's like these—these little white strings everywhere, all of them connected to each other like a web."

"Huh." Ralph frowned and tapped the end of a pen against his chin again. He stood up. "Wait here a minute, would you? I want to get something out of the evidence room that I think you should see."

Laura waited while he left, shifting uncomfortably in her chair. She didn't like this case. Everything about what happened to Kat Bishop was wrong. Her needless death. The mysterious fungus growing inside her. Normally, when Laura was faced with a medical mystery, her first instinct was to work at it obsessively until she had her answer. This was different. There was something repulsive about it that made her want to get away from it. The thought of something that shouldn't be there growing inside her body without her knowledge made her skin crawl.

To keep her mind off it, she examined at the three framed photographs that stood on Ralph's desk. The first was of Ralph and his wife Debra, a gorgeous woman with long black braids and a smooth umber complexion, holding their newborn baby Darius. Such a cute kid. Laura remembered how happy Ralph had been the day his son was born. He'd passed out cigars to everyone at the station like it was still the 1950s. Laura, never a smoker, still had hers in its wrapper in a drawer somewhere at home. The second picture was a candid of Debra on their porch swing. This picture was older; Debra's belly was still swollen with their son.

The last picture was of Ralph and his friends at Heuler's Tavern, a popular watering hole on MacLeod Avenue. The camera had caught them raising their pint glasses in celebration. Ralph was younger in this photo, all big smile and sparkling eyes, without any hint of the weight of the world in his face. On a TV in the background, colorful graphics announced the Boston Red Sox had won the 2018 World Series, and Laura's heart sank when it dawned on her what Ralph would have been celebrating in 2018. His and Debra's first pregnancy, the one that had ended in a miscarriage. Ralph's face had changed after that. The lines etched into his skin had remained ever since.

Something caught her eye, and Laura lifted the photograph off Ralph's desk for a closer look. In the background, she saw herself standing by the bar. The used-to-be her of five years ago. She held a glass of red wine in one hand, and next to her was Booker, head turned her way, listening to something she was telling him. She remembered inviting him to the party, which was maybe the second or third time they'd gone out together. He looked younger without his goatee, and there was a hint of a smile on his lips as though Laura had just said something witty. He'd always photographed well, but the sight of her next to him made her wince. Laura was of Welsh descent, which meant she was normally as pale as a sheet, but in the photograph her cheeks were already flushed from the wine, her brown eyes wide like a startled horse's, her chestnut hair a shaggy mess. She looked awful. It was a wonder he hadn't dumped her that night.

Instead, he dumped her a year later, over the phone from California. No, that wasn't exactly fair. After he moved across the country, splitting up had been a mutual decision, as much as those decisions could be. It wasn't his fault, and it wasn't hers either. Life simply took them on separate paths. Now he was back, and she wasn't sure how she felt about it.

Her phone buzzed. It was Adam texting her.

U COMING OVER TONIGHT? THOUGHT WE COULD ORDER IN CHINESE AND WATCH THE YANKEES ORIOLES GAME.

Always the romantic, she thought. Did she want to be with Adam tonight? Normally, she would have said yes. Adam wasn't the brightest, and it was unlikely they had a future together, but it beat sitting alone at home, and to be honest the sex wasn't bad. But today the thought didn't appeal to her. Performing an autopsy on a seventeen-year-old girl and seeing Booker again had her feeling all twisted around. She doubted she'd be good company.

She wrote back, NOT TONIGHT. IT'S BEEN A LONG DAY ALREADY AND IT'S NOT EVEN LUNCH. LET'S TALK LATER.

He texted back right away, HUH? THOUGHT U LIKED COMING OVER.

I DO, JUST NOT TONIGHT, OKAY? I JUST WANT TO GO HOME AND GET SOME SLEEP.

He texted back, WHATEVER, and she could feel the bitterness coming through the screen. It was the first time she'd turned Adam down in the two months they'd been together, and he was acting hurt and pissy about it. What the hell was his problem? Did he think she didn't have a life outside of him?

Ralph came back into the office, and Laura slipped her phone back into her pocket. Ralph had put on latex gloves and was carrying a sealed plastic evidence bag. Inside it was a book with a purple velour cover.

"We took this from Kat Bishop's bedroom in the course of our investigation," he said as he sat down.

He opened the bag and removed the book. He put it on the desk before him and flipped carefully through it with his gloved hands. Laura bent over the desk and saw each page was filled with pencil and charcoal drawings.

"She was an artist," Laura said.

"What you said before about strings connected to each other like a web reminded me of something I saw in here," he said. "We found the sketchbook lying open on her bed. We think she might have been drawing in it the night she died. If she was, this is the last thing she drew."

He lifted the sketchbook and turned it around so she could see. On the page was a hastily drawn outline of a woman in pencil. A self-portrait, perhaps, or the start of one, but instead of details like clothing and facial features, the outline Kat had drawn was filled with a web of dark lines. They spread from head to feet, intersecting and crisscrossing. The resemblance to the filaments Laura found inside the girl was eerie, but what caught her eye were the handful of lines that began inside the body but extended beyond its borders. They moved confidently outward across the empty whiteness of the page, and then off the page altogether, into the unknown.

5

Jeff Miller didn't feel well when he returned home that night. The shy, gangly fifteen-year-old was dizzy and nauseous, and his skin itched. He closed the front door and trudged up the stairs to his bedroom.

"Is that you, Jeff?" his mother called from the living room. "Don't track dirt onto the carpet, honey."

The sounds of a sitcom—sarcastic dialogue and canned laughter—accompanied her voice. He heard his father chuckle distantly from the couch.

Jeff was too tired to take off his sneakers, or to respond to his mother. At the top of the stairs he entered his room, closed the door behind him, and flipped on the lights. The full-body poster of the pop singer Lavender X greeted him from the wall next to his bed. A young woman in her early twenties, she wore a revealing red bikini and tall, matching boots. She caressed a microphone with long, elegant fingers while a fallen lock of her lavender-dyed hair obscured one eye. Jeff's mother had been skeptical about letting him put up the poster in his room, but she finally relented. Truth be told, he didn't like Lavender X's music all that much, but he liked the poster. He liked the poster *a lot.*

A heavy rain started outside, battering the window as he flopped onto his bed. He'd left the violin in its case on the covers, and now it bounced dangerously toward the edge. He contemplated letting it fall. Maybe if the violin broke, he wouldn't have to take lessons anymore. It was hard to connect with other kids his age when he had to go to his violin teacher's house after school every day. Unfortunately, summer didn't offer any escape. Day after day, it was the same thing. Today, his parents had only dragged him to that stupid town hall meeting because it was close to his violin teacher's house and they didn't want to have to drive back and forth. He hated the meeting—although it'd been pretty funny when that old guy stood up and started swearing—and he hated having to bring his violin with him. He was sure everyone was laughing at him behind their hands. He was convinced that even Laura—Dr. Powell—who'd always been nice to him, and whom he'd had a crush on for years, was only pretending to be interested because she didn't want to lose business as their family doctor.

Jeff rescued the violin case before it fell and placed it gently on the floor. As much as he hated the stupid thing, he knew his parents would kill him if he broke it. It was expensive, and they made sure he knew it every chance they got. He wished his parents understood that he didn't want to be a musician. He hated every minute that his teacher made him saw out Beethoven's "Ode to Joy" or Ferdinand Küchler's "Violin Concerto in D Major" on the violin strings. His parents would never listen, though. They both loved classical music and had always dreamed of playing in an orchestra, but since they couldn't it was up to him. It didn't matter what *his* dreams were.

His parents didn't understand him. Nobody did. He didn't get invited to his classmates' parties. None of the girls at school liked him, or even knew he was alive. He had no idea where he fit in. Sometimes it seemed like everything was part of one massive choreographed dance. Everyone knew the steps but him. Like in a nightmare, he was the only one fumbling through the dance, making it all up and hoping no one noticed.

He thought taking on a community garden project with some classmates this summer might help him make friends, but once the others saw how dedicated he was to tending their plot, they bailed and left it all on him. Typical. Still, it gave him something to do that wasn't violin practice, so after dinner he'd biked to Dradin Park to see how his class's vegetables were faring. Only, all the plants were dead, as though some biblical blight had struck them. He was going to have to call his faculty advisor in the morning and tell her what happened. Probably, he'd get the blame for it, too. That would be perfectly on-brand for his life.

The rain drummed against his window. His arms itched again, and he scratched them madly. He saw little red dots on his skin, but the more he scratched the redder his skin got and the dots were swallowed up.

The floor undulated under his feet like the stomach of some enormous, breathing creature. He moved his feet off the floor, and his legs smeared across his field of vision, leaving slow-motion trails in their wake. He found this odd but not alarming. More like funny. Laughter bubbled up from his chest. The sound of the television drifting up from downstairs changed, altering itself into the smooth, drawn-out notes of a stringed instrument.

Lavender X stood in the middle of his room playing a violin that looked just like his. Her slender fingers moved with confidence up and down the neck, caressing it like she caressed the microphone in the poster.

She was naked except for the red boots that came up to her shins. Her bikini was gone, and he wondered for a moment if she'd left it behind when she stepped out of the poster. She looked just as he imagined she would on the nights he stared at the poster and rubbed himself to sleep. Her breasts were plump and pointed, tipped with nipples like small rosebuds. Her eyes were dark, focused pools behind her fallen locks of lavender hair. The hair between her legs was lavender too.

His arousal strained at the front of his pants. The pressure was unbearable. With each draw of the bow across the strings, her breasts quivered and shook and he thought his erection was going to tear its way through his zipper.

Long, pale arms pulled him off his bed and onto his feet. More women surrounded him, as naked as Lavender X—and he realized they *were* her. Different versions of her, Lavender Xs from different worlds, different realities. Each of them had a second face beneath theirs, pushing and yearning to break through, something inhuman and unknowable. In their eyes, the whole of the cosmos waited. An overwhelming feeling of connection came over him, a connection to all the women, to all the world, and to something larger, some guiding force beyond his comprehension. The women danced around him in a circle, his hungry eyes drinking in the swaying curves of their breasts, their hips, their lavender public hair. Something stretched inside him like a rubber band, stretching until it snapped, and a tidal flood of semen burst out of him in endless spurts.

Jeff laughed and joined the dance. He finally knew the steps.

6

Ralph Gorney poured coffee into the travel mug his wife had given him for his birthday, the one with the words Chief of Police printed on the side, only with Police crossed out and My Heart written under it. It was hokey, but he loved it. He didn't even care if the guys at the station saw it or gave him a hard time about it. It was from Debra, and it meant something to him that she still loved him after everything they'd been through. The morning sun streamed through the kitchen window and painted a square of light on the counter to one side of the coffee machine, a spotlight missing its mark.

"Sorry, baby, I have to leave early today," he called down the hallway. "Lisa Miller rang the station. Something's wrong with her boy."

Sipping his coffee and smoothing his tan uniform shirt with his free hand, he started down the hallway back to the bedroom, where he'd left Debra still in bed. As he passed the door to the nursery, he saw she had gotten up and was sitting in the rocking chair in the corner of the room, feeding the baby. Darius, three months old, lay tiny and swaddled in her arms, greedily slurping formula from a bottle.

He's drinking too fast, Ralph thought. *He's going to choke.*

He forced the panicked thought aside. Memories of the miscarriage made it hard for him not to be nervous about every little thing.

Except nervous wasn't the right word. It didn't feel big enough to encompass what he felt. Neither did fear. It was bigger than that. It was bigger than anything else.

The miscarriage hadn't been anyone's fault. No one did anything wrong. Debra took her folic acid supplements every day and saw her doctor regularly. She didn't smoke or do drugs. She stayed away from caffeine and fish just to be on the safe side. But none of that mattered in the face of a simple chromosomal abnormality. At twenty-one weeks, the embryo stopped developing, and that was it. Intrauterine fetal demise, the doctor called it. Ralph and Debra knew it by another name. Stillbirth.

Debra looked up at him from the chair. Her face was still puffy from sleep, but she'd never looked more beautiful to him. "Did you say something, baby?"

"I said I have to go," Ralph replied. "Adam is picking me up in a squad car."

"Okay, be careful," she said. She tossed her long black braids over her shoulder and returned her attention to the baby.

Ralph hovered in the nursery doorway, drinking his coffee and watching the two of them. He was lucky and he knew it. Lucky to have such a beautiful, healthy child. Lucky to still have Debra in his life.

They'd kept it together for almost two months after the miscarriage. Almost two months of semi-normal, semi-sane living after the most devastating tragedy of their lives. There'd been tears and mourning and the occasional soul-crushing dream that the baby had been born healthy and happy, but there'd also been a strong need to move forward, to put it behind them as best they could. It was easier said than done.

One day, for reasons he no longer remembered, Ralph had opened the door to the nursery and stood looking into it, just as he was now. Back then, they'd talked about changing it back into a guest bedroom, but it was just talk. Neither of them wanted to touch it. Ralph had looked around the room, still full of toys in their boxes, gifts in their wrapping, a spotless changing table against one wall, an empty crib against the other, and he'd lost his mind. He didn't remember any of it. He had to be told afterward that he'd torn the crib to pieces with his bare hands, shredded the blankets, and stomped the toys to bits. When Debra found him, he was smashing the drawers from the changing table against the wall and screaming like an animal.

It had almost ended their marriage. So had a dozen other crazy things each of them did in the aftermath of the miscarriage, but the day he tore the nursery apart was the worst of it. He'd flown into a blind rage at the reminder of what they'd lost, at a vacant room that held only broken promises and crushed dreams. Knowing he had that kind of fury inside himself scared him. It scared Debra, too. She never said it out loud, but he saw it in her eyes that day when she talked him down.

It took them so long to get back to where they'd been before the miscarriage, so long to get to the point where they wanted to try again, that Ralph couldn't help feeling guilty every time he left them alone to go to work. What if something happened while he wasn't here? What if the baby fell, or went under the water too long during bath time, or let his curiosity get the better of him about an electrical socket they'd forgotten to baby-proof? They hadn't forgotten to babyproof any sockets, or the rest of the house for that matter, but the thoughts haunted him. A part of him kept insisting he ought to stay home. Just in case.

The three worst words in the world. *Just in case.*

A car horn from outside pulled him from his thoughts. "That's Adam. I'll call you later to check in."

Debra gave him a reassuring smile. "We'll be fine, Ralph."

He nodded. Of course they would be fine. There was nothing to worry about. Mother and child were both happy and healthy. He would call anyway.

Outside, he found Officer Adam Patterson waiting for him in a squad car at the foot of the driveway. Ralph skirted around the puddles from last night's rain and got into the passenger seat.

"Morning, Chief," Adam said.

He was a young white man with short cropped hair and a square jaw. A good-looking guy. Ralph could see why Laura was dating him, although he wasn't sure he approved. Laura was one of his closest friends, and Adam, well, he suspected there was a cruel streak in the man. It didn't show its face often, but it was there, just beneath the surface, waiting to twist someone's arm a little too hard, push someone against the squad car a little too forcefully. Adam was gung-ho about the job, and Ralph got the sense he was a little too at ease with the power that came with it. But those were his own issues with Adam. He knew enough to stay out of Laura's personal business.

"How's the family?" Adam asked as Ralph put the travel mug in the cup holder and connected his seatbelt.

"Everyone's good." Ralph peered through the windshield at the house as if he could see through the walls like Superman. Everyone *was* good. He had to learn to relax. Focusing on the job was a good start. "Let's go. The Millers are waiting for us."

Adam drove them through the sleepy residential streets. The morning sun shone through the trees and dappled the lawns and sidewalks. Everything was quiet. The clock on the dashboard read 7:04 AM, still too early for morning commuters to be on the roads. The only signs of life were a handful of joggers and people out walking their dogs. They turned onto Foxglove Road, and a young woman jogged up the sidewalk wearing nylon running shorts and a sports bra. Adam turned his head to watch her run by.

"Eyes on the road, Officer," Ralph said.

"Just looking," Adam said with a grin. "Nothing wrong with looking, is there?"

"You'll have to ask Laura about that," Ralph said. *If you cheat on her, I'll make your life a living hell*, he added silently.

Adam clenched his jaw, his mood shifting on a dime. "Laura's ghosting me, Chief. I know it. We were supposed to get together last night, but she canceled on me at the last minute. Said she just wanted to go home. She's *never* canceled on me before."

"I don't think that's what ghosting means," Ralph said. He wished they weren't having this conversation. It wasn't his business, and he didn't want it to be.

"You know Laura better than anyone," Adam said. "You don't think she's seeing someone behind my back, do you?"

"Come on," he said. "That's not what she's like. You know that."

"Do I?" Adam's grip on the wheel tightened until his knuckles turned white. "All I know is, she better not be cheating on me."

Ralph shook his head. "Aren't you the one who was just staring out the window at another woman?"

Adam didn't answer him. He just drove and stewed.

They turned off Foxglove and onto Grove Hill Road. The Millers' house was in the middle of the block, and Ralph felt an immense relief that the ride with Adam was over. He saw Lisa Miller waiting by the mailbox. She looked anxious and impatient, and when she saw the squad car approach she waved her arms frantically, as if Adam would have driven by her otherwise. Adam parked the squad car at the curb, and he and Ralph got out.

"Thank God you're here," Lisa Miller said, bustling toward them. "We didn't know who else to call."

"Where's your boy?" Ralph asked. It was a hot morning, and he drew an arm across his forehead to wipe away the beads of sweat.

"Jeff's inside." She led them to the house. The still-wet grass of the lawn was slippery under Ralph's shoes. "I don't know what's wrong with him. I don't understand why he's doing this."

"Doing what?" Ralph pressed.

"I don't know how to explain it," she said, fidgeting in agitation. "You'll see."

She opened the front door and led them inside. Her husband, Paul, stood at the foot of the stairs to the second floor.

"Thanks for coming," he said. His voice had none of the alarm his wife's did. "Can we make this quick? I have to be at work soon."

Lisa shot her husband a dark look, then said to Ralph, "Jeff is upstairs."

She led the three of them up the steps. Halfway up, Ralph heard a muffled thudding coming from somewhere above them. It grew louder as they ascended. At the top of the stairs, Lisa brought them down a hallway to the door at the far end, which was barricaded by a table that had been dragged in front of it. The thumping came from behind the door, which shuddered in its frame each time, as if someone were throwing themself against it from the inside.

Lisa held her hands to her mouth. "There's something wrong with him."

"That's Jeff in there?" Ralph asked. The boy's mother nodded mutely, as if she couldn't believe it any more than he did. "When did this start?"

"Last night," Paul said. "He started acting crazy after he came home from his shift at the community garden. He kept trying to leave the house, even when we told him he couldn't. He got violent about it and tried to take a swing at me. We had to lock him in his room. He's been banging on that door all night."

"Hold on," Ralph said. A connection was forming in his mind. "He was at the community garden?"

"Yeah, it's some kind of school thing," Paul said. "Why?"

Another thump came from the bedroom, the loudest one yet. The door cracked down the middle. A voice shouted from inside, "Let me out!"

"Like I said, he's been at this all night. You ask me, he just wants attention." Paul checked his watch. "I don't have time for this. I have a meeting I need to be at this morning."

His wife shot him another angry glare. "Will you shut up about your damned meeting, Paul?" She turned to Ralph. "Please, do something."

"All right," Ralph said. "You're going to need to stand back."

The parents moved to the far end of the hallway. Ralph and Adam cautiously approached the bedroom door. Another thump, and the crack lengthened. *Jeff must be really putting his shoulder into it,* Ralph thought. Adam drew his gun and aimed it at the door. Ralph put a hand on his arm and made him lower it, shaking his head angrily.

"He's just a kid, Adam."

Adam holstered his gun. "If you say so, but he doesn't sound like just a kid to me."

"Let me *out!*" Jeff screamed.

Ralph gripped the table blocking the door. "On three. I'll move the table, you grab him if he makes a break for it."

Adam assumed a wrestler's stance, ready to catch Jeff if necessary. "You got it."

"One," Ralph said.

The door shook in its frame under another thunderous blow of the boy's shoulder.

"Two."

Another thump, and a splinter from the door jamb dropped to the floor.

"Three."

Ralph dragged the table away. The door flew open under the weight of Jeff's assault, slamming into the table and pinning Ralph to the wall. Jeff ran shrieking out of the bedroom. He was a mess, his hair disheveled, his shirt half untucked, and with only one shoe on. In his hand was a violin, which he smashed into Adam's face like a club as Adam tried to grab him. The instrument made a horrible hollow, twanging sound as the wood and strings broke.

"Jeff, no, your violin!" his mother shouted in anguish from the end of the hall.

The kid just hit a police officer, and all she cares about is the violin? Ralph shoved the table away, freeing himself.

"I have to go to it!" Jeff yelled, skirting around Adam.

"You're not going anywhere, you little shit," Adam said. His face wasn't bruised from the violin strike, but it was red with anger. He got his arms around Jeff and lifted the boy off the floor, then slammed him down on his back hard enough to knock the wind out of him. At the other end of the hallway, his mother gasped and let out a sob. His father looked pale, but neither of them intervened. Adam kneeled on Jeff's chest with one knee. The boy scrabbled and wriggled beneath it, trying to get free.

"You hit me, you prick!" Adam snarled at him. "I ought to pound you into a stain on the rug!"

"Easy now," Ralph said, coming over. "Like I said, he's just a kid."

"The son of a bitch tried to coldcock me!" Adam said, glaring at the boy.

The cruelty Ralph had noticed in him before was back. He could see in Adam's eyes how badly he wanted to hurt the boy in retaliation. Break his arm, bloody his nose. He was itching for it, but Ralph knew this situation required finesse, not brute force.

"I saw. Keep your cool, okay?" Ralph crouched next to the pinned boy. He pried the broken violin out of Jeff's hand and placed it on the floor out of the boy's reach. "What's the story, Jeff? What's all this about?"

"It's calling to me," Jeff insisted. "Can't you hear it?"

"I don't hear anything, Jeff," Ralph said.

"The little shit's on something," Adam said.

Ralph agreed. The boy's pupils were dilated. He waved Jeff's parents forward. Lisa hurried to him, her hands balled in anxious fists. Paul groaned, rolled his eyes, checked his watch, and stamped over.

"Do you know if Jeff took anything?" Ralph asked them. "Pills? Alcohol?"

"How should we know?" Paul said. "It's not like we can watch him every second."

"He better not have!" Lisa said. "He's supposed to be practicing for his recital. Not that he'll be able to play now that he's *ruined* his violin!"

The two of them looked down at their son with very different expressions. Lisa was upset about the broken violin. Paul was impatient for this to be over with so he could start his day. Neither seemed all that concerned about Jeff's well-being. The thought infuriated Ralph. Didn't they know how lucky they were have a child at all? If they knew what he and Debra had gone through, they wouldn't take their son for granted.

He swallowed his anger. Now wasn't the time. "Was he acting like this when he came home from the park?"

"I don't know," his mother admitted. "He went right up to his room, but the ruckus didn't start until later."

"Okay, what I'd like to do is take Jeff to the station and administer a drug test," Ralph said. "But because he's a minor, one or both of you is going to have to come with us."

Paul threw his hands in the air. "Great. Just great. I don't have time for this."

"What, and *my* day is less important that yours?" Lisa snapped. "Tell them you're going to miss your meeting, Paul. We're *both* going with our son to the police station."

Jeff didn't make it easy for them. When Adam let him up, he tried to bolt again. This time, Ralph caught him, and much to the parents' chagrin, he was forced to handcuff the boy's arms behind his back in order to walk him out to the squad car. Back in the heat of the summer sun, Paul called his office to let them know in the pissiest voice possible that he was going to be late, while Lisa walked with her arm around her son so their neighbors wouldn't see he was in handcuffs.

Adam loaded Jeff into the back of the squad car, and then he got in behind the wheel. Ralph took the passenger's seat again. In the side mirror, he saw Paul and Lisa Miller get into their own car to follow them to the station. Adam pulled away from the curb, and almost immediately Jeff started to squirm and kick in the back seat.

"Cool it back there!" Adam yelled.

Jeff twisted around and kicked the door. It didn't budge.

"I said cut it out!" Adam yelled.

"You don't understand," Jeff said. "Can't you hear it?"

"Hear what?" Ralph asked.

"It's calling to me."

Ralph and Adam exchanged glances. Adam shook his head and rolled his eyes.

"What's calling to you, Jeff?" Ralph asked.

Jeff stared out the window. His eyes remained fixed on some distant point only he could see.

"God," he said.

7

When Laura got out of the shower, there was a voicemail message from Ralph asking her to come to the police station right away to help with a drug test. The subject, he said, had been sedated upon arrival at the station. She listened to the message a second time to make sure she'd heard that right. *Sedated?* Since when did Ralph need to sedate anyone?

She dressed quickly and drove to City Square. At the station, she parked in the police lot and hung the placard off her rearview mirror. She got out of her car, and as she approached the door, she saw Adam Patterson come out of the building.

"Hey, girl," he said.

He snaked an arm around her waist and pulled her in for a kiss. She turned her head so he only kissed her cheek. She was still annoyed with him for reacting so obnoxiously yesterday when she told him she didn't want to come over.

"What's with the cold shoulder?" he said.

It wouldn't be smart to get into it now. She was expected inside, and she knew as soon as she brought up how she felt, his temper would flare, and before she knew it they would be in a full-fledged argument.

"I'm here on business," she said, because she needed to tell him something. "Ralph called me in to draw blood for a drug test."

"Yeah, it's that Miller kid," he said.

Surprised, Laura said, "*Jeff* Miller?"

"Yeah, the scrawny kid. He's acting real weird," Adam said. "You ask me, he's definitely on something. The little shit attacked me. He hit me with his violin."

Laura frowned. That didn't sound like the Jeff Miller she knew.

"Hey, how about we make up for last night by getting together at my place later?" he said, pulling her close again. "I'll make it worth your while."

"Not tonight," she said, gently releasing herself from his embrace.

The disappointment was evident on his face, and a hint of anger, too. It put her on edge.

"That's what you said last night. What's the matter?"

"There's just a lot on my mind right now," she said.

"Right. A lot on your mind," he said, clenching his jaw. "I heard Booker Coates was in the station yesterday. Guess your ex is back in town, huh?"

"I called him in," she said. "I needed his help with something. It was no big deal."

"Right. No big deal. Whatever." His face darkened. "I don't want you hanging out with him."

She looked up at him sharply. "What?"

"I don't like the idea of him sniffing around like a dog," he said. "He needs to know you're with me now."

Laura's blood went hot. She couldn't believe what she was hearing. "I'm not your property, Adam. You don't get to tell me who I can and can't talk to."

"The hell I don't," he insisted. "Either you're with me or you're not. Which is it?"

"This is ridiculous."

She turned on her heel to continue toward the station. Adam's hand clamped around her elbow.

"Hey," he barked. "I'm talking to you."

The memory of Adam yelling angrily at the woman in the supermarket flashed through her mind, and she yanked her arm free from his grasp. "Let go of me."

"Fine," he said, putting up his hands. Not sorry, just *fine*. She doubted he even understood what he'd done wrong.

"Ralph is waiting for me inside," she told him and continued toward the door.

"You know what, if you don't want to come over, then don't come over," he called after her. "You don't have to be such a bitch about it."

The word cut her like razor, sharp and hot. She paused on the steps and turned back to him. "Don't call me again, Adam. Whatever this was, it was a mistake. It's over."

She continued up the stairs and through the front door into the air-conditioned interior.

"Whatever!" Adam called after her. "Who needs you, you fucking cu—"

The rest of his words were cut off by the door swinging closed behind her. Laura took a deep breath. Rather than feel upset about her blowup with Adam, she was relieved. If she was being honest with herself, she was never that into him. She hadn't dated anyone for a long time after Booker, and when Adam pursued her with such determination her loneliness got the better of her. The relationship never would have worked out in the long run, especially with Adam's temper. She rubbed her arm where he'd grabbed her. It was for the best that she ended it now, before things got any worse.

Ralph was waiting in his office when she got there. Some chairs had been brought in so that the Miller family could sit together along one wall. Lisa and Paul sat on the ends, and between them was Jeff, slumped in his chair with one hand cuffed to the chair's arm. Lisa looked mortified, her face as red as a fresh tomato, while Paul snuck glances at his wristwatch. Ralph filled Laura in on everything that happened that morning.

"Once we got Jeff to the station, we had to give him gabapentin to sedate him. It took two doses before it had any effect," Ralph said. "We've already got a urine sample from him for the tox screen. You missed *that* bit of fun. Sofia's analyzing it as we speak. Now we just need you to draw some blood."

"It's getting louder," Jeff slurred. His mother shushed him.

"What's that about?" Laura asked Ralph.

Ralph shrugged. "He's been like this all morning, claiming something is calling to him."

"Not something," Jeff said sleepily. "*God* is calling me. Why can't you hear it? It's so loud."

"You see what we're dealing with," Ralph said.

Lisa Miller looked pleadingly at Laura. "I don't know why

he's acting like this. He must have taken something."

The signs were definitely there. Jeff's eyes were bloodshot and his pupils were dilated. He was clearly in an altered state, and not just from the gabapentin. Judging from the story Ralph told her, he was acting erratically, too, completely unlike himself. Still, she found it hard to believe that the Jeff Miller she knew, that awkward and talented boy who'd been too shy to even look at her yesterday, was taking drugs.

But she'd thought the same about Kat Bishop, hadn't she? She never would have pegged the girl for a drug user, and yet there'd been psilocybin in her system when she died. Maybe she didn't know either of them as well as she thought.

"Why won't you let me go?" Jeff mumbled. He looked around the room with dull, glassy eyes. "Won't stop calling... until I go."

"Stop it, Jeff," his mother said. "You're embarrassing us!"

"I'll go get a syringe," Laura said. "I'll be right back."

"Let me step out with you," Ralph said. "Paul, Lisa, can I trust you to keep your son under control while I'm gone?"

"Just be quick," Paul snapped. "I've had enough of this nonsense."

Ralph escorted Laura out of the office, closing the door behind him. Once they were in the hallway outside, he said, "Two kids on drugs in two days. Back when my father was on the force, he had a saying: Once is a fluke, but twice is a trend. I'm starting to think he's right. If there's two, there's more."

"I don't understand it," Laura said. "Kat was a good kid with a bright future. So is Jeff. It doesn't make sense. All the warning signs for drug use in teenagers point to antisocial behavior, emotional issues, big personality changes like depression or aggression. These kids were leading charmed lives."

"I'm not so sure about that," Ralph said. "You should have seen Jeff's parents back at the house. Lisa was more concerned about his violin than about the boy himself, and Paul thinks this is all one big inconvenience for him. Neither of them is thinking about their son. It's infuriating."

"I know." She could guess what was on Ralph's mind. After the miscarriage, he'd leaned on her for support, bending her ear over a pint at Heuler's. Later, she'd bent his ear just as hard when Booker left. It had formed an iron bond between them. "How are Debra and the baby doing?"

Ralph smiled, something she didn't see often. "They're doing great, but it's getting harder to leave them every day. I don't want to miss anything. His first steps. His first word."

"I get it," she said. "Maybe some time off would do you good."

"Not a chance," he said. "Not if someone in Sakima is selling drugs to these kids. Go get your equipment. I want to know what the hell is going on."

Ralph returned to his office, and Laura went to the Science Wing to get what she needed from the medical supply cabinet. When she returned, nothing had changed. Jeff was still slumped in his chair, looking half asleep.

Laura put on a pair of nitrile gloves and wrapped a rubber tourniquet around Jeff's left arm. He watched her as she swabbed the area just below the inside of his elbow with alcohol.

"You're not you," he said.

"I'm not?" she asked, humoring him as she discarded the cotton swab.

"No," he said. "None of us are who we think we are."

"Who are we then?" she asked.

"That's the question, isn't it?" He smiled weakly, a string of drool dangling off his bottom lip. There was something wrong with his eyes, like he wasn't all there. "Did you know that every part of your body is covered with microbes? Every part of you, your skin, your fingernails, your eyes, your mouth, is *teeming* with life. There are more microbes in your body than your own cells. More bacteria inside you than stars in the sky. We're not individuals. We're plural. Collectives. It makes you wonder, doesn't it?"

Laura removed the cap from the plastic syringe. "What does it make you wonder?"

"Are we in control?" Jeff said. "Or are they?"

Laura paused. His eyes didn't look so sluggish anymore. There was a spark in them now, a sign of intelligence.

"Can we hurry this up?" Paul asked. "They pushed my meeting back to ten o'clock, and I really need to be there."

"Paul, stop it," Lisa said sharply. "What must they think of us, hearing you talk that way?"

Laura shot them a look but didn't say a word. She could imagine the expression on Ralph's face behind her. She wondered if he was bothering to hide it from them.

With the needle, she pierced the median cubital vein in Jeff's arm and let his blood flow until she'd filled two plastic collection tubes. When she was done, she pulled the needle gently out of his arm...and blinked in surprise. A bead of blood formed at the venipuncture site, which wasn't unusual, but there was something else there, something so small she almost missed it.

White and fibrous, it looked like one of the filaments she'd found inside Kat Bishop's body. Hyphae, Booker had called them, the organic material that made up the subterranean body of a fungus. The thin white strand poked out of the tiny needle hole in Jeff's arm, groping and swaying, and then quickly withdrew back beneath the skin.

8

After breakfast, Booker went out to the back yard of his new house. He needed to clear his head. Last night had been mostly sleepless because he couldn't stop thinking about the dead girl with the fungus inside her. Not in her lungs and orifices, where it might make sense, but on her organs, her bones. As much as he tried to figure out how it got there, he couldn't come up with a satisfying answer.

There'd been a heavy rain overnight, but the air still felt hot and thick with humidity as he walked the length of the back yard. At the far end, a gate had been built into the tall white privacy fence that surrounded his yard. He opened the gate and stepped through onto the trail that led into the woods behind his house.

Access to the forest in back was why he'd bought this house. Ever since he was little, he'd felt most at home among the quiet stillness of the trees and moss. The only child of a working single mother, he'd had to learn to entertain himself for long stretches of time. Unfortunately, he was never very good at making friends, so he spent much of his time alone, exploring nature in his childhood back yard. His interest in the things that grew from the earth was what eventually led him to study botany. Although after he'd been awarded his Ph.D., he never dreamed the degree would lead him back to Sakima, teaching Earth Science at the same high school he'd attended as a kid. The universe acted in mysterious ways.

The leaves on the trees were still wet with the rainwater they'd collected. Muddy earth sucked at his shoes. Booker tried to distract himself by mentally fine-tuning his lesson plans for the fall semester, but try as he might, his thoughts kept returning to the dead girl, Kat Bishop. The only dead bodies he'd ever seen were elderly relatives at open-casket funerals, but this was different. She was so young. It was a horrible sight, made worse by seeing her torso splayed open mid-autopsy. And that web of hyphae inside her... Yet the strangest part—What was he saying? *All* of it was strange—was that the fungus wasn't what killed her. If Kat hadn't gone through a window and died, Laura wouldn't have found the fungus at all.

The thought of Laura made him pause and lean against a yellow birch. If he was being honest with himself, it wasn't just the mystery of Kat Bishop that was stuck in his head. It was Laura, too. He couldn't stop thinking about her. Hearing from her yesterday had caught him off-guard. He always knew it would only be a matter of time before they ran into each other now that he was back in Sakima, but he hadn't been prepared to hear her voice again. He definitely hadn't been prepared for how beautiful she still looked to him. Had it shown in his face? Did she know she still took his breath away after all this time?

Did he *want* her to know?

They'd been together for nine months. Nine *amazing* months. He'd fallen for her hard and fast, and had even started imagining a future with her, but when the opportunity arose to fulfill his dream of earning his doctorate degree, he was torn. The university was in California, all the way on the other side of the country, far from Laura, who, as much as she wanted to stay together, didn't want leave Sakima or her growing family practice. In the end, she urged him to go, telling him she would never forgive herself if she was the reason he didn't follow his dreams. Moving to California and leaving her behind was one of the hardest things he ever did. They tried to stay together as a long-distance relationship, but eventually he got busier with his studies, and she got busier with her practice, and then...

Then it was over.

Drops of water dripped off the tree branches above, splashing on his head like a reminder to keep moving. He left the yellow birch and walked deeper into the woods, listening as the sounds of nature grew louder. Birds sang. Squirrels chittered in the trees. Something moved through the canopy overhead, shaking the branches and showering more rainwater onto the forest floor. Whether it was a bird, an animal, or just the wind, he couldn't say. For all the knowledge humankind had about the world after centuries of exploration and study, nature still excelled at keeping some things secret, as though they weren't meant for human understanding.

Not long after he'd returned to Sakima, he ran into Sofia Hernandez at a coffee place on MacLeod Avenue. She told him Laura was seeing someone, a police officer by the name of Adam Patterson. He felt an instant pang of jealousy, though he kept it from showing. He shouldn't be surprised that Laura had moved on. Four years was a long time. During those same four years, he'd been on exactly two first dates with two different women in California. There'd been no second date with either. There was nothing wrong with them; they were attractive, smart, and accomplished, but they were missing something he couldn't define. Maybe it was as simple as the fact that neither of them was Laura.

The plan to clear his mind obviously wasn't working. Booker sighed and turned around, heading back along the path toward home. As he reached the gate in his fence, he noticed a fallen tree in the woods. Protruding from its side was the wide, rounded cap of a mushroom like a Frisbee half buried in the wood. The mushroom was new, coaxed out by last night's rain. The gills beneath its cap would be filled with spores, he knew, which the mushroom would expel into the air to be carried on the wind, or on the bodies of forest animals, until they found places to settle and grow whole new fungi. Meanwhile, inside the fallen tree itself, the mycelium would be feasting.

Fungi were eaters of the dead. They broke down decaying matter using incredibly powerful acidic enzymes, then absorbed the leftover nutrients through their hyphae. Fungi also played a role in the decomposition of animal life, including humans. Normally, you could expect a postmortem interval of three to seven days before any fungal growth appeared on a human corpse, and yet Kat Bishop had been dead for less than twenty-four hours. So where had the fungus come from? Booker shook his head in frustration. His thoughts were circling right back to where they'd started.

His phone rang. It was Laura calling. After yesterday, he'd added her name and number back into his contacts. Just so he'd know it was her when she called with an update, not for any other reason. At least, that was what he told himself at the time. He answered the call.

"Laura?"

"Hi, Booker," she said. There was a slight hesitation in her voice. He wondered if he sounded the same way. "Am I interrupting anything? Is now a good time to talk?"

"Now's fine," he said. "Did you find something?"

"Kat Bishop's tox screen came back positive for psilocybin," she told him. "It's a psychedelic drug produced by certain types of fungi."

"I know what it is." Booker opened the gate and walked into his back yard.

"Right, obviously," Laura said. "That reminds me, am I supposed to start calling you Dr. Coates now that you've got your Ph.D.?"

He chuckled as he crossed the lawn to the back deck of his house. "That's Professor Coates to you, Dr. Powell."

"Well, *Professor Coates*, there's more," she said. "Another student from the high school, Jeff Miller, just tested positive for psilocybin as well. Ralph thinks there's a drug dealer in town, someone whose selling hallucinogens to schoolkids."

Booker tipped the small puddle of rainwater out of one of the patio chairs arranged around a glass-topped table and sat. "Did the kid say where he got the drug from?"

"He won't answer any questions," she said. "He just keeps talking about how something is calling him and he has to go to it. He got very agitated about it."

"Calling him?" he asked. "What does that mean?'

"I don't know. He's probably having a bad trip." Laura paused. When she spoke again, her voice was different, laced with worry. "Booker, I—I saw something. At least, I *think* I did. Maybe I imagined it."

He leaned forward in the chair. "What was it?"

"After I took Jeff's blood, something came out of the hole in his arm. I could have sworn it was a hypha, just like we found in Kat Bishop's body. And it…it moved. It looked like a little worm, wriggling around. Just for a second, and then it was gone." She laughed nervously. "I must sound like I'm the one who's on drugs."

"No, not at all. I'm sure you saw what you saw," Booker said. *Two* people in town with a fungus growing inside them? Was it possible? Did it mean there were more?

"Thanks, I've been half convinced I'm going crazy," she said. "There's a fungus growing inside Jeff, isn't there? Just like the one inside Kat. That poor kid. Why would it do that? What's it *doing*?"

"I wish I knew," he said. "Fungi are decomposers, but what we saw inside Kat's body didn't look like it was breaking down her remains. Her organs and muscles still looked healthy and intact. If I didn't know better, I'd say it looked more like the fungus had formed a symbiotic relationship with her."

"Is that possible?" Laura asked.

"I don't know," he admitted. "Some fungi are symbiotic, like the ones that combine with algae to form lichen, but they always form composite organisms for a reason. What would be the reason for a symbiotic relationship between a fungus and a human being? What kind of composite organism could they possibly create? I can't see how either of them would benefit from it."

An army of small black ants crawled across the wooden planks of the deck. They spread out, as if they were searching for something.

"What about the psilocybin mushrooms they took?" Laura asked. "There's got to be a connection."

"It would be one hell of a coincidence if there isn't, but I can't figure it out. Typically, psilocybin mushrooms are dead and dried before they're eaten. Even if they weren't, the stomach acid would completely destroy them. There's no way they could survive to create a whole new mycelium inside someone who ate them."

He thought back to the fallen tree being devoured from

within by a fungus. He couldn't shake the feeling he was missing something. Something he couldn't see.

"It turns out Kat Bishop and Jeff Miller were both tending the high school's plots in the community garden this summer," Laura said. "If there *is* a drug dealer, Ralph thinks he must operate somewhere in the park, probably not far from the community garden. He sent Adam to the park to check it out."

"Adam?"

"Officer Patterson," she said.

Right. Patterson. The guy she was dating. The jealous pang returned like a bitter tide, but he forced it away and changed the subject.

"What about the kid?" he asked.

"Jeff Miller? He's recuperating at home," she said. "I would have preferred to quarantine him for observation, but his parents wouldn't allow it. I think they're spooked enough as is."

"I would be too, if it were my kid," Booker said. "Will you let me know if you learn anything else?"

"Of course." Laura sighed heavily. "Now I have about ten minutes to eat breakfast before my first patient of the day. I didn't get to eat before. It's been a crazy morning."

Booker smiled to himself. "A yogurt and strawberry smoothie, right?"

"What can I say?" she replied. "I'm a creature of habit."

"I remember."

Laura was quiet a moment. He wondered if she was lost in her memories like he was.

"I guess I'm predictable," she said.

That got a laugh out of him. "Never. You always kept me on my toes, Laura. That was something I liked about you."

She laughed too. The sound of it made him feel lighter inside somehow.

"I'm glad the memories aren't *all* bad," she said.

There were a thousand things he wanted to say to her then— that he missed her, that he wished things had turned out differently, that he regretted not trying harder to make their relationship work after he moved—but what he said was, simply, "None of them are bad."

She exhaled through her nose, a sound she often made when she was amused by something. How many times had he heard that sound? He never realized how much he missed it.

"I really should go, Booker. Let's talk again soon, okay? Maybe we can get together for coffee sometime and catch up."

"I'd like that," he said. There was an awkward silence between them, an empty space full of promise and possibility in which neither of them wanted to hang up. Then, before he could stop it, the words escaped his mouth like floodwater, "I heard you were seeing someone. That Patterson guy."

Oh God, I sound like a dick, he thought. *I should've just hung up.*

"Not anymore. We weren't a good match," she said. "Anyway, how did you know about Adam? Have you been checking up on me?"

"I promise I'm not a stalker," he said. "Sofia told me when I ran into her."

"She does love to gossip, that one," Laura said. "Take care, Booker. I'll call you if I hear anything else."

"Thanks."

After he ended the call, the smile was slow to fade from his face. He felt like he was coming alive again, waking from a long, numb sleep.

Something she said stuck with him. If someone was selling drugs in the park, he knew who he had to talk to next. Booker found the name in his phone and tapped the contact. The ants on his deck swarmed chaotically, a swirling mess of tiny black dots. Whatever they were looking for, they hadn't found it yet.

"What?" Victor Cunningham answered tersely. It was how he always answered the phone, expecting it to be either a sales call or the IRS.

"Victor, it's Booker."

The old man's tone of voice changed instantly. "Hey, son. How's it hanging?"

Victor had called him son for as long as Booker could remember. It was a nickname, but it was something more than that, too. Booker never really knew his father, although he had flashes of memories of the man. He was four years old when his father went to fight in the Gulf War in 1990 and took an Iraqi bullet outside Kuwait City. Victor had served with him during the war, and when he came back he acted as a kind of surrogate father for Booker, a role that continued throughout Booker's life. He couldn't remember when Victor had started calling him son, but he didn't mind it.

"Hey, did you hear what happened at the town hall yesterday?" Victor asked. "I ran that big-city ratfucker out of the room!"

Booker chuckled. "Oh, I heard. It's the talk of the town. If you weren't a crazy old recluse, you'd be everyone's hero."

"Story of my life," Victor said. "So to what do I owe the pleasure of this call?"

"I need your help with something," he said. "I can't give you too many details because there's an ongoing police investigation."

"I already don't like the sound of this," Victor said.

"You wouldn't happen to know anything about someone selling magic mushrooms to high school kids, would you?"

There was a moment of silence, and then Victor said, "You really think I would do something like that? Just because I grow 'em, you think I'm enough of a rat bastard to sell 'em to kids? You're out of your fuckin' mind. You know me better than that. They're for personal consumption only."

"I know, I know," Booker said, trying to calm him down. "I'm not saying it was you."

"Good, because I haven't sold drugs outside the high school since '82."

Sometimes Booker didn't know if Victor was joking or not. The old man had led a life Booker only knew the half of. Most people considered Victor nothing but a junkie, just another waste-case vet so strung out he didn't know up from down. They thought of him with pity or disgust, if they thought of him at all, but Booker saw a darker truth under all the drug use and bravado. He was convinced Victor had experienced something during the war, maybe seen something or done something, that made him want to blow his mind with drugs in the hope of forgetting. Booker never asked what it was. He doubted Victor would tell him if he did.

"I just thought you might have heard something, Victor," he said.

"There's a reason I live all the way out in the woods, son. I don't like other people. So no, I haven't heard anything, because that would involve having conversations with them. Also, just FYI, at the top of the list of the many, many people I don't like are cops. I can't say I'm thrilled you're working with them."

"Laura needed my help," he said.

"Laura?" Victor said. "Shit, you never could say no to that girl."

"I was just helping her out," he said. "It was professional courtesy."

Victor snorted. "Sure it was. Listen, son, like I said, I don't talk to people much, but if I hear anything about some pigfucker selling drugs to kids, I'll let you know."

"Thanks, I appreciate it," Booker said. "Take care, Victor."

"Keep on keepin' on."

Booker ended the call. The ants scuttled back and forth across his deck. Then, suddenly, they formed an orderly line and marched off, as if something were calling them.

9

It had been two months since his wife Isabella passed on, and Kenneth Dalpe knew the only way to get through the pain of missing her was to keep himself busy. The trouble was finding ways to do it. He'd only gone to the town hall yesterday to hear Sean Hilton, the vice president of Bluecoal, talk about developing Dradin Park because it was something to take his mind off the depressing memories of Isabella wasting away in her sick bed. Yet even among the crowd he'd felt alone. All he could think was what Isabella would make of it all. Luckily, Dr. Powell had found him. Laura, as she always insisted he call her, had been kind enough to let him sit with her, and then that crazy old recluse Victor Cunningham had made a scene. Kenneth enjoyed it, felt more alive than he had in ages, but the feeling didn't last. Once the meeting was over and he went back home, the memories of Isabella were everywhere, and loneliness took a bite out of him again.

He remembered sitting beside the bed holding her frail hand, the oxygen tube under her nose like a gag mustache from a joke shop. Age and illness had made her so small and withered she was almost lost in the sheets. Laura was her physician in those final days. When she told Kenneth there wasn't much time left and he ought to say goodbye while he had the chance, he didn't. He refused. Instead, he held Isabella's hand and told her he was coming right behind her, that it wouldn't be long before they were together again. Two months had passed since then, however, and his damned eyes kept opening in the morning. His cursed heart kept beating.

After spending all day at home today, Kenneth decided after an early dinner to visit Dradin Park. It was the place he and Isabella had loved to go together in younger, healthier days, and walking the park's curated paths made him feel closer to her again. He saw a few people in the park with him, nodding pleasantly to them as he walked by, but not many. Most were home for the evening by now, eating dinner or watching TV with their families. He hoped they knew how good they had it.

It didn't take long for his legs to get tired, a reminder that he wasn't as young as he used to be. He decided to sit for a minute on a park bench near the gate to the community garden. (It was the same bench where, had he been there two nights ago, he would have stumbled across Kat Bishop and her girlfriend Tasha necking, a sight that would have embarrassed him but not offended him, as he considered himself the live-and-let-live type.) Kenneth sat and watched the sunset.

A profound sadness swept over him again. He would miss this park when they turned it into condos. Then he would have even less to remember Isabella by. He felt so lost without her. A tear tickled the corner of his eye, and he wiped it away angrily. Hadn't he cried enough? How could there be any tears left? The thought of returning to his empty house filled him with dread. He couldn't go on like this.

A noxious odor came to him on the wind. He crinkled his nose and looked around. It seemed to be coming from beyond the painted wooden fence around the community garden. He got up and moved toward the tall wooden gate. It was carved with a design that depicted snaking vines sprouting with star-shaped leaves. An arch over it proudly displayed the words Sakima Community Garden.

The smell got stronger as he approached. Whatever the source of the foul odor was, he was getting closer. It smelled like rot. It smelled like death. He reached for the gate.

Something moved through the trees nearby, shaking the branches. Kenneth froze. Odds were good it was nothing more than a deer or raccoon. Still, there'd been a news report recently that black bears were making a comeback in the Hudson Valley, some of them bold enough to lumber right into people's yards. He backed away from the gate and started moving down the park path back the way he'd come. Kenneth wasn't about to take any chances. His days of being able to outrun a bear were long behind him.

A shape crashed out of the trees. It wasn't a bear, it was a man. Kenneth halted his retreat. The way the man was moving, something was wrong with him. Either that or he was drunk. He lurched and weaved across the grass.

"You okay, son?" Kenneth called out.

The man didn't answer. He was wearing the blue uniform of a police officer, only it was covered in dirt and leaves as though he'd been rolling on the ground. As the man came closer, Kenneth recognized his face, although it was streaked with dirt, and more leaves were stuck in the tangles of his hair.

"Officer Patterson?" Kenneth said. "Adam, are you all right?"

Adam's eyes were wide but his mouth was wider, stretching into a toothy grin. He laughed, and the sound of it made Kenneth step back. Something was definitely wrong with Adam, and Kenneth didn't feel safe. He took another step back and tripped on a twig, sending him off balance. Kenneth fell to the paved path, the hip and arm that he landed on both flaring with sharp pain. Adam loomed over him. His pupils were so dilated his eyes looked like black pools. He brought his hand up to his mouth and blew across his palm, and a dark cloud of something that felt like powder struck Kenneth's face.

He coughed and choked as the powder went into his nose, mouth, and throat. His skin itched and burned where it touched him.

"What—what was that?" he rasped. His eyes watered. His throat was tight and dry. He could barely get the words out between hacking coughs. "What did you do to me?"

Adam stood over him, the delirious grin still on his face.

Frightened and confused, Kenneth watched as more dark figures emerged from the trees.

10

A loud banging woke Booker. His room was pitch dark when he opened his eyes. No light came in through the blinds he'd drawn over the window. Dazed and only half awake, he reached for his phone on the bedside table and saw it was only a little after two in the morning. The banging came again, and this time he realized it was coming from the front door downstairs. Who the hell was pounding on his door at this time of night?

He got up and put on a robe over his pajamas. More banging, furious and insistent. Whoever it was, they sounded like they weren't going to stop anytime soon. Booker left his bedroom, then thought better of it and returned to grab the aluminum baseball bat out of his closet. He crept down the stairs, holding the bat in both hands like he was ready to knock a curveball out of the park. He wondered if he was being foolish. This was Sakima, after all, where the crime rate was so low most people didn't bother locking their doors at night.

But Booker did. Locking his door was a habit he'd picked up in California, and right now, as someone outside continued pounding their fist against the door, he was glad he did. When he reached the bottom of the steps, he switched on the light.

"Who is it?" he shouted. "You ever hear of a doorbell?"

No answer, just more banging. He inched toward the door until he was able to look through the peephole. It was too dark outside to see anything other than the outline of a man, but when the figure turned slightly, the moonlight glinted off a brass badge on his chest.

The police? His first thought, his *only* thought, was that something had happened to Laura. He quickly unlocked the door and opened it.

Bathed in the light that spilled from inside, the police officer who stood in the doorway didn't look right. He was smudged and spattered with dirt. His uniform was disheveled, with his shirt half untucked. He had a lunatic grin on his face and eyes that looked right through Booker. Something was very wrong with him. Booker knew right away he'd made a mistake opening the door.

The officer lifted his cupped hand to his pursed lips. Booker didn't hesitate. He swung the bat and knocked the officer's hand aside. A dark brown powder spilled from his palm and dispersed into the air. The officer's thumb was bent at a strange angle, possibly broken from the strike of the aluminum bat, but he didn't look or act like he was in any pain. He didn't seem to feel it at all. Booker reached to slam the door closed, but the officer was inside before he could.

"You shouldn't have done that, Booker," he said. His voice was high, as though he were on the verge of laughter.

Booker cocked the bat, ready to swing again if he had to. "You know me?"

His eyes went to the metal name plate under the officer's badge. It read Patterson.

Adam Patterson. Laura's ex. What the hell was he doing here?

"You better leave now," Booker said, shaking the bat.

Adam advanced slowly. He smelled of mud and dirt and dried leaves. "Are you a churchgoing man, Booker? Have you read your Bible?"

"I'm not going to warn you again," he said.

"In the Book of Genesis, when Onan spilled his seed upon the ground, he was judged a sinner for it and slain." Adam looked at his empty hand, his crooked thumb. "You've gone and spilled an even more important seed, Booker. Divine seed. You know what the punishment is."

Adam leapt at him. Booker swung the bat, but Adam blocked it with his forearm. The blow was hard enough to fracture his ulna, but no pain registered on Adam's face. He yanked the bat out of Booker's hands and tossed it aside. Booker tried to run, but Adam tackled him to the floor. The officer's gritty, dirt-crusted hands wrapped around Booker's throat.

"You're a dog, Booker. Sniffing around what doesn't belong to you. Trying to take what's mine. You could have been something more. You could have been one of us." Adam squeezed his neck hard. "I'll be visiting Laura next. Maybe she'll put up a fight like you. I hope she does. I wouldn't mind teaching her a lesson or two before bringing her into the fold. The bitch has got it coming."

Booker gasped for air and slapped at Adam's face. The officer's eyes were bloodshot. His pupils were so dilated Booker couldn't tell what color his eyes were normally. Thin, white strings dangled wormlike from the corners of Adam's eyes, near the tear ducts.

Booker fought to breathe, but it was a losing battle. Adam's grip on his throat was tight and unyielding. Booker's fingers grasped for the handle of the baseball bat that lay just out of reach. His vision started to dim as his brain struggled with the lack of oxygen. In another few seconds, he would pass out, and if Adam kept up the pressure on his throat he would die. His fingers inched across the carpet, desperate to reach the bat. His fingertips brushed the cool metal knob at the base of the handle, then closed around it.

He slammed the bat into Adam's side. He was weak and the angle was wrong for the blow to do any real damage, but it was enough to knock Adam off him. Booker scrambled to his feet as quickly as he could. Adam was already rising from the carpet, ready to spring at him again. Booker swung the bat like he was swinging for the bleachers, and the aluminum barrel struck Adam in the side of the face with a satisfying crack. Adam spun around, spitting blood, and crumpled to the floor. He didn't get back up.

Breathing hard through his aching throat, Booker crouched beside him and felt his neck for a pulse. Adam was still alive. He stood again. What the hell was all this about? Attacking him, talking about the Bible, threatening Laura? Adam must have lost his mind.

A noise behind him caught his attention. He turned, realizing he'd left the door open. Another figure stood in the doorway, an older man, stooped and gray. He chuckled to himself as though he'd seen something funny.

"My wife, Isabella, she's come back," the old man said. A long string of drool hung from his lower jaw. "Kenneth and Isabella, together again. Don't you see her? She's right there."

He pointed into an empty corner of Booker's living room.

"It can give you anything you want, you know," Kenneth said. "Just like it gave Isabella back to me. All you have to do is let it in."

From behind, Adam shoved past Booker and ran out the door. Booker cursed himself. He let the old man distract him and didn't see Adam regain consciousness. Booker ran to the door. Outside, in the moonlight, he saw Adam and Kenneth run across the street, heading for Dradin Park opposite Booker's house.

They weren't alone. More figures sprinted through the dark toward the park, coming from all directions. Among them was a small, skinny boy dragging the remains of a smashed violin behind him.

Was that Jeff Miller, the boy Laura had told him about who tested positive for psilocybin? And were the two adults running behind him his parents?

What the hell is going on?

Booker closed and locked the front door. He went upstairs to the bedroom, taking the aluminum bat with him, and called Ralph Gorney's cell. He sat on the edge of the bed and listened to it ring.

"Come on, pick up the damn phone," he muttered. He went to the bedroom window, pulled aside the shade, and looked outside. The figures were gone. They'd disappeared into Dradin Park.

"Hello?" Ralph's tired voice came through the phone.

"Ralph, it's Booker," he said.

"Booker? What are you doing? Do you have any idea what time it is?"

"Ralph, listen to me," he said. "Officer Patterson was just here. He was acting strange, saying some really weird shit, and then he attacked me."

"Wait, what?" Booker heard the sound of sheets rustling as Ralph came to full attention. "Adam *attacked* you?"

"I don't know what the hell is going on, but he threatened Laura, too. He said something about going after her and teaching her a lesson."

"Christ," Ralph said. "He and Laura just broke up, and now her old flame is back in town. I should have seen this coming. He's too impulsive, too jealous."

"I think it was more than that," Booker said. "There was something wrong with him, Ralph. *Really* wrong. He was filthy, his uniform was a mess, and he was rambling, quoting the Bible at me. There was someone else with him, too, an older man. He called himself Kenneth."

"Kenneth Dalpe?" Ralph said. "What was he doing there with Adam? I've never seen the two of them together before."

"After Adam attacked me, they both ran into the park," Booker said. "There were others, too. I saw them, maybe a dozen more people, all running into the park at the same time."

Ralph was silent a moment, thinking. "I've been trying to reach Patterson all day. I sent him to the park to follow up on a lead, but I never heard from him afterward."

"Well, he's back now," Booker said, rubbing his sore neck. "Look, if he's part of some kind of cult or conspiracy—"

"Whoa, whoa, whoa," Ralph interrupted. "This is Sakima. There are no cults here."

"Fine," Booker said. "Whatever it is, the park must be where he and the others gather. You've got to close it. Don't let anyone inside until you've got a handle on this."

"That's going to be hard to do," Ralph said. "People love that park, and keeping them away from the community garden ..."

"You've got to, Ralph. If they attacked me, they're going to attack others. The park isn't safe as long as those people are in there."

"Okay," Ralph said with a groan. "It'll be a shit show, but I'll see what I can do."

Relieved, Booker tried to let himself relax, but his body continued to tremble from the adrenalin. "He threatened Laura, Ralph. Do me a favor and make sure she's okay, will you?"

"I'll call her and send a car to her house. They'll keep an eye out for Adam or anyone else."

"Thank you." Booker went to the window again and pushed the blinds aside to peer out into the night.

Ralph lowered his voice so the baby wouldn't hear him swear. "Shit, Booker. This is my city. I'm responsible for it. What the fuck is going on?"

Across the street, Dradin Park was a vast, dark emptiness.

"I wish I knew," he said.

11

The more Booker thought about his violent encounter with Adam Patterson, the more he was convinced his aluminum bat wasn't enough to keep him safe. There was no guarantee Adam or any of the others he'd seen running into the park with him like a pack of wolves under cover of night wouldn't come back for him, especially since he lived right across the street from the park. The sharp ache in his throat was all the proof he needed that these people weren't fucking around. If they came back, he would need better protection. He needed a gun, and he knew just where to get one.

In the morning, Booker left his house, looking across the street at the park, which was now fully visible in the sunlight. His was a side view of the park, mostly of the brick wall that surrounded it and the treetops that towered over the wall. Were Adam and the others still in there? If so, what were they doing? At the park entrance, which he could only partially see from his house, interlocking steel barricades has been set up, and two uniformed officers stood guard. Ralph had been true to his word and closed the park to the public, but would two officers and some portable steel barricades be enough to contain the group he'd seen last night? There'd been a dozen of them, at least.

Booker walked to his SUV parked in the driveway, got in, and drove toward Victor Cunningham's house on the outskirts of town. On the way, he passed a house with police tape over the door, then another, and a third that had a police cruiser parked in front. Booker slowed as he passed by, but he couldn't see anything through the house's windows.

It was clear he wasn't the only one who'd been attacked

last night. He counted seven houses marked as crime scenes by police tape over their doors, and that was just along the street where he drove. Who knew how many others there were throughout Sakima? A police cruiser zipped by him, lights flashing, presumably on its way to yet another crime scene.

Why had they attacked people last night? What were they trying to do?

You could have been one of us.

Victor's house stood at the end of a dirt road in the woods, a rustic wooden split-level that wouldn't have been out of place in the Old West. Victor loved the solitude and isolation that came from living so far from town, but it made Booker nervous as he got out of the SUV. He looked over his shoulder at the trees. There were plenty of places for Adam and his buddies to hide in the woods, and no one around but Victor to come to his aid if they attacked again.

He shook it off. There was no reason to believe they would come this far out. All the houses they'd targeted were closer to the center of town. Closer to the park.

Booker rapped on the front door. He knew Victor would be home—the old man didn't go anywhere if he could help it—but since it wasn't noon yet, the only question was whether he was awake.

He was. Victor opened the door in a pair of white shorts and a navy-blue short-sleeved shirt with little sailboats on it.

"Booker!" he said. "What are you doing here, son?"

"I need a gun," Booker replied.

Victor nodded stoically. "Then you'd better come inside."

Booker stepped into Victor's living room, which was as messy as ever. Bookshelves were filled to overflowing, while the floor was crowded with stacks of more books that couldn't fit. Novels by Henry Miller, Ayn Rand, George Orwell, William Styron, and Tom Wolfe were scattered among books like *The Anarchist Cookbook*, *A People's History of the United States*, and *Pedagogy of the Oppressed*. The coffee table and couch were strewn with newspapers, some of them weeks old, in which select paragraphs had been circled in pen and handwritten notes were jotted in the margins. A tattered and charred American flag from

Victor's tour of Iraq hung framed on the wall. Next to it was a photograph of Hunter S. Thompson with the quote: "I hate to advocate drugs, alcohol, violence, or insanity to anyone, but they've always worked for me."

"So what do you need a gun for?" Victor asked, closing and locking the door.

"Because people have lost their damned minds," Booker said. "Someone attacked me in my own home in the middle of the night. Look at this."

He pulled down the collar of his shirt so Victor could see the bruises on his neck. The old man winced and shook his head.

"Looks nasty," he said.

"It wasn't just him, either. There's a whole group of people acting crazy."

"That's nothing new. People have been acting crazy since 1974," Victor said. He brought Booker deeper into the house, through the living room and into the hallway that led to the kitchen. "I blame the Republicans."

"What happened in 1974?" Booker asked.

"Ford pardoned Nixon," he said. "That was the day our political class learned they could do whatever they wanted without consequences. No charges, no trials, no removal from office, no jail time. What kind of message do you think that sent everyone else? It told 'em nothing matters. Do what you want. Have at it. 1974, son. That was when the whole country took a nosedive into the loony bin."

Victor opened a closet door in the hallway. Inside, the narrow space was cluttered with brooms, mops, and other cleaning equipment. He pulled a shotgun out of the back.

"You keep a shotgun in your broom closet?" Booker asked, although he shouldn't have been surprised. Victor lived off the grid and as far out of view of the government as he could. Part of that was due to his lifestyle, using and growing his own illegal drugs, and part of it was paranoia. He was convinced that because of the things he'd seen during the first Gulf War, the government would come for him one day. He wanted to be ready.

"If you think a shotgun in the broom closet is funny," Victor said, "you should see what I keep in the kitchen cupboard."

He handed the shotgun to Booker. It wasn't as heavy as he expected it would be, and it sat perfectly balanced in his hands. It was a nice-looking weapon, with a walnut stock, a nickel-plated bolt on the side, and a gold-coated trigger. Dual bead sights stood like soldiers at the end of a twenty-eight-inch barrel.

"She's a classic Remington Model 11-87 Sportsman, twelve-gauge," Victor said. "Holds four shells at a time, and it's autoloading, which means no pumping necessary. There's no learning curve here, son. She's about as point-and-shoot as you can get."

He reached up to the shelf in the closet and pulled a box of three-inch shotgun shells from behind a bottle of laundry detergent.

"You'd better take these too," he said, handing the box to Booker. "No point in waving a gun around if you can't back it up with some buckshot."

"Thank you," Booker said. "I feel better already."

"Outside of New York City, you're not required to have a license to own a rifle or shotgun in this state, so don't worry about that," Victor said. "I've got plenty more I can give you if you want."

"This will be fine," Booker said. "I probably won't even have to use it, but better safe than sorry."

"Words to live by," Victor said. "Now, if there's nothing else you need, I ought to get back to tending to my boys downstairs." He gestured over his shoulder at the basement door just past the kitchen.

"You mean your magic mushrooms," Booker said.

"Don't be a square, son. No one has called them that since the Sixties," Victor scoffed. "Shrooms, maybe. You're not going to accuse me of selling them to children again, are you?"

"No," Booker said. "You haven't heard anything about who might be selling them, have you?"

"Not a peep," Victor said. "Can you see yourself out?"

"Sure thing. I'll have the gun back to you soon, I'm sure."

"Take your time," Victor said. "Plenty of fuckers out there who could benefit from staring down the barrel of a shotgun every now and then. Close the front door behind you, would you? Had a raccoon sneak in here a couple weeks ago. The ass-hole stayed under my sink long enough I could have charged him rent."

Victor turned and walked toward the basement door. His shoes left dark, dusty tracks on the floor. Something about it looked familiar to Booker.

"What's on your shoes?" he asked.

Victor looked down at the prints he'd left on the floor behind him. "That? Mushroom spores. My boys are fruiting. Damn stuff gets all over everything."

Booker crouched down and picked up a pinch of the spores from the floor. He rolled the fine, brown powder between his thumb and forefinger. Immediately, he realized where he'd seen it before. It was the same powder Adam Patterson was holding before Booker knocked his hand away with the bat.

Why would Adam come to my house with a handful of mushroom spores?

He thought of the psilocybin in Kat's and Jeff's systems, and the mycelium growing inside Kat's body. It was inside Jeff's body, too. Laura had seen it. And Booker saw it last night, didn't he? The strings dangling from the corners of Adam's eyes were hyphae. The fungus was inside Adam. Was it inside Kenneth Dalpe, too? What about the group of people he'd seen running into the park?

It can give you what you want, you know. Just like it gave Isabella back to me. All you have to do is let it in.

"Shit!" Booker stood up, letting the spores drop to the floor. They left a stain like cocoa powder on his fingertips. He hoisted the shotgun over his shoulder, letting it hang there on its woven paracord shoulder sling, and ran out the door. He pulled out his phone and called Laura.

"Booker?" she said when she picked up. "Are you all right? Ralph said Adam attacked you last night!"

"I'm okay." He got into the driver's seat of his SUV and slammed the car door closed. "I need you to meet me at my place, Laura. I think I know what's going on."

12

Laura ran out of her house to her car. Booker's phone call had sounded urgent. She was surprised, and yet also not, to see Melanie Elster opening the door of Laura's mailbox and sliding something into it.

"What are you doing here, Melanie?" Laura said.

The old woman looked up at her in surprise, her wrinkled face scrunching in disdain. "Oh, you're here. I might as well give this to you." She removed the note from the mailbox and held it out to Laura. "It's about your trash containers. When you put them out for pickup last night, they were in the wrong spot. They're not supposed to be touching the sidewalk, but the corner of one of them—"

"I don't have time for this," Laura said, walking past her. She got into her car. Through her windshield, she saw Melanie waving the note like the flag of a conquering army.

"Leaving your trash containers in the wrong area makes the streets dirty!" the old woman shouted. "Only bad neighborhoods have dirty streets! You don't want this to turn into a bad neighborhood, do you?"

Laura rolled her eyes and drove away. Let the old bat take it to the homeowners' association if she wanted. Laura had more important things to worry about than whether her trash containers were accidentally touching the sidewalk.

Her route to Booker's house brought her past Dradin Park, where she saw two police officers stationed by the barricaded entrance. Hiding somewhere inside the park was Adam, a man she thought she knew but obviously didn't. Ralph called in the middle of the night to tell her Adam had gone berserk, broken into Booker's house and physically assaulted him, and then fled into the park. She was horrified but relieved that Booker was okay. She kept thinking about the way Adam grabbed her arm yesterday when she tried to walk away from him. She knew he would be angry after she broke up with him, but to go after Booker, who had nothing to do with it? She never would have imagined him doing such a thing.

Ralph told her other people were involved, too, who'd also fled to the park, Kenneth Dalpe among them. It was hard for her to believe the old widower could do anything violent or criminal. He'd always been so gentle and introverted. A lot of people had been acting out of character lately. Taking drugs. Crashing through windows. Attacking people. Booker said he had an idea what was happening, and she was eager to hear it.

The GPS informed her she'd arrived at the address he gave her. She parked her car at the curb, got out, and walked the flagstone path that cut through a large, green lawn to the front door. Booker had bought a modest two-story house, painted a slate gray with white trim. Not bad for a high school science teacher. She rang the bell and waited. There were scuff marks in the wooden door as though someone had been really pounding on it. Was that Adam? Had he tried to break it down?

Booker opened the door, and Laura threw her arms around him in a tight hug. He was as surprised as she was. She hadn't intended to do that. She broke away and said, "Sorry, I'm—I'm just glad you're okay. It must have been so frightening!"

"I'm fine," he said. "Just a little bruised. Come in."

As soon as she was inside, Booker locked the door, and she made a mental note to start locking her own door too, at least until Adam was in custody. Booker showed her into the living room. It was bright and airy, with a white sofa that matched the painted white bricks of the fireplace, but the room wasn't complete. The built-in shelves sat empty, and three cardboard moving boxes were acting as a makeshift coffee table.

"Sorry about the mess," he said. "I've ordered some more furniture, but it hasn't come yet."

"I'm the one who should apologize," Laura said. "I think Adam coming here was my fault. He's a jealous, possessive man, but I never thought he would do something like that."

"It's not your fault," he said. "And I don't think that's what brought him here. Not entirely, anyway. That's what I wanted to talk to you about."

He gestured for her to sit on the couch, then disappeared into the kitchen. When he returned, he was holding two opened bottles of Fat Tire Belgian Ale.

"You remembered my favorite beer," she said with a grin. "But it's kind of early for a drink, isn't it?"

"I think you're going to need it," he said, passing one bottle to her. "I think we both are."

She put the bottle down on one of the boxes. "What is it?"

Ralph sighed, sat down next to her on the couch, and took a swig from his beer.

"I made a mistake, Laura. I've been looking at it all wrong," he said. "All this time, I thought Kat Bishop took psilocybin mushrooms before she died and the mycelium inside her was somehow a side effect of that. But I got it backward."

Laura took a sip of her beer. She got the sense he was struggling with what he wanted to tell her, as though he thought she wouldn't believe him.

"I don't think Adam was in full control of himself when he came here," he said. "I don't think *any* of them were in control. I think they were under the influence, just like Kat and Jeff were."

"Psilocybin?"

"Yes." He took another swig of his beer, then put it down. "Except I think it's coming from spores. Fungal spores. They're airborne, which makes them particularly hard to trace, but I think they're coming from somewhere in the park."

"What makes you think it's spores?" she asked.

"Because last night Adam was carrying a handful of spores with him," he said. "I think he was going to do something with them before I knocked them out of his hand. I think he was going to do something to *me*. If I'm right, I bet the other people I saw were carrying spores too, taking them to other houses."

"I don't understand," Laura said. "Why would they?"

"To infect people, the same way they're infected." Even though what he was saying sounded outlandish, she could tell he was serious. "I think it's the spores that are responsible for the fungi growing inside each of them, and it's those fungi that are pumping their systems full of psilocybin. There's no drug dealer. No one sold those kids mushrooms. They were infected by the spores."

"Even if that's true, why would they want to infect others?" she asked.

"Reproduction." He took another drink. She could tell he was stalling. "I know this is hard to believe, but hear me out. When I said those were under the influence, I meant it literally. I believe they're being manipulated by the fungi inside them."

"You're joking," she said. "Fungi can't really do that, can they? *Manipulate* people?"

Booker stood up and went to the living room window. He looked out at the park across the street with such intensity she wondered if he was trying to see through the brick wall.

"Have you ever heard of the *Massospora* fungus?" he asked. His eyes stayed focused on the park as he spoke. "Cicadas spend seventeen years underground when they're in their pre-adult form. When they finally burrow to the surface as adults, some of them encounter *Massospora* spores in the soil. Those spores enter the cicadas' bodies and grow into a fungus that takes control of them from within. It floods their brains with psilocybin to keep them drugged and docile."

"Like you think *this* fungus is doing," Laura said. "But David Miller was hardly docile. They had to give him a sedative at the police station just to calm him down. It doesn't sound like Adam was very docile, either."

He turned away from the window to face her. "It gets worse. About a week after the cicada's initial infection, things turn gruesome. The bottom half of the cicada falls off, including its genitals. In its place is a white plug of fungal spores, which the cicada proceeds to sprinkle on other cicadas like a salt shaker, repeating the cycle of infection. The fungus also forces adult male cicadas to try to mate with everything they encounter, whether it's another cicada or not, whether it's female or not, but since their genitalia are gone, all they do is shake more deadly spores onto their unwilling partners. An infected cicada won't live long. Just long enough to spread the spores to more cicadas and continue the fungus's lifecycle."

Laura thought a moment. "So the fungus drugs the insect with psilocybin so it won't put up a fight, and the mycelium attaches itself to the insect's muscles in order to control its actions, make it fly around and spread its spores."

Booker returned to the couch and sat beside her. "Sound familiar?"

It did. It sounded horribly familiar.

"You're thinking of what we found inside Kat Bishop's body," she said.

"Not just Kat. The same kind of fungus is in Jeff, Adam, Kenneth, and who knows how many others," he said. "It's pumping them full of drugs and using them to spread its spores, just like the *Massospora*. What I don't understand yet is why. There are plenty of other ways, much *better* ways, for a fungus to reproduce that don't involve humans."

Laura realized she was biting her nails and made herself stop. The bottle of beer sat untouched in front of her. It was all too awful to contemplate. Booker was wrong. There had to be some other solution, something that made more sense.

Booker finished his beer and brought the empty bottle back to the kitchen. When he returned, Laura said, "Has this ever happened before? To people, I mean, not cicadas."

"No," he said. "Not that I know of."

She chewed it over, trying to solve it like a riddle. "The infected cicadas must be operating on instinct, that's all. A fungus can't just manipulate another living thing to do its will."

"It's not as uncommon as you might think," he said. "Let me show you something."

He pulled one of the boxes out of its place in the make-shift coffee table. It was filled with books, which he rummaged through until he found a science textbook. He brought it over to the couch, sat beside her, and flipped through the pages until he found what he was looking for. It was a magnified photograph of a reddish-brown ant holding a segment of a green leaf in its mandibles.

"This is a leafcutter ant," he said. "They live mostly in South and Central America. Believe it or not, next to humans they form the largest and most complex societies on Earth. Their nests can contain up to eight million individuals. However, what most people don't know about leafcutter ants is that they don't eat the leaves they cut off the trees. They actually get their nutrients from drinking leaf sap. What they do with the leaves is bring them back to their nest and feed them to the *Lepiotaceae* fungus they keep there."

Laura studied the picture. The ant held the leaf cutting in its mandibles surprisingly gingerly, as though it were of supreme importance, an acolyte delivering a sacrifice to its god.

"They're gardeners," she said.

"More like servants," he said. "They feed and protect the fungus, and give it shelter in their nests. Scientists discovered the ants can tell when the fungus doesn't react positively to certain kinds of leaves and change up the menu accordingly. Think of it, eight million servants all tending to its needs. In return, the fungus acts as a renewable food source for the ant larvae. Basically, it allows a small part of itself be eaten in order to ensure that the larvae will grow up to continue feeding and protecting it. This relationship between ant and fungus has been going on for fifteen million years, a lot longer than we've been around."

She turned to him. Their faces were so close together she could smell the beer on his breath. Even with everything that was on her mind, she couldn't resist studying his face for a moment, refamiliarizing herself with it. His lips, which were slightly parted; the line of his jaw where it met the dark, curly hair of his goatee; the smooth, brown expanse of his slightly rounded cheek; the adorable way the top of his right ear bent outward just a bit. She'd forgotten about that.

She straightened and scooted away from him on the couch. What was she doing? She needed to focus.

"I thought you were a botanist," she said. "I didn't know you had an insect fetish."

He grinned. "When you're a scientist, they don't call it a fetish, they call it an area of interest."

"Anyway, what you described sounds like a mutually beneficial relationship between the ants and the fungus," she said.

"The ants aren't being manipulated."

"Are you sure?" He looked at the photo of the leafcutter ant again. "Who do you think is calling the shots in that relationship? The fungus, which spends its life being tended to in the safety of the nest, or the ants, who work all day to feed and protect it?"

"But it's not drugging them and taking control of their bodies like the *Massospora* does to the cicadas, right?"

"That's right."

"So how does the fungus communicate with the ants? How does it tell them it's dinnertime and they'd damn well better have some leaves for it?"

"No one knows," he said. "Scientists have been trying to unlock that mystery for years. It could be something as simple as a chemical signal, or it could be something more complicated. A form of communication we don't understand yet."

"This is ridiculous," she argued. "People aren't ants, they can't be controlled by a fungus. And how could a fungus control someone anyway? It doesn't have a brain. It doesn't even have a central nervous system. It's not intelligent."

Booker closed the textbook and put it back in the box.

"For centuries, we've judged the intelligence of other life forms by measuring them against our own," he said. "Maybe that was arrogant of us. How do we know there aren't other forms of intelligence in the world, ones that are completely alien to us? Ones we don't understand yet? Maybe it's time we expanded our definition of intelligence."

Laura picked up her bottle and took a long drink. Booker was right, she needed it.

"Look, I get it. I know it sounds far-fetched," he said. "It's just a hypothesis. I don't have any proof yet. When a fungal spore attacks a cicada, it takes a week for the mycelial network to spread through the cicada's system and overtake it. What happened to Adam and the others took a lot less time. A matter of hours, maybe. But that doesn't make sense. Humans are larger and more complex organisms than cicadas. If anything, it should take *longer*."

"Okay, let's think this through," Laura said. "If this has

never happened before *and* it's not happening in a manner consistent with its closest correlation, then we have two possible answers. The first is that the hypothesis is wrong. No offense."

"None taken," he said, closing the box and pushing it back with the others. "I'd actually be relieved if I was wrong."

"The other possible answer is that we're not dealing with a normal fungus, but with some kind of mutation," she said. "One that grows at an accelerated rate."

He looked up at her. "What could cause a mutation like that?"

It was Laura's turn to get up from the couch and walk to the window. Outside, Dradin Park looked quiet. What was happening on the other side of that brick wall? Was Adam still in there?

"Everyone knows the park used to be a landfill," she said. "There's hundreds of thousands of tons of garbage and who knows what rotting away under the ground. If some of that waste was toxic..."

Booker came up behind her. She felt him there, felt the heat of his body, before she saw his reflection in the glass.

"Fungi love decaying garbage, it's the perfect environment for them. They can eat to their hearts' content," he said. "But even if there were toxins in the garbage, it wouldn't be enough to cause a mutation this extreme. Fungi can adapt to whatever food source is available. Some were recently discovered breaking down polyurethane plastics. Another fungus was found in the fuel tanks of aircraft, digesting crude oil. No, there would have to be a catalyst, something from outside the existing ecosystem that acted as a mutagen. I'm guessing it would have to be recent too, if this fungus has only just started affecting people."

"How do we find out?" she asked.

"That's the other thing I wanted to talk to you about," he said. "I want to take some samples from the park for analysis."

She turned around, putting the window at her back. They were standing close together again. She didn't move away this time.

"I'll go with you," she said. "I want to help."

"It's too dangerous. I don't want you to risk getting infected like the others," he said. "Ralph's got the park locked up tight. I was hoping you could talk to him and convince him to let me go in."

"You can't do this alone," she said. "If you're right about the spores, you'll need protective equipment to make sure you don't get infected, and I'm pretty sure you don't have any PPE here. On the other hand, I do. I'm the medical examiner in this town, remember? So if you want to use that equipment, I'm coming with you."

"I just don't want anything to happen to you," he said. "Laura, if you got infected…"

He trailed off, not wanting to finish the sentence. Laura's gaze dropped from his eyes to his mouth, his full, exquisite lips. She wondered what his reaction would be if she leaned forward and kissed him. Was that really what she wanted? Or was it just the comfortable familiarity of the moment that put the thought in her head? They'd stood close like this so many times.

"I don't want you to get infected either," she said. "That's why we need the PPE."

He sighed. "There's no talking you out of this, is there?"

"Nope." She pulled the phone out of her pocket. "Let me call Ralph and see if he'll let us in."

She stepped out the front door for some privacy and made the call, keeping one eye on the park across the street. When Ralph picked up, she explained their need to get into the park, but he turned her down flat.

"Booker's the one who suggested I close it off in the first place, and he was right," Ralph said. "It's too dangerous to let anyone inside. Adam and the others still haven't come out. What does Booker want with samples anyway?"

"He's got a theory there's an infection moving from person to person like a virus," she said. "Only it's not a virus, it's fungal spores from somewhere in the park. It might be what's making people act crazy all of a sudden. Taking samples would help prove it, maybe even help us find a way to stop it."

"Even if I wanted to, I couldn't let you," Ralph said. "Sean Hilton from Bluecoal agreed with me about closing the park. He doesn't want anyone going in there either."

"Who gives a damn what he says?"

"That park is Bluecoal's land now," Ralph reminded her. "They bought it from the city. They get final say."

Laura sighed. "So what are we supposed to do?"

"My advice is to leave it alone," Ralph replied. "Like I said, Adam and the others are still in there somewhere. They're liable to attack anyone who enters the park just like they attacked folks last night. But we won't be waiting much longer for Adam and his friends to come out of their own accord. Mayor Harvey wanted us to hold off for a bit and see if they'll surrender themselves. He's worried about how a police raid will look during an election year."

"It figures," she said.

"Yeah, but I got him to give us the green light for first thing tomorrow morning. If they're not out by then, the whole damn police department is going in after them."

"You can't!" Laura said. "Please, at least let us make sure it's safe first. If Booker's right about the spores—"

"Sorry, but no," Ralph said. "Stay out of the park, Laura. You may only be a part-time police employee, but I'm the chief and an order is an order."

"Ralph," she said, but he ended the call. "Shit."

Laura went back inside. Booker was standing in the middle of the living room, waiting expectantly.

"What did he say?" he asked.

"He won't allow it," she told him. "He says it's too dangerous with Adam and the others still in there. Also, he's sending officers into the park tomorrow morning to go after them."

"Tomorrow? But the spores..."

"I know."

"What do we do?"

"We go in anyway." Laura took a deep breath. "We'll have to do it after dark, when no one will see us. Just in and out, real quick. Sofia can sneak the PPE out of the station for me. She owes me a favor."

"We'll never get inside the park," he said. "There's only one entrance, and the police are guarding it."

She smirked. "That's where you're wrong, Professor Coates. I know another way in."

13

Heather Bishop, mother of the deceased Kat Bishop, lifted a framed photograph of her daughter off the top of the living room credenza and tipped it to better catch the golden afternoon light from the windows. She held it close and ran her fingertips gently over the glass. The photograph had been taken when Kat was in seventh grade, and of course her daughter hated everything about it: the way her hair looked frizzy in her ponytail, the way her smile exposed the braces on her teeth. Heather thought she looked beautiful, like an angel. This was how she wanted to remember her daughter, still young and innocent.

Yesterday, Chief of Police Gorney had phoned to tell her they found drugs in Kat's system. Heather tuned out the rest of what Ralph said. She was too furious to listen. It was her worst fear confirmed: Her baby was doing drugs. It was a slap in the face, and that wasn't even the worst of it.

Not long after Ralph's phone call, the second shoe dropped. One of the other mothers from the high school called to offer her condolences, and when Heather asked how she knew Kat, the woman said Kat and her daughter were dating. Her *daughter*. She said it like it was no big deal, like this kind of thing happened all the time, but Heather's heart broke into sharp, angry pieces. Kat was dating another girl. Some dyke named Tasha. It was impossible. Tasha must have manipulated Kat into it. Filled her head with all sorts of radical, rebellious nonsense that Kat had gone along with just to hurt her parents. Well, it had worked. Mission accomplished. Heather and her husband George were already devastated by their daughter's death, but this news only crushed them further.

Tasha must have given Kat the drugs. Her daughter's dyke

drug dealer. Maybe it was the drugs that had turned Kat into a lesbian. Maybe Tasha had drugged Kat and forced herself on her.

Heather put down the picture of her daughter from happier, more wholesome times. George still wasn't home. She looked out the living room window, hoping to see his car pull into the driveway, but there was no sign of him. He should have been back from the funeral home by now. She'd insisted he go without her. It was still too soon; she couldn't bear the idea of making plans to bury her daughter. No parent should ever have to do such a thing, but George, bless him, was stronger than her. A man of fortitude and brass tacks. He would soldier through it.

She moved into the kitchen and filled the tea kettle with water. The thought of Kat's funeral filled her with dread, but not just because it would be her baby in the casket. There was no way she would be able to keep that bitch Tasha from showing up, and then everyone would know the truth. She could already imagine what everyone would say. They'd pretend to offer their condolences, but inside they would be judging her, wondering what kind of mother she was that her daughter had turned into a lesbian.

Worse, a lesbian *drug addict*.

She'd rifled through Kat's copy of last year's yearbook to find a picture of Tasha. The girl looked exactly how Heather expected: hefty, short hair, no makeup, a pierced eyebrow and a ring through her nose. She looked like trash. How could Kat be interested in someone like that? Where had she and George gone wrong? Where had they failed?

Heather put the filled kettle on a burner. Before she could light it, she heard the front door open.

"George?" she called.

She went back into the living room and froze. It wasn't George. Heather gasped and put a hand over her mouth. Two men creeped through the open door, dirty and disheveled. One she recognized as Rithvik Panchal, the Indian man who owned the parking lot on MacLeod Avenue. The other was Walter Monahan, who ran the green grocer. She'd never seen either of them like this before. They wore maniacal expressions on their dirt-smeared faces, their eyes wide, their mouths stretched in exaggerated grins. She backed away from them. A third figure came through the door behind them.

Heather stopped her retreat. Anger made her fear dissipate.

"You," she spat. "I know who you are! How dare you come here? You're the reason Kat is dead!"

Tasha grinned back at her. She was smeared with dirt, just like the other two. She wore a ripped and smudged men's bowling shirt with the name Norton written in cursive on the breast. Heather's anger boiled over. Was the filthy dyke on drugs right now? Were all three of them on drugs?

The ring in Tasha's nose caught the sunlight as she crept closer. "Kat isn't dead, Mrs. Bishop. No one is ever really gone. We're all connected. We're all one."

Something dark ran under Tasha's eyes. At first Heather thought it was drips of dark mascara, but as Tasha came closer, Heather saw it was blood. Her eyes were dark red and bleeding from the corners.

"Join us," Tasha said, reaching for her. "Serve with us, and it will give you whatever you want."

Heather spun and ran as quickly as she could into the kitchen. Tasha, Rithvik, and Walter ran after her, laughing like it was all just a big joke. Heather's heart pounded in her chest. This wasn't normal. Something was very wrong. Tasha's hand caught her shoulder near the stove. Heather wriggled out of her grasp and snatched up the tea kettle, wishing she'd had time to turn on the burner before they showed up. Boiling-hot water to the face would teach these people the right lesson. Instead, she swung the kettle like a club, the water inside it sloshing as Tasha ducked and the kettle struck Walter in the face. He reeled back. Blood streamed from his broken nose, but he didn't react. It was like he didn't even feel it. Heather ran for the screen door at the far end of the kitchen. She threw it open, ran outside, and hurried down the small staircase to the driveway out front.

George stood in the middle of the driveway. He wasn't alone. A group of people from town were with him, even the funeral director in his dark suit. They all had the same expression on their faces that Tasha did. A few of them were stained with dirt and grass. Heather froze. Someone in the crowd laughed. It wasn't a sane laugh.

"It's okay, Heather," George said, walking toward her. "It's okay."

"George?" she said. "What's—what's going on? Who are these people?"

"Everything is going to be okay," he said. "You'll see."

He hugged her, pulling her into his comforting embrace. Behind her, she could hear Tasha and the two men coming down the stairs from the kitchen.

George only had one arm around her. Heather thought that was strange, to hug someone you've been married to for so many years with only one arm. George had never hugged her like that before. She pulled away from him. He brought his free hand up to his mouth.

"You'll see," he said again, and blew a cloud of gritty, burning spores into her face.

14

Once the sun was down, Laura and Booker walked to Dradin Park under cover of darkness. They approached the park from the back, where there was less of a chance of being seen. The rear of the park faced an abandoned cluster of old warehouses from back when Sakima was an active port for cargo ships on the Hudson. If anyone *had* spotted them, they would have been surprised to see two people in full hazmat suits sneaking along the brick wall that surrounded the park, one of them with a shotgun strapped over his shoulder.

It had taken some doing for Laura to convince Sofia to bring her two disposable full-body protective suits from the police station. Unfortunately, they were bright white in color, and even in the twilight she was worried they stood out like sore thumbs. Adam or anyone else hiding inside the park would be able to spot them easily. It was a wonder they'd made it from Booker's house to the back of the park without drawing attention.

They didn't have a choice. If Booker was right about the spores, they couldn't risk exposure. In addition to their suits, they wore foot protection over their shoes and nitrile gloves on their hands. Under their full pullover hoods, they wore goggles and N95 respirators, which Laura had shown Booker how to properly fit so that minimal leakage would occur around the edges. She hoped it would be enough protection. They didn't know enough about the spores to be sure.

"There it is," Laura said. "The other way in."

She pointed to an old, gnarled tree that grew out of the sidewalk. About halfway up, one thick branch stuck straight out like a plank, passing over the wall and into the park. She and her friends used to sneak into the park this way all the time when she was a kid.

"We're going to have to climb it," Booker said, his voice muffled by his respirator. He adjusting the shotgun strapped over his shoulder.

She wished he hadn't brought the gun. If his theory was right, Adam and the others were sick and not in control of their actions. They needed help, not violence, but Booker wasn't taking any chances after Adam tried to kill him.

"Let me go first," she said. "I've done this before."

He turned to her, his eyes showing surprise under his goggles. "You have? When?"

"The last time was probably twenty years ago," she said. "But it's like riding a bicycle, right? You don't forget. At least, that's the theory."

Booker stood back as she scaled the tree. She hugged the trunk and shinnied upward, her feet remembering where to find knots in the bark that her conscious mind had long forgotten. She let her muscle memory guide her as she climbed up to the first layer of branches. She grabbed the closest branch and hoisted herself onto it. She would have to be careful amid the branches. Even the slightest rip in her protective suit would leave her vulnerable to the spores. When she reached the thick branch that extended over the wall, she moved cautiously down its length on all fours. Once she cleared the wall and was inside the park, she looked for a safe place to jump down. But as kids they hadn't needed to jump, had they? She remembered now that there was a boulder under the branch that they used to lower themselves down to easily, and then it was just a matter of climbing down the boulder, which wasn't very high. She was relieved to find the boulder still there, waiting for her all these years later. When she was back on the ground, she felt a surge of pride that she was still able to do something in her mid-thirties that she'd done as a kid. Or maybe it was just that the tree wasn't all that hard to climb.

A thought occurred to her then, one that sent a chill through her. If they could use the tree to get into the park this easily, who's to say Adam and the others weren't using it to get out of the park just as easily. No one would see them, not at the back of the park where the old warehouses were. They could leave any time, return any time, and no one would know. Only the park entrance was guarded.

As Booker made his way along the branch overhead, Laura got the feeling they weren't alone. Was someone watching them, or was she just scaring herself? She looked around the darkened grounds but didn't see anyone.

Booker climbed down the boulder. When his feet were on the ground, he said, "Let me see your suit."

"My suit? Why?"

"We need to check each other's suits to make sure there are no tears," he explained.

He went first, running his gloved hands over the back of her suit, and then along her legs. She was only wearing underwear beneath, and it felt unexpectedly intimate to feel his hands moving over the thin fabric, practically touching her skin. He did a visual check of the front of her suit—she supposed using his hands there would have been *too* intimate—and then it was her turn to do the same for him. The feeling of closeness and familiarity returned to her as she ran her hands along the smooth material of his bodysuit. She was surprised how much she could feel through her gloves. Like her, Booker was only wearing underwear beneath, and she could feel the muscles of his chest and arms through the fabric, the curve of his thigh. When she was done, she stepped quickly back. It took her a moment to find her voice.

"We have to be quick. We don't want to get caught."

The same words teenage lovers might say as they fumbled in the dark. She put the thought out of her mind. The past was the past. She and Booker were just friends now. Colleagues. That was all.

"Where did you want to take the samples from?" she asked.

"The community garden," he said. "Kat and Jeff both had a connection to it, so the garden might be where they were first infected. There's just one problem."

"What's that?"

"I can't remember where it is," he admitted. "I haven't been here in years."

She laughed under her respirator. "I'll lead the way."

They moved deeper into the park, walking on the grass like visiting aliens in their full-body protective suits. When they came to a paved path, it led them through a small grove of trees to the white gazebo that stood at the heart of the park. Laura remembered that she and Booker had been here before. Years ago, on their second date, they'd stood inside the gazebo and looked up at the stars. Fueled by the wine they'd had with dinner, and with no one else there to make them feel self-conscious, they'd kissed for the first time.

Laura looked back at Booker to see if he was thinking about that night too, but his expression was one of focused concentration. He had one thumb hooked under the shotgun sling, ready to pull the gun off his shoulder if anyone attacked them.

In another few minutes, they reached the painted fence that surrounded the community garden. As Laura opened the carved wooden gate, an awful stench came to her, strong enough to reach her through the N95 respirator. Booker smelled it, too.

"What is that?" he asked.

"Smells like something's rotting," she said.

They passed under the arch and into the garden. Three acres of Dradin Park were dedicated to the community garden. That was enough space for dozens of ten-by-ten plots arranged in neat rows. Laura remembered when the garden first opened how those plots had been marked off with simple wooden slats. Now, the slats had been replaced with more ornate, decorative borders of stone, cement, or iron work. People took pride in their plots. This was more than just a garden. It was the heart of Sakima.

The odor was even stronger within the garden's walls. It came from every direction. Laura walked along the gravel path between plots, keeping an eye out for the brass spigots that rose out of the ground at intervals where gardeners could hook up their hoses.

As her eyes adjusted and the dark plots came into focus, she saw where the stench was coming from. Everything was dead. The lettuce and zucchini. The asparagus and carrots and peppers.

Tomatoes on the vine looked like dark, shriveled stones. In plot after plot, everything was withered and limp.

"What happened here?" Laura asked.

Booker knelt beside a plot. With his gloved hand, he inspected a rotting zucchini that hung limply off its dead plant. "Come here, look at this."

She crouched next to him. Booker brushed his fingertips over the zucchini and showed her the brown, dusty smear left behind on the fingers of his gloves.

"Spores," he said. "It's covered with them."

Booker moved to the next plot and brushed his fingers across the ridged exterior of a wilted head of lettuce. His gloved fingertips came back coated with more of the same fine powder.

"The spores are everywhere," he said. "We must be near the source."

Laura stood and looked around the garden. She couldn't see all of it in the dark. There were shadows everywhere, and the farthest end seemed to disappear into an inky void. Was the fungus somewhere in here, growing in one of the plots? She pictured its mutated mushroom—in her mind a twisted, bulbous monstrosity—pushing up out of the dirt and pumping the air full of poisonous spores.

She froze. Something moved in the distant shadows.

"Booker," she whispered. "I thought I saw something over there."

He stood up and squinted into the darkness. He took the shotgun off his shoulder and pointed it into the night.

"Is someone there?" he called. "Show yourself!"

Only the sound of nighttime insects answered him. Laura waited, holding her breath, listening for a snapping twig, the crunch of gravel underfoot, any sound that meant someone was lurking in the dark. Nothing came. Finally, Booker lowered the shotgun.

"I don't like this," he said.

"Me neither," Laura said. "Let's get the samples and get out of here."

Booker plucked the zucchini free and placed it carefully into one of the plastic evidence bags Sofia had brought along with the PPE. Laura sealed the bag while he pulled the head of lettuce out of the soil and put it into another one. Once both were sealed tight, they turned on the nearest spigot and rinsed off any spores that had stuck to the outside of the bags. They did the same to their gloves, and then they left the garden.

They walked quickly back the way they came. As they passed the gazebo, Laura felt like she was being watched again. The feeling was stronger this time, more urgent than before. She turned and looked behind her.

Was that movement she saw in the trees? Were there shapes in the darkness? When she tried to focus on them, they were gone. A shiver crawled up her spine, and she continued with Booker toward the tree that would take them over the wall and out of the park.

15

When they got back to Booker's house, Sofia was waiting for them in the driveway, leaning against the side of her car and scrolling through something on her phone. The light from the screen lit her face from beneath, accentuating her high cheekbones and reflecting off her glasses. Laura was relieved to see she was still there. She'd asked Sofia to wait for them, but their expedition to the park had taken longer than expected and she was worried Sofia would be gone when they got back. The lab tech looked up at them, turned off her phone, and slid it into her coat pocket. Then, as Laura had instructed her, she put on her own N95 respirator.

"Jesus, look at you two," Sofia said. "You look like you walked out of that Dustin Hoffman movie with the escaped lab monkey."

"Thanks for waiting for us," Laura said. "Did you put on the gloves, too?"

Sofia lifted both hands and wiggled her fingers to show she was wearing blue nitrile gloves. "Done and done."

"Good," Laura said. "And the bag?"

Sofia opened the car door and pulled a large blue insulated storage tote out of the back seat. She put it down on the driveway, unzipped it, and then stepped back a few feet from it, another precaution Laura had asked her to take. Laura placed the two evidence bags into the tote.

"What are those, plants?" Sofia asked. "Ugh, is that a head of lettuce? It looks rotten."

"They're from the community garden." Laura zipped the tote closed and stepped back so Sofia could approach it again. "We think the garden might be the epicenter."

"Epicenter of what?" Sofia asked.

"We were hoping you could tell us," Laura said. "We need you to analyze these samples as soon as possible."

"You mean at the forensics lab?" Sofia asked. "Look, it's bad enough I brought you the PPE and evidence bags, but if I get caught with these samples I could be in serious shit, especially since Ralph told you not to go in the park."

"Did he?" Laura asked. "We had a bad connection. I couldn't hear him."

Sofia shook her head. "This is a lot to ask, Laura. I know I owe you big time for your help with getting my stuff out of Chuck's place, but..."

"Please, Sofia," Booker said. "It's important."

"You heard about all the break-ins last night," Laura said. "People are acting crazy, not like themselves at all. The answer might be right here. It could help us stop what's happening, but we need your help."

Sofia looked down at the storage tote at her feet and sighed. "I know I'm going to regret this. I'll go to the lab early tomorrow morning, before Ralph gets in. I'll call you as soon as I have the results."

"Thanks," Booker said. "But just to be safe, I wouldn't bring the samples home with you. Maybe leave them in a secure spot in your lab first."

"And when you analyze them, be sure you're wearing PPE," Laura added. "Don't get anything on your skin, and don't breathe it in."

"What the hell have you gotten me into, Laura?" Sofia asked.

"Thanks for doing this," Laura said. "You're a lifesaver."

"Don't mention it," Sofia said, loading the tote into the trunk of her car. She slammed the lid down. "I mean it. Especially not to Ralph."

Sofia got into the car and drove off. Laura watched her go until she couldn't see her taillights anymore. She hoped they were right and analyzing the spores would be the key to stopping the infection. Otherwise, she was risking their job for nothing. Sofia's, too.

"Come with me," Booker said.

He led Laura around the side of the house and through a gate into his back yard. In the center of the yard, he'd set a metal wheelbarrow, a bottle of bleach, and a hose. Booker began undoing the hood of his protective coverall suit. They'd agreed earlier that it would be safest to remove their contaminated PPE before entering the house. Laura couldn't wait to get out of hers. The material didn't breathe at all, and her whole body was soaked in sweat. She undid her hood and pulled it back. The night breeze felt refreshing on her hair and scalp.

Booker loosened the elastic cuffs around his wrists and pulled down the long, single zipper that ran the length of his suit, from chin to crotch. He wiggled out of it, emerging in only his boxer briefs. Once he had the suit down around his feet, he loosened the elastic cuffs around his ankles so he could step out of it. Still wearing his gloves, he picked up the suit and placed it in the wheelbarrow. He removed the protective coverings from his shoes and tossed them in as well.

Laura paused with her hand on the zipper of her suit, feeling suddenly self-conscious. She didn't know why. It wasn't like she and Booker hadn't seen each other's bodies before. They'd been lovers, for crying out loud. She knew every inch of his body, and she was sure he knew every inch of hers. Or *used* to know. That was the issue, she supposed. They weren't the same people anymore. Four years had passed. In a way, he was a stranger now, someone she needed to get to know all over again.

"It's okay," Booker said, picking up on her hesitation. "I can turn around if you want."

"Thanks," she said.

He turned around. His naked back was as smooth and muscled as she remembered, but in the years since they'd been together he'd grown softer around the middle. She supposed she had, too.

Time makes ruins of us all, she thought.

Laura undid the zipper down the front of her suit, grateful for the privacy afforded by the tall white fence that surrounded the yard. She stepped out of the suit and put it in the wheelbarrow on top of Booker's, along with the coverings from her shoes.

Standing there in their underwear, shoes, gloves, goggles,

and N95 respirators, she thought they looked so ridiculous she couldn't help laughing. Booker turned around, surprised.

"What's so funny?" he said.

"If anyone were to see us now, they'd think we were seriously kinky," she said.

He laughed, which only made her laugh harder, and she realized she didn't care that she was standing in her underwear in front of him. She felt comfortable. Safe. It felt almost like old times.

"Go on inside. I'll take care of this," Booker said. He picked up the hose and the bottle. Hot water and chlorine bleach would kill any spores still clinging to the protective equipment.

She dumped her gloves and goggles into the wheelbarrow, but kept the N95 respirator on. They still weren't sure how airborne the spores were, or if inhaling them could lead to infection. She walked up the steps to his back deck and entered the house. Once she was inside, she finally took off her N95 respirator, disposed of it, and washed her hands thoroughly. She made her way to the bathroom, where she stripped out of her underwear and took a shower, one final precaution to make sure she was free of spores.

She could smell Booker everywhere around her, the same musky aftershave she remembered, the same nutmeg-and-vanilla-scented soap that she now lathered over her body. The smell of him opened a Pandora's box of memories, and suddenly she was back with him on that sailboat on the Hudson River. It had been one of the best days of her life, the two of them lying close to each other on the padded bench as the boat lolled on the waves, kissing under the perfect blue sky. She remembered holding him close, holding him tighter than she ever had before, as if she could keep him from leaving.

When Booker came inside, he took a shower too, and afterward they sat in his living room, back in the clothes they'd worn before changing into their PPE. He poured them each a glass of wine.

"Do you remember that day we took a sailboat out onto the river?" Laura asked, cupping her wineglass in both hands. "I was thinking about it earlier."

"Sure I do," he said with a smile. "We brought wine and cheese and crackers with us. We only rented the boat for three hours, but the time went by so fast we joked about stealing it and raising a pirate flag, remember? It was a good day."

"The best." She looked down at her wineglass again. "I almost asked you to stay that day. To just stay and not go to California."

She had promised herself she would never tell him that. It was easy enough to keep that promise when she thought she would never see him again. But here he was, here they both were, and it felt good to finally let it out. She hadn't realized the weight of what she was carrying until she released it.

Booker paused with his wineglass half raised to his lips. "Really?"

"Everything felt so perfect and so right, I thought about asking you to put your doctorate on hold and stay with me," she said. "I didn't, obviously. I knew it wouldn't be right to. It was selfish, and I didn't want you to think I was holding you back."

He put his wineglass down on the cardboard box coffee table. "I wouldn't have thought that, Laura."

"Yes, you would have," she said. "Of course you would have. If the roles were reversed and you asked me to put my dreams and goals aside for the sake of our relationship, eventually I would have come to resent it. You would have, too."

"Laura…" He shook his head, having trouble finding the right words. "What happened wasn't your fault. It was mine. I should have tried harder."

"No, it was my fault too," she said. "My father abandoned us when I was little. He couldn't handle my mother when she was off her meds, which happened a lot. Then, when I was away at college, she… You remember, I told you how she took all those sleeping pills."

His put his hand over hers. "I remember."

"After she was gone, I was all alone at just twenty years old," she said. "Over the years, I got used to relying only on myself, and in a way that made me feel like I didn't have to fight to keep our relationship alive. I was so used to being on my own that it almost felt like that's how things were supposed to be."

He gave her hand a reassuring squeeze. She smiled at him. It was a relief to finally talk about this.

"In the end, there was nothing either of us could do, not realistically," she said. "We were on opposite coasts. Your studies were taking up more and more of your time, and my practice was picking up in town. What happened was inevitable."

He picked up his wineglass again, but instead of drinking from it he stared into it like it held the answers, the oracle at Delphi breathing in the vapors. "I wanted to email you when I got back."

"Why didn't you?" she asked.

"Because I didn't know if you would want to hear from me," he said. "And because there was a part of me that didn't want to know if you were seeing someone, or if you'd gotten married." He looked up from his glass, his eyes meeting hers. "I didn't think I could handle it."

"Booker," she said.

"I never stopped thinking about you," he said. "I never stopped caring about you. I had my choice of jobs after I was awarded my doctorate. Museum jobs, private laboratories, government research, but I chose to be a high school science teacher because it was the job that would bring me back to Sakima. Back to you. But once I was here I—I chickened out. I couldn't even send you a goddamn email—"

She kissed him, cutting him off. She put her hand gently on his cheek. His skin was warm, flushed either from the wine or the kiss. At the base of her thumb, she could feel the prickly hair of his goatee near the corner of his mouth. He kissed her back, putting a hand on her waist and drawing her closer. But then, suddenly, he pulled away.

"Wait," he said. "Are you sure about this, Laura? With everything that's going on…"

She answered him with another kiss. Yes, she was sure. She was very, very sure. Booker didn't pull away this time. He kissed her deeply, and his hands slid up from her waist to her back to draw her against him.

They went to his bedroom upstairs and collapsed in a tangle onto his bed. She felt warm and alive and wanted more of his touch. She unbuttoned her blouse, pulled it off, and threw it onto the floor. Her bra followed, and then his hands and lips were on her and the warmth she felt turned to a burning heat. She unbuttoned his shirt and pulled it off of him. She ran her hands over the smooth skin of his shoulders, arms, and chest. She went for his pants next, undoing his belt and pulling his zipper down over the straining bulge behind it. She slid his pants down, and then his underwear down to free him fully. Booker kicked them the rest of the way off, then turned his attention to her, undressing her until she was as naked as he was.

He kissed her again, his tongue sparring with hers, and then kissed his way down her body—her breasts, her stomach, and then between her legs. She surfed the waves of pleasure that pulsed from her core, breathing through it faster and faster, letting it build inside her until her whole body trembled in climax. She guided him back up to her, grabbed him by the hips, and pulled him into her.

The sensation coaxed a gasp from her throat. She wrapped her arms and legs around Booker and threw herself into the feeling. Everything else melted away. There was only this moment, the delicious push and pull of it, drawing sounds from her throat she hadn't made in so long they sounded alien to her. She felt the pleasure building again, her legs quivering, every muscle tightening like a gun about to go off, a dam about to burst, and she cried out as the pressure exploded and was released. Booker's body went rigid as he climaxed, his breath catching in his throat.

Afterward, they lay naked in bed together, spooning and half asleep. They hadn't thought to draw the curtains over the bedroom window earlier, and it was too late now. Neither of them wanted to get out of bed. She could tell from his breathing that Booker had fallen asleep behind her. She pulled his arm tighter around her. Outside, Laura could see the treetops of Dradin Park like dark spires in the night sky and was overcome with the same feeling she'd had in the park—that there were people hidden in the darkness, watching and waiting. But waiting for what? Orders? From whom? The fungi inside them, as Booker thought? She shivered, thinking about the hypha she saw sticking out of Jeff Miller's arm, and the words he'd said.

God is calling me. Why can't you hear it? It's so loud.

It. Not Him, which was the pronoun she'd heard used most often for God. Not Her, which was the pronoun Laura's mother had liked to use. *It.*

A disturbing thought came to her. She was tempted to disregard altogether, but her medical training wouldn't allow it. It made her face the thought instead of pushing it away.

There's something in the park. That's why Adam and the others went there. It's not just the fungi inside them that's manipulating them, there's something else. Something in the park that they call God.

16

Ralph got home late from the police station to find Debra watching the news in the living room. The worries hit him instantly: What had he missed while he was gone today? Had Darius rolled over on his own? Strung together new sounds? Finally laughed out loud? It was a daily ritual, torturing himself with these thoughts. They stuck in his mind no matter how hard he tried to shrug them off, stubborn as sticky burdock seed pods.

"Hi, baby," he said, kissing Debra hello.

"Darius is down for the night if you want to say goodnight," she said.

"I do." He went into the nursery and stood over the crib. Darius was sleeping on his back, his tiny mouth open, his hands in loose fists up by his ears. Ralph smiled. He'd give anything to sleep that soundly again.

In the bedroom, he took off his uniform and placed his brass police chief's badge in its box on top of the dresser. His sidearm went in the pistol safe next to it. When Debra got pregnant that first time, she'd insisted they get a safe for his gun, pressing the point that she didn't want to raise a child in a house where he might accidentally come across a loaded weapon. It was clear she had the whole speech prepared, citing statistics and news stories. He didn't have the heart to interrupt and tell her he'd ordered one already. Had ordered it, in fact, the very same day her pregnancy test came back positive.

Ralph changed into jeans and the threadbare old New York Rangers t-shirt he'd owned since college. He went to the kitchen, grabbed a beer out of the fridge, and joined Debra in the living room in front of the TV. She leaned her head against his shoulder.

"Did you eat already?" she asked. "I can heat something up."

"I'm good. I got takeout earlier."

"Long day?"

"You have no idea," he said. "We took in five people today, and every one of them was acting crazy. Entering homes without permission. Chasing after folks. It's like everyone's lost their damned minds."

"Five?" Debra sat up and pushed a long black braid behind one ear. "You don't usually take in that many people in a *month*."

"Don't I know it," he said. "Remember Walter Monahan, the green grocer?"

"Sure. I bought that bok choy from him last week."

"He was one of them." Ralph took a swig from the bottle, still trying to make sense of the day he'd had. "We got a call that he was wandering on Foxglove, trying people's doors, rapping on their windows, talking crazy. Mrs. Brewer said he had a handful of dirt or dust or something that he threw right in her face. When we caught up to him, Walter wasn't in his right mind. I've never seen him like that. Delirious, laughing at everything. He got violent when we tried to restrain him. He kept saying we should join him. Join *us*, he said. Be one with *us*."

He took another drink of his beer and found he'd drunk the whole bottle without realizing it. Debra knew him well enough to know something had really gotten under his skin. She turned off the TV.

"I put Walter in the holding cell with the others," he went on. "I asked them straight up if they'd taken any drugs, but they didn't answer me. I asked them if they were involved with Adam and the others, and they didn't answer that, either. They didn't answer anything I asked, they just laughed at me. That laughter...I've never heard anything so frightening." He reached for the bottle again, remembered it was empty, and let his hand drop. "I thought I would try to shake them up. Get them talking, you know? I told them we were going to raid the park tomorrow morning. Take every officer I've got and round up Adam and the others, bring 'em in and charge 'em. That got their attention. That got them talking. Except..."

"Except?" Debra pressed.

"Walter said it wouldn't matter," he told her. "He said there were enough of them now."

"Enough of them for what?" she asked.

The lights in the living room snapped out. The whole house went dark as if they'd lost power. Ralph got up and went to the living room window. Outside was only darkness and stars. The whole street had blacked out.

"What's going on?" Debra asked.

"I don't know. There's no storm—"

Three heavy knocks sounded on the door, interrupting him.

"Who could it be at this hour?" Debra got up and started toward the door.

"Don't," Ralph said.

In his mind, he saw Walter Monahan and the other four ragged figures in the holding cell again, staring silently at each other. He had a bad feeling about this, as he had about everything that had happened over the past twenty-four hours.

A rock smashed through the window and rolled across the living room floor, trailing shards.

"Debra, go to the nursery and shut the door!" he said.

"Ralph, what's happening?"

"Go!" he said.

Debra ran to the nursery and closed the door. There was no lock on it, they'd taken it off when they babyproofed the house, but Ralph couldn't let himself think about that now. He dashed into the bedroom and went to the pistol safe on the dresser. There were four buttons on the front of the safe that he could just make out in the dark. He tried to enter the electronic opening code, but another round of banging rocked the front door and caused him to slip, pressing the wrong key at the wrong time. The safe beeped a warning and remained locked.

Something moved outside the bedroom window. A shape slinking through the dark.

The handle on the front door rattled. Someone was trying to force their way in. How long would the lock hold? He wasn't sure, and he didn't want to put it to the test.

Ralph entered the code again, getting it right this time, and the safe popped open. He pulled out his sidearm and slammed a magazine into the grip.

A tapping at the bedroom window, the sound of fingernails on glass. He spun with the gun raised, but whoever had been there was gone, melting back into the night.

Something big thudded against the front door, hard enough to rattle it in the frame. The lock wasn't going to hold much longer.

Ralph moved as silently as he could down the hall, past the closed door of the nursery. Somewhere behind it, Debra was protecting their baby. She was the second line of defense. He was the first.

He went to the front door, holding the gun in both hands, and shouted, "Whoever's out there, you best rethink your plans! I've got a gun, and I've got no qualms about using it to protect my family!"

Another kick to the door, strong enough that it cracked the wood of the doorjamb.

"Maybe you didn't hear me," Ralph called. "I said—"

One of Ralph's own garbage cans smashed through the already broken living room window, slamming into the couch where he and Debra had been sitting just minutes before. More shards of glass showered the floor. The lock on the front door finally gave, and the door burst open.

Shapes swarmed into the house through the doorway and the window. He recognized their faces even in the dim light. They were people he knew, people he saw every day, people from church and the supermarket, but they were different now. Changed. Ralph backed up. There were so many of them, all with creepy, delirious grins on their faces. The same grin Walter Monahan had when they arrested him earlier today.

Ralph raised the gun. He couldn't let them get to Debra or hurt Darius. He aimed it at the nearest person and saw it was Dahlia Mintz, the desk officer from the station. She was still in her uniform. He paused with his finger on the trigger.

"Dahlia?" he said.

Hands grabbed his arms, his gun. Heather Bishop, mother of Kat Bishop, yanked the weapon out of his hand. Behind her, her husband George grabbed at the collar of Ralph's Rangers t-shirt.

"Why fight, Ralph?" Dahlia asked. "It's so much easier to become one with us. It's so much better, too. You've never experienced anything like this before. This connection. This feeling. Join us. Serve with us. Worship with us."

"No!" Ralph pulled himself free of George Bishop's grasp, the neck of his t-shirt tearing,

He ran down the hallway to the nursery, where he intended to make his stand and protect his family, but a small group of people had gotten by him already. They dragged Debra out of the nursery. Darius was cradled in her arms, crying furiously at being woken up, not understanding what was happening.

"No!" Ralph yelled. "Leave them alone!"

"Ralph, I'm sorry," Debra said. Tears streamed down her face. "I tried...I couldn't stop them..."

Ralph looked frantically around the hallway for Heather Bishop, desperate to take his gun back from her, but more and more people were cramming into the house, laughing, groping for him, insisting he become one with them. There were too many. He struggled, trying to reach Debra and the baby, but writhing, creeping forms crowded the space between them, pushing and grabbing. He was spun around and pawed at until he lost sight of Debra and Darius.

"Debra!" he shouted.

"Debra! Debra!" the others shouted, mocking him, laughing at him.

A young boy of twelve approached him. Ralph didn't recognize him at first because his features were obscured by what Ralph thought was paint on his face. As the boy drew closer, Ralph saw it was Jeff Miller, the boy who'd attacked Adam with his violin, and whose parents had barricaded him in his room. Only now his parents were with him, shoving in with the rest of the crowd.

His eyes, Ralph thought. *What's wrong with his eyes?*

Jeff looked up at him with eyes so swollen and red there were no whites visible. What Ralph had thought was paint was actually blood spilling from the corners of his eyes and running down his cheeks. Jeff hardly seemed to notice or care. He smiled, lifted his hand, and blew a cloud of spores into Ralph's face.

17

Laura woke up to the feeling of Booker kissing her bare shoulder. They were still spooning in bed just as they had been when they fell asleep, with Booker's arm around her waist. He pulled her against to him.

"Hm," she said with a smile. "Good morning, Professor Coates."

"Good morning, Dr. Powell," he replied.

She twisted around and kissed him as his hand moved up her body to caress her breast. His touch lit a fire inside her. Her blood ran hot as their tongues intertwined. She reached down below his waist—

A shrill, panicked scream came from somewhere outside, followed by the screech of tires and the sound of a vehicle crashing into something.

"What the hell?" Booker leapt out of bed and went to the window. "Oh my God..."

Laura got out of bed, wrapping the top sheet around herself and joining him at the window. Outside, a car was up on the sidewalk, its front end smoking and crumpled against the base of a streetlight. People were running on the street, some dashing into and out of houses, others sprinting for their cars. More people chased them, grabbed them, blew handfuls of spores at them. There were fistfights, screams, cars swerving and screeching as they tried to drive away, only to be swarmed by a crowd.

"Where the hell are the police?" Booker said.

Laura scanned the mayhem, looking for uniforms. She spotted two officers in the thick of it, but her heart sank when she saw they weren't trying to stop anything. They'd joined the ranks of the infected, chasing people down and blowing spores at them.

"Oh, God…" Laura said. It had started. Whatever the infected were waiting for, the time had come.

Someone pounded on the front door. More than one person. From the sound of it, they were trying to break it down.

"We have to get out of here," Booker said.

"How?" she asked. "Look at it out there, Booker. We won't get far. We're safer staying inside."

The pounding on the door grew louder, heavier.

"They'll get in eventually. We shouldn't be here when they do," he said. "All we have to do is get to my car, and I can get us out of here."

They threw on yesterday's clothes and hurried down the stairs from the bedroom. At the bottom of the steps, Booker grabbed the loaded shotgun he'd propped up next to the door and slung it over his shoulder by the strap. The door rattled in its frame under the onslaught of fists and shoulders from outside. Laura and Booker dashed into the living room, where he picked up a box of shotgun shells.

A face appeared at the window. Laura gasped. It was Adam. He banged on the glass, his eyes big and red, his mouth twisted into a lunatic grin.

"You don't have to be such a bitch about it!" he shouted at her, laughing. He sounded insane, stuck on a single looping thought. "You don't have to be such a bitch about it! *You don't have to be such a bitch about it!*"

Booker grabbed her hand and together they ran into the kitchen. He looked out the window into the back yard to see if any of the infected had jumped the fence. The yard was empty. The wheelbarrow was still there, and their protective gear was inside it, soaking in bleach-laced water and useless to them. Without PPE, they were vulnerable to the spores, but as the pounding on the front door worsened, she realized Booker was right. If they stayed here and the infected broke in, they were cornered. Their chances of escape were better outside. She just wished they had protection. All they could do was hope no one blew any spores at them.

Booker opened the door to the back yard, and they raced

down the patio steps to the grass. Behind them, Laura heard the glass of the living room window shatter. Adam had broken through.

Booker unlocked the gate that led around the side of the house to the front, and they made a break for the SUV in his driveway. A group of four infected townspeople who were gathered at Booker's door turned and chased after them. Adam joined them, one fist bloodied from putting it through the living room window.

More of the infected came running at them from the street. Laura sprinted for the SUV. Kenneth Dalpe came around from the other side of the vehicle. The old widower's eyes were as red and swollen as Adam's. Laura and Booker skidded to a halt.

"Isabella's angry with you, Dr. Powell," Kenneth said. "She says you didn't try hard enough to keep her alive. I'm inclined to agree, but once you're one of us it won't matter."

Booker took the shotgun off his shoulder and aimed it at the old man. "Get out of the way, Kenneth."

"All sins are absolved by the God of Dirt," Kenneth said. "Come worship it. Serve it, as we do."

"I'm warning you," Booker said, his finger on the trigger.

"Don't!" Laura pushed the shotgun down. "He's not in control of his actions. He's sick. They *all* are. They need help."

"We're going to need help in a minute," Booker said, glancing over his shoulder.

The infected group from the house were almost upon them, and the infected from the street weren't far behind. Booker launched himself at Kenneth and shoulder-checked him away from the SUV, then ran around the front to the driver's-side door. He yanked it open, jumped inside, and closed it again.

Laura threw herself into the front passenger seat and slammed the door closed as Booker hit the Engine Start button on the dashboard. They engine roared to life. He pulled out of the driveway seconds before the group from the house reached the SUV. He swerved through the crowd on the street, hands viciously battering the sides of the SUV and grabbing at the door handles.

Laura realized her window was open and hit the power

window control switch in the door handle. The glass began to rise with a mechanical whirring sound. Adam appeared at the window, startling her. He opened his uninjured hand to reveal a heap of fine, brown spores and blew them at her. She screamed and flinched back. The window reached the top of its frame just as the spores hit the glass, leaving a brown stain.

"Shit!" Laura exclaimed.

Booker glanced at her in a panic before returning his eyes to the road to maneuver through the crowd. "Did any of it get inside?"

"I don't know! I don't know!" Laura touched her face, her arms. She looked at her clothes and her surroundings. She didn't see anything, but that didn't mean they were safe. A single spore could be microscopic, too small to see with the naked eye, and yet one spore was all it would take to infect her. Or Booker, if it had drifted far enough into the SUV.

He kept driving, swerving and skidding around the infected. A middle-aged, gray-haired man in a disheveled suit bashed a stone against his window, cracking it but not breaking it. A teenaged girl jumped onto the hood, grimacing with a mouthful of braces, her eyes filled with crazed determination, but she couldn't keep her grip and was thrown off.

"They're trying to kill us!" Booker said.

Laura wasn't so sure. Kenneth Dalpe had said he wanted them to join him in serving and worshipping their god. The spores were meant to infect them, drug them, but not kill them. It wasn't about changing them; it was about converting them. The infected were missionaries, evangelists for their God of Dirt.

Booker turned off his street, passing by the entrance to Dradin Park. The police who'd been stationed there were gone, already infected. The metal barricades were down, as though they'd been pushed over from the inside. It reminded her of a cattle ranch fence after a stampede. How many had been inside the park? How many were there now? Their numbers already seemed to be in the hundreds, because the other streets they drove on were no better off than Booker's. The infected were everywhere, streaming into people's homes or chasing them down. Booker swerved around several cars abandoned in the road, their doors still open. One had flipped over near the sidewalk, its shattered windshield spattered with red.

"Where are we going?" Laura asked.

"I have to make sure Victor's okay." Booker gritted his teeth as he yanked the steering wheel to one side to prevent running into two children who stood in the middle of the road, holding hands and laughing like they didn't have a care in the world. "Jesus fucking Christ!" He took a breath and got a hold of himself. "If Victor's all right, his place in the woods is far enough away that we should be safe there."

Watching the horror unfold around them, she found it hard to imagine any place was safe.

She pulled out her phone and called Ralph. He needed to know what was going on, if he didn't already, but the call went right to voicemail. *Damn it, where are you?* She left a message telling him to call her right back, then tried the direct number to his office at the station. There was no answer. She tried his home number next, hoping she could at least reach Debra, but she only got voicemail there, too. She put down her phone and took a deep breath. Ralph was the chief of police, surely he already knew what was going on. He was probably busy right now trying to restore the peace and that was why she couldn't reach him. He would call her back when he had the chance.

They passed a house where a group of a dozen infected townspeople were gathered outside. They surrounded a young father and two small children on the lawn. The mother, young like the father in her late twenties and wearing a yellow sundress, came storming out of the house. She waved a pistol at the crowd, yelling something Laura couldn't hear. The infected didn't respond. Some blew spores at the husband and children, while the rest of them lunged toward the mother, grasping for her. She fired a warning shot into the air, but it didn't deter them. She let out a sobbing shriek and put the gun to her own temple.

The SUV was past the house when Laura heard the gunshot ring out. She bit her fist to keep from crying, or screaming, or both. Booker drove on, focused on the road in front of them. He swerved onto Grove Hill Road, where Laura saw two houses on fire. One of them was the Miller house. She hoped Jeff and his parents were okay, but the thought stopped half formed in her mind. She already knew Jeff wasn't okay. He had the fungus in him. It was likely his parents did by now, too.

From Grove Hill Road, Booker turned onto MacLeod Avenue, driving so fast the wheels squealed on the pavement. Normally this was the busiest part of town, where shops and restaurants drew customers day in and day out, but now the sidewalks were eerily empty. It was like a ghost town. Store windows were smashed, the Chinese takeout was on fire. How had it all happened so quickly? Last night had been quiet. A matter of hours—was that all it took for the whole city to fall apart? Laura was frightened, yes, but more than that, she felt unmoored. If civilization was really so fragile it could be shattered in the blink of an eye, then they'd been lying to themselves for thousands of years. Lying about who they were, and what it meant to be human. Lying to themselves that they were anything more than animals under the skin, waiting to be let loose again, waiting to go for each other's throats.

Laura gasped as she saw a man come running out of the parking lot of the Great Eastern Motel up ahead. He wore a blue pinstriped suit with a red tie loosely knotted around the collar of his white dress shirt. He looked familiar, but Laura couldn't place him. He dashed across the street from the motel, stopped in front of a donut shop, and screamed for help, waving his arms at the SUV.

"Shit!" Booker said. He looked like he wanted to ignore the man and keep driving, but some more compassionate part of him made him slam on the brakes. The SUV skidded to a halt in front of the donut shop.

Out her window, Laura saw a crowd rushing out of the motel parking lot, heading right for them, yelling and laughing crazily. She yelled, "Hurry up! Get in!"

The man in the blue suit yanked open the back door and threw himself into the SUV's back seat. "Drive! For God's sake, drive!"

Booker hit the gas, and the SUV screeched away from the

curb, leaving the crowd from the motel to watch them speed away.

Laura turned in her seat to look at the man. He was breathing hard and red in the face from exertion and fear. "Are you okay?"

"What the *fuck* is going on?" he said.

She realized then why he looked so familiar. The man in the back seat was Sean Hilton, vice president of Bluecoal. She'd seen him at the town hall meeting just three days ago, trying to convince everyone that turning Dradin Park into luxury condos would be a good thing.

"You're from the developer, right? What are you still doing in Sakima?" she asked. "I thought you would be back in New York City by now."

"I was supposed to leave today," he said. "Instead, when I went to check out of the motel, there was a mob waiting for me. At first I thought it was a bunch of radicals who were against developing the park and wanted to string me up—"

Sean paused as Booker gave him an icy look in the rearview mirror.

"Anyway, they—they came after me and tried to throw dirt or sand at me," he continued. "I don't know what the fuck that was all about. I hid in the breakfast room until I could make a break for it, but they were between me and my car so I ran for the road. If you two hadn't come along, I don't know what would have happened."

Laura noticed he still hadn't said thank you, but decided not to push it. The circumstances were extenuating, to say the least.

"Did they get any spores on you?" Laura asked.

"Spores?" he said. "Is that what that shit was?"

"They're spores from some kind of fungus," she explained. "At least, that's our working theory for now. The spores infect people and cause them to try to infect others. So we need to know, did any get on you?"

Sean looked at his arms, his hands, his suit jacket, and seemed satisfied. "No, I didn't."

"Did you breathe any in?" Booker asked, looking at him in the rearview again.

Sean shook his head. "No, I don't think so."

"You don't *think* so?" Booker pressed. He shot a quick, concerned glance at Laura. Laura knew what he was thinking. She was thinking it herself. Maybe picking up a stranger was a mistake.

"No, I'm sure of it, I didn't breathe any in," Sean said. "So where are we going? I assume we're getting the hell out of this shit hole."

Laura bristled at this stranger from downstate referring to Sakima, her home, the city she'd spent her whole life in, as a shit hole, but once again chalked it up to the stress of the situation.

"Not yet," Booker told him. "I need to check on someone first. I need to make sure he's okay."

Sean leaned forward from the back seat. "Bad idea, pal. If you're smart, you'll just keep driving until this clusterfuck is behind us."

"We're not going anywhere until I make sure he's okay," Booker insisted. "If you don't like it, I can drop you off right here and you can take your chances on your own."

Sean leaned back again with an exasperated sigh. "Fine, but you're making a big mistake. We need to get the fuck out of here. Whoever this guy is you want to check on, there's nothing you can do for him anymore. The shit's already hit the fan. If it were me, I wouldn't stop driving until we're over the bridge in Kingston, or up north in Rhinebeck, and then I'd tell the cops there to nuke this dump from orbit."

"Booker," Laura said. "He might be right. You have to prepare yourself for the possibility—"

"I have to see him," Booker said, his jaw set tight. "I'm not just going to abandon him."

Before Laura could answer, Sean said, "You can kiss those fucking condos goodbye, I'll tell you that much. The property value around here just took a nose dive into the crapper." He reached into his inside jacket pocket, and his face dropped. "Shit. I left my phone back in the motel room. Have either of you already called the police?"

"I tried, but I couldn't reach anyone," Laura said. "I'm sure they know what's happening by now, though. They have to."

Sean leaned forward again. She could tell he was trying not to panic, masking his fear with anger instead. "You mean you don't know for sure? Fuck." He fell back in his seat and slapped his hands in frustration against the upholstery. "Fuck!"

Booker drove on.

18

The SUV skidded to a halt in front of Victor's house in the woods, the wheels kicking up dust clouds on the dirt driveway. Laura got out, careful not to touch the brown stain on the outside of the window. The sight of it drew a shiver from her. If she'd been one second slower to close the window...

Everything happened so quickly after they left Booker's house, she hadn't had time to process that it was Adam who tried to infect her with the spores. Her ex-boyfriend, the man she'd dated for two months. She thought she knew him well, warts and all, but this morning she hadn't seen anything of Adam left in his eyes. He was unrecognizable, an imposter wearing Adam's face.

Booker hopped out of the driver's seat and slung the shotgun over his shoulder. Sean slid out of the back and adjusted his tie.

"We're not staying long, are we?" Sean said. "We're just checking in, and then we're getting back on the road, right?"

"I don't know yet," Booker said. "If it's safe to hole up here, that's what we'll do."

"Safe?" Sean scoffed. "We won't be safe until we leave Sakima far behind, and you know it."

Laura didn't want to hear them have the same argument over again, so she left them behind and walked to the house. The front door burst open before she got there, and Victor Cunningham scowled out at them from the doorway. His angry expression was in direct contrast with his cheerful Hawaiian shirt. His eyes were hidden behind the sunglasses he always wore.

"What the hell's going on? Pullin' into my driveway like

a bat out of hell!" Victor yelled. Then he noticed Laura and a ghost of a smile crept onto his face. "You again."

"Hi, Victor," she said, relieved to find him all right.

Booker had taken her to meet Victor only once when they were dating. He wanted her to meet the man who helped raise him in his father's absence, but when they arrived, it was clear Victor had snorted a mountain of cocaine beforehand. The drug made Victor charming and energetic, but also unpredictable and quick to anger. When the pot roast he cooked for them didn't turn out right, he dumped everything out of the pot into the garbage, and then threw out the pot for good measure. Booker had been too mortified to bring her back after that. She wondered if Victor remembered that night, or if the memory had disappeared in a drug-induced haze.

"Are you two back together now?" Victor asked her. "I hope so, because Booker's been a real shit ever since..." He trailed off, his gaze moving off of Laura and landing on Sean. "The fuck is *he* doing here?"

"Oh, Christ, not this guy again," Sean groaned. "This is the asshole who interrupted my presentation at the town hall!"

"You had it comin'!" Victor said.

"Enough, everybody get inside," Booker said.

Victor grudgingly stepped aside to let Sean into the house. After everyone was inside, Booker made sure to lock the door.

"Are you okay, Victor?" he asked.

"Yeah, son," Victor said. "What's happening? Why are you here?"

"It's not safe out there," Booker said. "Everyone's lost their minds. Acting crazy, going after each other."

"Shit. They put something in the water, didn't they?" Victor said. "I always knew this day would come. It's MK-Ultra all over again."

Sean laughed and covered his face with his hands. "Holy crap, he's out of his mind. I should have known at the meeting!"

"It's not the water," Booker said. He took the shotgun off his shoulder, pushed aside some of the newspapers on the couch, and sat down. "We think it's fungal spores. Half the town's already infected."

"Maybe more by now," Laura said.

"Spores?" Victor said. "The hell are you talking about?"

"I'd like to know, too," Sean said. "I saw what those people turned into. How can mushroom spores do that?"

Booker filled them in, telling them the same things he told Laura about the cicadas and leafcutter ants. Laura couldn't stand to hear it again. It was too creepy. She went to the living room window instead and looked outside. Booker's SUV and Victor's dusty, mud-spattered Ford Fiesta from the '90s sat in the driveway, and beyond them the woods loomed dark and foreboding. Were they far enough from town to be safe here? She didn't feel safe. Every nerve in her body was on high alert. Each branch that swayed in the wind was Adam, back to finish the job. She shuddered.

Sean's voice drew her out of her thoughts. "You really expect me to believe this bullshit?"

"I know it's hard to believe, but it's the only explanation that fits," Booker said.

"It's not so hard to believe, son. Not so hard at all," Victor said. "I've seen it before, or something like it."

He took a stack of magazines off a chair and sat down facing Booker. Laura sat on the arm of the couch. Sean remained standing, crossing his arms defiantly.

Victor said, "This was years ago when I was down in South America, in the Amazon rainforest, back in my tree-hugging days, fighting against illegal loggers and the like."

"Of course you were," Sean muttered, but no one paid him any mind.

"I saw something in the rainforest I've never forgotten," Victor said. "Ants, hundreds of them, hanging like ornaments all over the trees and plants. They were dead, and they had mushrooms growing out of their heads and thoraxes. We had a local guide named Joao who called 'em zombie ants. He said if just one spore from a particular kind of fungus landed on an ant, it would infect the ant's body in a matter of days, spreading through it and taking control. It drugs the ant's brain with psilocybin, just like you were saying about the people in town. The ant is compelled to climb up a tree or a plant to a spot where the light and humidity are just right, and then it clamps down with its pincers and roots itself in place. The ant dies, and the fungus's mushroom bursts out of its carcass to send out more spores. Joao said an entire ant colony could be wiped by just one fungus this way."

"People aren't ants," Sean insisted. Laura had said the same thing once, and now she felt embarrassed for it. "We're not going to suddenly start climbing trees and growing mushrooms out of our heads."

"No, the details may be different, but the principle is the same," Booker said. "Fungi use their spores to control other life forms. It's real, and we're seeing it play out on a scale no one has ever seen before."

"Son, you said those people were carrying the spores around with them, right?" Victor asked. "Well, that's good news, at least."

"How do you mean?" Booker asked.

"I may not be as smart as you, but I know something about mushrooms," Victor said. "Spores come out of a mushroom's gills. They're designed to be so small and light they're picked up by the wind and travel far away from their source. If these infected folks have to bring the spores with them, that means the spores aren't carried on the wind, or at least don't get very far. Maybe they're bigger or heavier than other spores, but whatever the reason, they need *help* being dispersed."

"Which means they're not fully airborne," Laura said. "I should have realized that right away. That's why they have to blow the spores at people. The wind can't spread them on its own."

"How much time do we have before this whole city is infected?" Victor asked.

"Not long, I think," Booker replied. "It'll spread at an exponential rate."

"It won't stop with Sakima, either. It'll spread to other cities," Laura said. "Kingston. Rhinebeck. Connelly. It's like a virus, city borders don't mean anything to it. It'll just keep spreading outward for as long as it's allowed."

"Jesus," Sean said. "So why aren't we driving the fuck out of here? We're wasting time."

"Because they need our help," Laura said. Her annoyance

with Sean was turning into anger, but she tried to keep a lid on it. Things were bad enough as they were, and they didn't need any added tension. "If we can find a way to treat people or inoculate them, we can stop the spread before it leaves the city."

Sean let out a groan and ran his hands through his hair. "For Christ's sake, wise up! There's nothing we can do! We should get out while we can!"

"You're free to start walkin'," Victor told him. "Or you can man up and start thinkin' about people other than yourself for once."

Sean's eyes narrowed. "Fuck you. Don't pretend you know me."

"Oh, I do know you," Victor said. "I've known your kind all my life. Stuffed shirts. Pencil pushers. Political appointees who've never seen a battlefield in their lives but have no problem ordering others to their deaths. Men like you act tough, you think you're smarter than everyone else, you think you have all the answers, but at the first sign of trouble you cut and run. You're an empty shell, Sean Hilton. You're the worst kind of backseat driver. The kind that judges other people's actions without ever risking your own neck."

"Victor," Booker warned him.

Sean glared at Victor. "You want to start something with me, old man? Try me."

Victor chuckled. "You know what they say about the dog that barks the loudest..."

"That's enough, both of you," Booker said. "We have to work together if we're going to get through this."

Victor and Sean glared at each other.

Laura stood up and broke the silence. "What we need is a plan."

"Well, you're welcome to stay here as long as it's safe," Victor said.

Sean rolled his eyes. "Great. Thanks. And what do we do once it's *not* safe?"

"Glad you asked. Follow me." Victor led them through his small, cluttered kitchen to a door at the far end. It opened onto a flight of wooden steps that led down to the basement. Victor switched on the stairway light. "I've got something to show you."

As they descended into the basement, the air grew cooler, dropping a good ten degrees. Laura guessed the house's original stone foundation still stood behind the drywall, locking in the cool, humid air. A rank odor assaulted her nose halfway down the steps, forcing her to breathe through her mouth instead. Sean, true to form, played up the theatrics, making gagging sounds and cringing.

"What's that awful smell?" he asked.

Victor laughed. "I gave my boys breakfast earlier. Composted manure, their favorite. Resist the temptation to ask where I got it."

"Your boys?" Laura asked.

When they reached the bottom of the steps, Victor spread his arms proudly and said, "My boys!"

Two tables were set up against the far wall, both covered with a collection of fourteen-by-sixteen-inch, high-sided wooden trays. Each tray was filled with dirt, and from out of the dirt poked mushrooms, dozens and dozens of them, in various shapes and sizes.

Sean reeled back. "Are you out of your mind? We were just saying mushroom spores are making people act crazy, and you've got the fucking Kingdom of the Mushrooms down here!"

"Relax," Victor said. "My boys aren't like that. They're good boys."

Laura and Booker followed Victor to the tables, but Sean hung back by the foot of the stairs. From his expression, Laura could tell he was masking his fear with anger again. It was starting to make her nervous.

Who was she kidding? Sean had made her nervous from the moment they'd picked him up outside the Great Eastern Motel.

"I grew 'em with the best Grow It Yourself kit on the market. Comes from a company called Myco Vault. See that first table?" Victor pointed to the wooden trays that sprouted mushrooms with long, thin stalks and pointed arrowhead caps. "Those are my boys, for personal consumption only. As many as I want. Myco Vault doesn't give a damn if I grow 'em, because you see that second table?" The mushrooms on the other table were different, a variety of shapes and sizes. "I used their kit to grow those, too, and as soon as they reach maturity I'll send 'em back to Myco Vault."

"What do they do with them?" Laura asked.

"R and D," he said. "They're a cutting-edge eco research firm. They're looking for ways to put fungi to sustainable, environmentally friendly uses—immunosuppressant drugs for organ transplants, anticancer drugs, antidepressants, they all come from fungal compounds. They're even looking into ways to build temporary structures out of fungus, military barracks or refugee housing that will decompose naturally when they're no longer needed. Biotechnology."

Victor looked over his mushrooms like a proud father.

"The future is fungus," he said.

From over by the stairs, Sean laughed derisively. "You sure you're not tripping right now?"

"Don't underestimate fungi," Victor said. "Four hundred and twenty million years ago, in the Paleozoic Era, the largest living things on land were fungi. *Prototaxites*, huge pillars of fungus up to twenty-six feet tall. They kept the title of largest living things on land for seventy million years." He quieted, and shook his head. "This world was theirs for a long, long time before we came along. We're no different from insects to them. We were arrogant to think otherwise."

Sean barked out a derisive laugh. "Now I *know* you're crazy."

Laura turned away. She didn't want to hear them argue anymore. Looking around the unfinished basement, she noticed a picture hanging on the drywall above a wide chest of drawers. It was a painting of a bacchanalia. Scantily clad figures danced and drank, and off to one side were the unmistakable tangled, naked bodies of an orgy. Standing at the center of the painting, holding a chalice and wearing nothing but a laurel of grapevines in his hair, was Dionysus himself, also known as Bacchus, the god for whom the bacchanalia was named. Most people knew Dionysus as the god of wine, but after studying the classics in undergrad, Laura knew he was also the god of insanity, of ritual madness and religious ecstasy. The bacchanalia wasn't simply a party. The cult of Dionysus drank until they passed out, danced until they collapsed, and fucked until they bled, all in worship of their god.

All sins are absolved by the God of Dirt. Come worship it. Serve it, as we do.

"Is this what it's like when you're on psilocybin?" she asked Victor.

He admired at the painting beside her. "In some ways, sure. It makes you feel happier than you ever have in your life, and I reckon the people in that picture are feeling pretty damn happy. It also gives you hallucinations. The walls and floor breathe. You see things that aren't there. Oh, and you laugh a lot. Everything is so goddamn funny."

Laura nodded. The infected townspeople were all laughing this morning, weren't they? Even as they tried to break into Booker's house, even as they chased after his car, they were laughing like maniacs. She'd never been so frightened by the sound of laughter in her life.

"'Course, there's any number of drugs that can give you hallucinations and a case of the giggles," Victor continued. "Psilocybin's different because it affects you on a philosophical level, too. You feel a connection to everything. Other people. Nature. God. That's one of the things I like most about it, that feeling of being connected to everything and everyone. Being one with each other, and with the universe."

"I thought you hated other people," Booker said.

"Oh, I don't mind feeling connected," he said. "I just don't like talking to 'em. People are idiots."

"Are we done fucking around here?" Sean said, coming over from the stairs. "When you said you had something to show us, I assumed it wasn't just your stash of illegal psychedelics."

"Fine, fine," Victor said. "I was getting to it."

On the wall opposite the mushroom tables was a large, metal cabinet. Victor punched a code into the keypad, then pulled the double doors open. Inside the cabinet were weapons, an unbelievable amount of weapons. On one side of the cabinet were six long guns—four rifles and two shotguns—while on the other side were shelves holding handguns, boxes of ammunition, folding combat knives, and a plain black metal box.

"Oh my God," Laura said.

Sean's eyes lit up. "Now this is more like it!"

"Jesus, Victor," Booker said. "I knew you had guns, but you never showed me this before."

"I stocked up for when the jack-booted thugs come for my stash," he said. "I never imagined using them to defend my home against psilocybin-crazed PTA members."

"I don't like this," Laura said. "Those people are sick. They're not responsible for what's happened to them. We should be finding a way to help them, not trying to kill them."

"I hear you. These are for a worst-case scenario only," Victor said. "But if it comes down to it, if it's life or death, or if those fuckers try to dose us, we're protected."

Sean reached into the cabinet, then stopped himself. "May I?"

It was the first time he'd shown any manners, Laura noted. Maybe seeing the guns made him feeler safe enough to relax.

"Sure," Victor said. "They're not loaded."

Sean pulled a long black rifle out of the cabinet. "This is a Ruger Semi-Automatic."

"You know your guns," Victor said. "Maybe there's hope for you yet, pencil pusher."

Sean held the rifle pointed downward and peered along the barrel like he was sighting a target on the floor. "I may be from the city, but my old man used to take me white-tailed deer hunting up in Allegany County when I was a teenager. He taught me all about guns."

Laura's phone rang in her pocket. She pulled it out, hoping it was Ralph finally calling back, but the number on the screen was Sofia's private cell. Laura's stomach dropped. Where was Ralph? Why hadn't he called her yet?

She answered the phone. "Sofia?"

Bursts of Sofia's voice came to her, mixed with static and silence. Laura looked at her phone and saw she barely had a signal down in the basement.

"Sorry, Sofia, I can't hear you, hold on a second." She turned to Booker. "I'm going to take this upstairs."

"Let me know what she says about the samples from the park," Booker replied.

Laura climbed the steps back to Victor's kitchen. The signal got stronger as she moved into the living room.

"Sofia, can you hear me?" she asked.

"Yes, can you hear me?" Sofia replied.

"I can now," Laura said. "Sorry, I'm out in the woods at Booker's friend Victor's place. Are you okay? Where are you?"

"I'm at the forensics lab," Sofia said, and Laura sighed with relief. She would be safe in the police station. "I brought the samples in last night just intending to leave them here before going home, but then I decided since I was already at the lab I might as well begin the analysis. I've been here all night."

"Thank you, I really appreciate it," Laura said. "What did you find?"

"Those are definitely fungal spores on the vegetables, but they're not like any I've seen before," Sofia said. "There are cells that resemble the *Armillaria mellea*, which is a common honey fungus, but its spores are white, not brown. Also, these spores are roughly twice as big. There are some other genetic markers I can't identify at all."

"So it *is* a mutation," Laura said. She turned to look out the window. Tree branches swayed in the wind.

"It looks that way, although I couldn't say for sure," Sofia said. "From what I can tell, you were right about the way the spores infect their victims. They have to touch bare skin, which includes breathing them into your nose or mouth. They release an acidic enzyme that allows them to burn through the epidermis or mucus membrane and enter the body."

"Would you be able to feel that when it happened?" Laura asked. "Maybe we could use it as a kind of early-warning system when a subject is infected."

"You would feel it, yes," Sofia said. "It would sting, maybe itch. You might mistake it for bug bites."

Something moved in the underbrush outside. Laura froze. Was it an animal? A person? The movement stopped. Nothing emerged from the forest. Probably, it was just the wind.

"Laura, I found something else in the samples, something that shouldn't be there," Sofia said. "Traces of an experimental herbicide called MCA 8564."

Laura caught herself chewing her nails and pulled her hand

away from her mouth. "What is that?"

"It was an herbicide designed for industrial use," Sofia said. "It was discontinued a few years back because it contained unapproved genetically-modified enzymes that were carcinogenic. Think about what happened with Roundup Weed Killer, only ten times worse."

"That explains why all the crops in the community garden were dead," Laura said. "Someone poisoned them. Who would do that?"

"I don't know," Sofia said. "But MCA 8564 is almost impossible to come by. It's illegal. You would have to have connections on the black market, or maybe someone on the inside at the company that manufactured it, but I can't think of anyone in Sakima with that kind of reach."

Laura's mind was reeling. It was too much to take in at once. "Have you heard anything from Ralph?"

"Nothing. I haven't even seen him today," Sofia said. "He didn't come in this morning, and then when everything went crazy, everyone went out on emergency calls. I've never seen the police station so empty. It's never like this."

Outside the window, there was another rustle in the forest. Something was definitely moving. Laura's heart sped up.

"Stay inside," Laura said. "It's safer."

"I don't think it is," Sofia said. "When I said the station is empty, I wasn't exaggerating. There's *no one* here. I'm the only one."

"That's impossible. What about the staff? The desk officer?"

"Beats me. They must have taken off. Maybe they're checking on their families."

Or maybe something happened while Sofia was locked away in the forensics lab, Laura thought.

"I think I'm just going to go home," Sofia said. "I'll feel safer there."

"No, I don't want you going outside alone," Laura said. "We're going to come get you."

"When?" The relief in Sofia's voice was audible. It was clear she didn't want to be alone, even if she didn't say it out loud.

"We'll be there as soon as we can," Laura said. "Don't let

anyone else inside the building."

"I can't lock the front door. I don't have the key," she said. "But the door to the Science Wing is always locked. No one can get in if they don't have the key fob."

"I've got mine, I can get in," Laura said. "We'll come get you."

"Don't take too long, okay?"

"We won't. Just sit tight, and stay safe."

Laura ended the call and turned her gaze back to the window.

A figure stumble out of the woods. Laura froze. It was an older woman wearing a dirty, torn dress, but Laura couldn't see her face. The woman staggered into the side of Victor's Ford Fiesta, bounced off it, and collapsed to the ground.

19

Seeing the older woman lay motionless in the driveway, Laura's medical training took over. She raced for the front door, shouting, "Booker! There's someone outside!"

She unlocked the front door and rushed out to see if the woman was all right. Whoever she was, she might have escaped the infected townspeople like they had and been wandering the woods looking for safety. She was elderly; she could be dehydrated, exhausted, injured. When Laura reached the woman, she crouched over her. The woman was lying face down in the dirt. She was breathing, which was a relief. Laura put a hand on her shoulder, which felt frail and bony under the dress material.

"Are you all right?" Laura asked. "Ma'am, can you hear me?"

Come on, she thought desperately. She needed to know there were other uninfected people in Sakima, that not everyone had been taken by the fungus yet. *Please be okay!*

The woman stirred. It felt like a weight lifting off Laura's shoulders. *She's okay!* The woman pushed herself off the ground onto all fours. She lifted her head. It was Melanie Elster, the old woman who kept leaving passive-aggressive notes in Laura's mailbox.

"Melanie?" Laura asked, surprised.

The old woman let out a loud, raving laugh. Laura stumbled back, away from her. Melanie's pinched features were more relaxed now as the psilocybin flooded her system. Her eyes were red and swollen. She continued laughing as she got to her feet.

"You fucking bitch," Melanie spat. Her eyes began to bleed. Red rivulets trickled down her cheeks. "You keep putting your trash containers in the wrong place. You do it on purpose, don't you? You do it just to drive me crazy!"

Laura backed away from her. The blood coming from Melanie's eyes…she'd seen that before in other infected people. What did it mean? Why was it happening?

Melanie opened her wrinkled hands and looked at her stained, empty palms. "I'm all out. No spores for you. Sorry."

Laura paused but kept a distance between them, one arm extended in case the old woman rushed her and needed to be pushed away. "Melanie, are you okay?"

"Okay?" Melanie laughed, even as the blood streamed from her eyes. "I've never been better. I don't even care about your trash containers touching the sidewalk anymore, or your hedges being the wrong size. Well, maybe I do just a little." She laughed, a string of drool swaying on her wrinkled chin. "You can feel this way too, Laura. I can help you feel this way. You *want* to, believe me. It's like nothing you've ever known. We're all connected, Laura, and it's beautiful, it's so beautiful. You can be one with us, if you just come with me. Let me take you to Dradin Park. Let me show you something *wonderful.*"

"The God of Dirt?" Laura asked.

"Call it whatever you like. It will change your life. It will make you let go of everything that's holding you back," Melanie said. "You know what, Laura? Forget the homeowners' association. Forget the trash and the hedges. None of that matters. This is so much more important than anything you can imagine. Let me show you."

She walked toward Laura, reaching for her as if she wanted to take her by the arm and lead her back to the park like two old friends out for a stroll. Laura took a step backward, and a loud bang rang out. Melanie's head snapped back. A shower of blood and bone erupted from the back of her skull. She crumpled to the ground, a fresh red hole staining the center of her forehead.

Gasping, her eyes wide with horror, Laura turned around. Sean stood just outside the door, the Ruger Semi-Automatic rifle smoking in his hands.

"What did you do?" Laura demanded. She crouched over

Melanie, but it was clear there was nothing to be done. The old woman was dead.

The door burst open behind Sean, and Booker and Victor came running out of the house.

"What happened? Is everyone all right?" Booker said.

Sean lowered the rifle. "I saved her from one of them. The old woman was coming right for her." He looked Laura and added, "You're welcome."

Furious, Laura got to her feet again. "They're sick, Sean. I told you that. They need *help*."

"So you keep saying," he snapped. "She didn't look interested in your help, though, did she?"

Laura shoved past him into the house.

Booker followed her inside. "Are you okay?"

"She didn't have any spores with her, Booker." Her anger grew inside her, a fire fed by her frustration and feelings of helplessness. "She wasn't a danger to me or anyone. We could have helped her, but that—that asshole...!"

"I get it," Booker said. "I don't like it any more than you do, but we have to protect ourselves—"

"They're not monsters, Booker! They're our friends, they're people we know, people we work with!"

He nodded. "What I'm saying is, we have to protect ourselves until we find a way to help them. We don't know how yet. We don't even know if we can."

The sound of the front door lock engaging drew her attention as Sean and Victor came back inside. Laura glared angrily at Sean, who shrugged like he didn't see what the problem was.

"We moved her body into the garage," Victor said. "Didn't seem right to leave her in the driveway like that."

"*He* moved her into the garage," Sean said. He sat down on the couch, clutching his rifle next to him. "I didn't see the point. But then, none of you care what I think anyway. If you're so torn up about the old woman getting killed, maybe you should consider that if you'd listened to me from the start, we would have left town and she'd still be walking around."

Laura felt like her head was going to explode. Fuming, she stormed into the small kitchen off the living room. She needed to be away from the smug, selfish bastard for a minute, even if she couldn't put an actual door between them.

Booker followed her into the kitchen. "Hey. It's okay."

"It's really not," she said. "He's a murderer."

He didn't say anything. He just put his arms around her and tried to comfort her. She closed her eyes, wishing she could wake up from this nightmare. She took a deep breath and let it out slowly, trying to get her anger under control. Finally, she pulled away from him and leaned back against the stove.

"That was Sofia on the phone before," she said.

"What did she say?"

"That we were right, the fungus is a mutation, probably of a common honey fungus. She said the spores are twice as big as they should be, which fits with the theory that they can't travel far on the wind."

"Does she have any idea what caused the mutation?" he asked.

"No, but she mentioned there were traces of an illegal herbicide in the samples from the community garden. Something called MCA 8564. That's why everything in the garden was dead. If I had to bet, I'd say the herbicide's genetically modified ingredients are what caused the mutation, but I don't know how it moved from the plants to the fungus."

"Most likely the mycorrhizal connection," Booker said. "Fungi attach themselves to plant roots underground so they can exchange nutrients. The herbicide must have reached the honey fungus that way and altered its genetic makeup enough that it spawned a mutation."

"Why didn't it just kill the fungus instead?" Laura asked.

"Because that would have made our lives too easy," Booker said with a grin.

"Because fungi adapt," Victor said. He was standing at the kitchen entrance, listening to them. "It's what they do best. The fungi in Chernobyl adapted to feed off gamma radiation. If they can do that, they can adapt to eat the toxic shit you're talking about."

"So who poisoned the community garden?" Laura asked. "And why?"

"Who do you think?" Victor said, lowering his voice. "Who stands to benefit the most from destroying the community garden when it was the main focus of the opposition to developing the park?"

"Bluecoal?" Laura said. "You think *they* did it?"

"I can hear you, you know," Sean said from the living room. "That's quite an accusation!"

"It's true, though, isn't it?" Victor said, turning to face him. "You thought poisoning the community garden would destroy the opposition and let you build your precious development. Where'd you get a hold of the MCA 8564? Are you friends with the manufacturer? Buddy-buddy with the CEO, so he slipped you a container in secret?"

Sean scoffed. "You don't have a shred of evidence that Bluecoal was involved!"

"Gee, that sure sounds like something an innocent person would say," Victor said. "One question, Sean old boy. Did you poison the community garden yourself, or did you have some underpaid lackey do it for you?"

"If you can prove I had anything to do with it, then prove it," Sean sneered. "Anything else is slander, and I have a team of very good lawyers at my disposal. I'm sure they'd be happy to hear about your illegal drug setup downstairs, too."

Victor laughed. "You really think there are gonna be any lawyers left once those spores get out of Sakima? You think anyone's gonna give a shit about slander when they're acting like drugged-out zombies? You fucked the world, man, the whole goddamn world, just so you could build your condos where no one wanted 'em. We ought to kick your sorry ass out and let you fend for yourself."

"You wouldn't!" Sean turned to Booker. "You said yourself we have to work together."

"No one's getting kicked out," Booker said. "But it's clear we're not safe here anymore. If one infected person found us, others will too. We should move on."

"About damn time," Sean muttered. "If that old woman—"

"Her name was Melanie," Laura interrupted, glaring at him.

Sean ignored her. "If that old woman made it all the way

out here, it's not a good sign. For all we know, Sakima has been completely overrun."

"Fine, we'll hit the road," Victor said. "But we should take the guns with us. Sorry, Laura. I know how you feel. I just want us to be safe."

Laura didn't bother arguing. She knew she would only be outvoted. The four of them returned to the basement to start emptying the guns and ammunition from the cabinet. Victor paused in front of his tables of mushrooms and sighed wistfully.

"Sorry I can't take you boys with me," he said. "Be good until I get back."

Sean shook his head and muttered, "That crazy old man's going to get us all killed."

Laura didn't say a word, but the look she gave Sean would have withered a houseplant.

They got to work, starting with the rifles and shotguns, which they brought upstairs and loaded into the back of the SUV. The boxes of shells and cartridges went next, and then the handguns. They left the knives, since using them would require getting too close to someone who might be carrying spores. Finally, when they were just about finished, Victor took the plain black metal box out of the cabinet.

"What's in there?" Laura asked.

He opened it to show her. Inside were what looked like two green steel apples, only with metal safety clips and pull pins at their tops.

"They're M67 fragmentation grenades," he said. "I brought 'em back from Iraq in '91. No idea if they still work. They only way to test 'em would be to pull the pins." He closed the box and handed it to Booker. "Best to be gentle with these, just in case."

Booker brought the metal box carefully up the stairs. Laura went with him, one eye on the box, wondering alternately if the grenades were dead after all this time or if they were going to explode at the slightest jostle. Outside, Sean had stationed himself next to the SUV, keeping watch in case any more of the infected came out of the woods. Booker carefully put the box in the cargo area with the other weapons and closed the rear hatch.

"If that's everything, we should go," Sean said, his eyes still on the tree line near the house. "I don't want to stay here any longer than we have to."

"I'll go get Victor," Laura offered quickly. She didn't want to be left alone with Sean. Everything he said or did rubbed her the wrong way now.

She went back down into the basement, where she found Victor standing in front of the bacchanalia painting, his back to her. She saw the chest of drawers under the painting was open. Victor slid one of the drawers closed and slipped something she couldn't see into his pants pocket.

"Are you all set?" Laura asked.

Victor spun around, startled. "Yes, yes. I was just taking a look around to see if there's anything else I need."

"We should go," she said. "The others are waiting."

"Yep. Right behind you." She started toward the stairs, but Victor said, "Wait."

She turned around. "What is it?"

Victor took off his sunglasses. It was the first time she'd seen him without them. His eyes underneath were a light blue, and kinder than she imagined they would be. The crow's feet etched in the corners of his eyes made him look older, frailer.

"Are you gonna stick around?" he asked.

"What do you mean?"

"When all this is over, and if we're still in one piece, are you gonna stay with Booker?"

She shrugged. She hadn't expected him to ask something so personal. "I honestly don't know. We haven't had a chance to talk about it."

"Look, everything has gone to shit, so I need you to be straight with me," he said. "Are you gonna stick around?"

Her first thought was to tell him that this line of questioning wasn't appropriate right now. Her second thought was to tell him she didn't know yet what she wanted. Her third thought was to tell him the truth.

"Yes, I'd like to."

He nodded. "Good. You know, when Booker was a boy, he spent most of his time alone in the woods. He didn't know how to make friends, and sometimes I think he still doesn't. When it comes to other people, I can take 'em or leave 'em, but he's different. He needs someone to talk to. Someone to lean on. I was never very good at that."

"You're a good father to him," Laura said.

"Thank you," he said. "But sometimes fathers and sons don't talk about certain things. I know he would talk to you, though. He cares about you a lot. Even when you weren't together, I could tell he was suffering for it."

"You can be very sweet when you want to be, you know that?" she said.

"Don't tell anyone. I have a reputation to uphold." He sighed. "Look, his pop died in Iraq when Booker was just a little kid. His pop was my friend, my *best* friend. He had my back in the Gulf War, and when his number was up, I came home and returned the favor by helping raise his little boy. I did the best job I could, and so did his mama. But now she's gone too, and if something happens to me, he'll be all alone in the world. That doesn't sit right with me. So, if that happens, can I rely on you to make sure he's okay?"

"Nothing's going to happen to you," she said. "We're going to get through this."

Victor scoffed. "I'm an old man, Laura. I've been around long enough to know when I'm being tossed a few crumbs. So please, answer me for real. It's important to me to know he'll be all right. That he's got someone who'll look after him."

She nodded and put a hand gently on his arm. "I'll make sure he's okay. I promise."

He nodded and closed his eyes for a moment in relief. "You're a good person, Laura. He's lucky to have you back in his life, even if he doesn't know it yet."

"You really love Booker, don't you?"

"He knows I do," Victor said. "It's never something I needed to say out loud to him. He just knows."

"Maybe it's time you said it out loud," she said.

"Maybe." Victor put his sunglasses back on. "But it's like I said, there are certain things fathers and sons don't talk about."

They left the basement and joined the others in the driveway.

They piled into the SUV, Booker in the driver's seat, Victor in the passenger's, and Laura and Sean in the back seat. She didn't relish the idea of sitting next to him, but she knew it would be worse if it was Victor next to him instead. The bickering would never end.

"We have to swing by the police station," Laura said. "I told Sofia we'd pick her up. She's all alone there."

"Another stop?" Sean groaned. "You people are crazy. If you were smart, we'd be halfway to Albany by now."

"The station has protective equipment, too," she pointed out. "Masks, gloves, goggles. If we go there, we'll have better protection from the spores."

Sean seemed to calm down as he thought about it. "Okay, but let's be quick."

"Well, as long as we have your approval," Booker said. He started the car, and they pulled away from Victor's house.

They took the dirt road that led out of the woods. Soon, the dirt turned to asphalt, and soon after that the trees thinned and they were back on the city streets. They drove for five minutes on empty roads. Laura looked at her phone to see if she'd missed any calls. Nothing. Ralph still hadn't called her back. Her worry sat like a chunk of ice in her stomach.

When they turned onto MacLeod Avenue, Booker slammed on the breaks. The road ahead was crowded with people. As soon as they saw the SUV, they shouted and yelled and ran toward it. Some of them held pieces of wood or metal pipes like weapons, waving them in the air or hitting the ground with them as they ran.

"Shit!" Victor exclaimed. "Back it up!"

Booker threw the gear into reverse and floored the accelerator. The SUV flew backward. He yanked the wheel to one side, spinning the vehicle around so they could make their escape, but then he hit the brakes again. A second crowd just as large as the first rushed at them from that direction, screaming and yelling and laughing that awful, maniacal laugh. With infected townspeople closing in on them from both sides, they were boxed in.

20

Behind the wheel of the SUV, his fingers holding tight, his foot itching to step on the accelerator, Booker scanned the road for anywhere he could go and noticed a chain drug store on other side of MacLeod Avenue, its large parking lot open to the street. The crowd of infected townspeople in front of them closed in, waving their sticks and pipes. The crowd in back was almost upon them as well, shouting, laughing, screaming. He knew Laura was right, these people were sick and needed help, but they barely seemed human anymore. He couldn't let them reach the SUV. There were too many of them, enough to over-turn the vehicle if they wanted to.

Booker yanked the steering wheel in the direction of the drug store and stepped on the accelerator. The SUV rocketed across the avenue, over the curb, and onto the sidewalk, bounc-ing him hard in his seat. The guns rattled in the cargo area in back. He thought of the black metal box with two grenades inside and prayed the pins hadn't been jarred loose. He kept his foot on the gas and sent the SUV through a row of low hedges into the drug store parking lot.

There was a second exit on the far end of the parking lot that led out to a side street. Booker steered toward it. In the rearview mirror, he saw the two pursuing crowds merge into one and pour into the parking lot behind them. He returned his gaze to the road ahead—and slammed on the brake.

The second exit began to fill with more people, all of them running toward the SUV. Both ways out were blocked.

"Just fucking go through them!" Sean said from the back seat.

Laura yelled, "Booker, look out!" as a steel pipe smashed

the driver's-side mirror. Five people had run up on the SUV unseen, and now they surrounded the vehicle and battered the hood, roof, and doors with sticks and pipes. The passenger-side window shattered, sending cubes of safety glass spraying across Victor's lap. A stout teenaged girl with short hair and a torn men's bowling shirt with the name Norton scrawled in cursive across the breast reached in to grab Victor by the shirt. Beneath her pierced eyebrow, her eyes were red and bleeding profusely. The whole lower half of her face was slick with it. Victor cried out and struck her with his elbow. Booker heard her nose break under the impact, and more blood streamed down over her mouth, but it didn't slow her down. She laughed, blood bubbles swelling and bursting from her mouth as she tried to pull Victor out the window.

Laura screamed from the back seat as the window next to her shattered. A tall, lanky, dirt-smeared man reached in, grabbed her by the arm, and tried to pull her out. Laura punched him again and again, each punch fiercer and harder than the last, but the man was oblivious to the pain.

As more of the infected rushed toward the SUV, Booker spied an opening in the crowd. He stomped on the accelerator. The SUV roared forward. Victor and Laura were yanked free of their attackers' grasps, the collar of Victor's Hawaiian shirt tearing in the process.

The crowd of infected people approaching the SUV from the front didn't move out of the way. Booker had to fight his instinct to step on the brakes. The crowd watched the SUV speed toward them with a curious, amused look on their faces, as though they didn't believe it could harm them. The front of the vehicle clipped three men, knocking them aside. Booker heard and felt the impact as they bounced off the SUV's metal and fiberglass body.

"Drive! Drive, God damn it!" Sean shouted, as if Booker weren't doing just that. Sean rolled down his window and aimed his rifle outside, but the SUV bounced too much as it sped over the pavement. He squeezed off a shot that went low, plowing into the asphalt. "Shit!"

Booker gunned it out of the parking lot through the second

exit. The SUV's wheels screeched and the vehicle tipped pre-cariously as he made the sharp turn onto the side road. He kept his foot on the gas and careered up the street.

"Is everyone all right?" Booker asked.

"Just dandy," Victor said, inspecting his torn shirt. "Fuck. I've had this shirt since I bought it at a Jimmy Buffett concert in '94."

Booker glanced in the rearview and saw Laura was pale and shaking. "Laura?"

"The man who grabbed me, it was Paul Miller," she said. "Jeff's father. Did you—did you see his eyes?"

"Are you okay?" he pressed.

"Yeah, I'm okay." She paused to brush the pieces of safety glass off her lap. The wind through the open window blew her hair into a chaotic tangle. "Paul was so far gone, I don't think he even knew who I was."

"That's what I keep telling you," Sean said. "They're beyond help. We have to look out for ourselves now."

"We don't know that," Laura countered angrily. "It could be they need help now more than ever. I'm a doctor, Sean. I won't give up on them."

"Well, *Doctor*," he sneered derisively, "what exactly do you think *you* can do to help them?"

His tone of voice made Booker want to stop the SUV and punch Sean in the face, but instead he kept his eyes on the road in case any more people tried to ambush them. A glance in the mirror showed him Laura was thinking in the back seat.

"We're already know of several diseases caused by fungi growing in the body," she said. "Aspergillosis, candidiasis, fungal meningitis. This is technically the same, even if the symptoms are different. The other diseases are treated with antifungal drugs like voriconazole, itraconazole, or posaconazole, so maybe they would work on this one too. Kill the fungus inside them, the psilocybin will clear out of their systems, and ostensibly they're back to normal."

Sean gave her a skeptical look.

"It's worth a shot," she said. "If we can cure them, we have to try."

"Do you have any of those drugs in your clinic?" Booker asked.

"Not nearly enough, but I know who would," she said. "The CDC."

Laura pulled out her phone. In the rearview, Booker saw her try to scroll through her contacts, but her hands trembled too much. It was clear she was still shaken from the attack.

"Why don't you take a moment, Laura?" Booker said.

"There's no time," she said. She found the contact she was looking for, tapped it, and held the phone to her ear while she waited for someone to pick up. "I should have called them right away, when all this started. I just hope I'm not too late."

Booker stuck to the side streets as he drove. When someone from the CDC finally picked up, he could only hear Laura's side of the conversation.

"Yes, hello, this is Dr. Laura Powell calling from Sakima, New York. My physician's license number is…"

Booker scanned the road in front of him. Mostly, the streets were empty, but occasionally he saw people dart between houses or disappear into the woods. He hoped at least some of them weren't infected and were looking for places to hide, but when he saw the drunken way they moved, he knew better. Was anyone left who wasn't infected?

"Sakima, in New York State," Laura was saying. "We've had an outbreak of a fungal infection, and it's spreading very quickly. We need an emergency response team."

The streets were eerily quiet, except for the crackling of flames as they passed house after burning house. The sky grew dark with billowing smoke. He could taste ash in the back of his throat as the smoke drifted through the broken windows. Victor coughed into his fist. Sean waved a hand in front of his face.

"They're burning houses," Victor said. "I saw the same thing in Kuwait. They burn 'em to flush out anyone who's hiding inside."

"And then they're forced to decide whether to burn to death or get a face full of spores," Sean said. "It's evil. It's just plain evil."

"No, I—I can't send any samples," Laura said into her phone. "This is an ongoing emergency. We need help immediately."

Booker drove past a fiery three-story house, its windows bright with flames. The detached garage burned, too. He thought about the people inside, faced with the awful choice Sean had described. He leaned on the accelerator. He didn't want to be among the burning houses any longer than necessary.

From the back seat, Laura continued, "Yes, I would definitely say it qualifies as an epidemic. More than half the city is infected and it's spreading fast. We need thousands of doses of antifungal medication. We need doctors, nurses, public health experts, we need police and—and firefighters—" She paused, and then she said, "Hello? *Hello?*"

The panic in her voice made him look in the rearview again, where he saw Laura lower the phone from her ear and stare at it in horror.

"Laura, what is it?"

"The—the battery," Laura dropped the dead phone to the floor of the SUV, her eyes filling with tears of frustration. A moment later, she angrily wiped them away, determined not to give up. "Fine, I just need to call back, that's all. Does anyone have a phone on them?"

"Shit," Booker said. "I'm sorry, we ran out of the house so fast I left it behind."

"I never bothered owning one," Victor said. "Didn't like how easy it was to track."

"And mine's back at the fucking motel," Sean said. He rubbed his face with his hands. "Jesus, we're fucked, aren't we?"

Booker drove into City Square, trying to stay hopeful. Maybe Laura had given them enough information to go on. Maybe they would still come. He was surprised to find the streets deserted here, too. The normally crowded sidewalks in front of the library and government buildings were desolate. He'd never seen this part of town so empty. He couldn't shake how eerie it was. He parked the SUV at the yellow-painted curb in front of the police station, figuring parking violations were the least of the police's priorities right now, and stepped out into the heat. The humidity drew sweat from his pores almost instantly. The others got out of the SUV too, Victor fussing with his torn shirt, and Sean strapping his rifle over his shoulder. Laura exited last, her jaw set defiantly.

"They're coming, I know they're coming," she said.

"How do you know?" Sean pressed.

"They have the name of our city," she said. She started chewing her fingernails, then forced herself to stop. "I—I think they heard what was happening before the phone died. They'll come. They have to."

"How soon will they get here?" Booker asked.

"They would need to gather supplies first," she said. "But the first group of doctors could be here by late afternoon, early evening. The police and firefighters could get here sometime before that."

"That's *if* they're coming," Sean pointed out. "We don't know for sure that they are, which means nothing's changed. We're still neck deep in the same shit we were five minutes ago, and we're still on our own."

21

Laura led the others into the police station. The air-conditioning was still running, which she appreciated after being out in the heat, but true to what Sofia had told her, the station was abandoned. The public waiting area was empty. The floor was littered with scraps of paper, a couple of hastily dropped purses, and horribly, a single child's shoe. She half expected to see Dahlia Mintz sitting at the front desk as usual, but the far side of the dividing barrier was as empty as the waiting area.

The phone on the front desk was ringing and had been since before they came inside. Booker hurdled over the barrier and grabbed the handset off the cradle.

"Hello?"

Laura watched his facial expressions change from hopeful to confused.

"Hello? Is someone there?" He flinched and slammed the phone down again.

"Who was it, son?" Victor asked.

"I don't know. A man," Booker said. "He started laughing and didn't stop."

"You shouldn't have answered it," Sean said. "Now they know we're here."

"I doubt it," Booker replied. "Something tells me this guy didn't even know what number he was calling."

"You don't know that," Sean said. "Those freaks out there are looking for us, and I'd rather not get caught because you keep making dumb mistakes."

"Hey!" Victor interrupted. "Talk to him like that again and I'll throw you in one of the cells myself."

Sean swallowed whatever comeback he had in mind. "Let's

just find your friend and get out of here."

Booker opened the gate to let them in. Laura brought them through the interior door into the back of the station. She remembered how it used to smell of burnt coffee back here, how there was the constant noise of conversation and ringing phones. Now it was dead silent. It was *wrong* how quiet the station was. It made the sound of her own breathing too loud in her ears. As they passed Ralph's office, she glanced inside, hoping against reason that he was at his desk, working furiously on a plan, but his office was as empty as the rest of the station.

The door marked holding was open. Inside, at the end of a short corridor, she saw the holding cell was open, too. If anyone had been locked up, they weren't anymore.

Finally, they reached the closed door to the Science Wing. Laura hoped Sofia was still okay on the other side. Whatever had gone down in the rest of the station didn't look good. The infected must have forced their way inside. Maybe some had been here already, officers who didn't know what was growing inside them until it was too late, or detainees who'd been put in the holding cell before anyone knew what was wrong with them. She expected to see spores coating everything in a fine brown dust, but there was nothing, only overturned chairs and papers scattered on the floor. Everyone must have been dragged off to be infected elsewhere. The park, she supposed. Where the God of Dirt waited.

Come worship it. Serve it, as we do.

She used her key fob to unlock the Science Wing door and called, "Sofia? Are you here?" She walked down the hallway until she got to the forensics lab. No one was inside. She called out again, "Sofia? Where are you?"

"Back here!" The muffled voice came from farther down the hall.

Laura and the others continued to the morgue. Through the window in the hallway she saw Sofia inside, standing before the morgue refrigerator and dressed in the same clothes Laura had seen her in last night. Sofia reached for the handle of one of the eight doors in the stainless-steel refrigerator.

"Sofia, stop! What are you doing?" Laura called.

Sofia turned and looked back at her through the window. "After I tested on the samples, I remembered the fungus you found inside Kat Bishop's body. I wanted to inspect it again. The body's still in here, isn't it?" She reached for the door handle again.

"Wait, don't!" Booker said, but it was too late.

Sofia opened the refrigerator door. The space inside was packed wall to wall with dark, bulbous mushrooms and furry webs of hyphae, all of it growing out of Kat's decomposing corpse. For one horrifying moment, Laura thought the corpse moved, saw it stretch like a sleeper coming awake, but it was only shifting under the weight of the crowded fungi that spilled out the open door. A shower of spores fell to the floor as Sofia jumped back from the refrigerator with a gasp.

Laura banged on the glass. "Get away from there! Don't let any of it touch you!"

"I'm okay," Sofia said, catching her breath and backing away from the horrific sight of the mushroom-covered body.

"Did you breathe in any spores?" Booker called.

"I'm okay," she said again. She put her hand to her chest like she'd had a fright. "Jesus, I wasn't expecting that."

Laura pointed at a door in the morgue wall. "Go in there. There's a bathroom with a shower. You're going to have to wash off any spores that might have gotten on your skin or your clothes."

"I told you, I'm okay," Sofia insisted.

"Please, just in case," Laura said. "If you got any on you, you may be running out of time. We don't know how long it takes for the spores to affect someone."

Sofia nodded solemnly. "Okay, but don't leave without me."

"We won't, I promise," Laura assured her.

Sofia started unbuttoning her blouse and disappeared into the connecting bathroom.

Laura brought Booker, Victor, and Sean to a storage closet in the hallway. Inside was the remaining stash of PPE. There were no more protective bodysuits like the ones she and Booker had worn to gather samples in Dradin Park, but they were able to create makeshift suits from what was still on hand: long-sleeved gowns, scrub pants, boot covers, hair covers, goggles, nitrile gloves, and N95 respirators.

Laura pulled her gown and scrub pants on over her clothes. It was one thing to strip down to her underwear in front of Booker, who'd seen her in less, but there was no way she was going to do that in front of Sean. Not even if it would make the PPE more comfortable.

The others followed her lead, putting the PPE on over their clothes. As Booker pulled on his gloves, he said, "Victor, you've been quiet since we got here. Is everything okay?"

"Something on my mind, that's all." Victor put a hair cover over his bald head and tucked in his rat-tail braid. "I was reminded of something when Laura said this fungus could be a mutation of a common honey fungus. The largest known fungus in the world is a honey fungus out in Oregon. Its mycelial network spans three and a half miles. Scientists think it might be the largest living organism on the planet. It made me wonder how big *our* fungus is. As big as the park? Bigger? There's no reason to think its mycelial network underground will stop at the park's borders."

"Shit," Sean said, snapping a pair of goggles over his eyes. "Doesn't anyone have any *good* news?"

"I know the fungus you're talking about, Victor. It's over two thousand years old," Booker said. He sat on the hallway floor to pull the coverings over his shoes. "As far as we can tell, our fungus is still young. It only started releasing spores three days ago, if we can go by when the infections started. It couldn't have grown that big yet."

"Normally I would agree, but we're dealing with a mutation," Victor said. "We don't know how quickly it can grow. When you get right down to it, we don't know much about it at all. If it grows faster, if it expands past the park, what happens when it fruits again? Its mushrooms could come up anywhere in town, and their spores could infect even more people. Provided there's anyone left by then."

"A lot of the city is paved," Laura said from behind her N95 respirator. "That will limit where it can send up mushrooms."

"No, it won't," Booker said, standing up again. "Mushrooms

are made of hyphae, just like the mycelium, only packed tightly together, and hyphae can hold up to thirty thousand times its own weight. That makes mushrooms strong enough to break through granite."

A memory came back to Laura. One summer when she was a child, a small mushroom had appeared in the front walk of her childhood home, having pushed its way up through the concrete. It had inspired young Laura to see something so small overcome such insurmountable odds. She'd taken it as a lesson that nothing could stand in her way if she refused to let it, an Aesopian moral that size didn't matter, only determination. Now the thought of that mushroom breaking through the concrete made her shudder.

When they were finished putting on their PPE, Sofia still hadn't returned from the shower. Laura checked her phone. Half an hour had passed since they left her in the morgue's connecting bathroom.

"You guys go wait by the SUV," she told them. "I'll get Sofia. Be ready to leave as soon as we're back."

As the three men filed out of the Science Wing, Laura walked back in the direction of the morgue. Sofia appeared at the end of the hallway. She was still naked and wet from the shower, as if she'd only just stepped out of it. Laura hurried toward her.

"Oh my God, I'm sorry, I should have left some clean clothes for you," she said. "Let's get you into some PPE. The others are waiting outside."

"What?" Sofia said. "Where—where am I?"

"Are you okay?" Laura said. "You're in the Science Wing. Don't you remember?"

Sofia closed her eyes and shook her head, her wet hair spraying water on Laura. "Something's wrong. I can't think straight. I'm seeing things. I thought there were snakes in the shower. It's—it's happening to me, isn't it? The same thing that happened to the others."

Laura put an arm around Sofia's bare, wet shoulders and guided her toward the forensics lab. "I've got you. Let's get somewhere safe and we'll figure out what to do."

Her words sounded confident, but inside she was grasping

at straws. A spore from Kat's body must have gotten on Sofia and burned its way through her skin before she got in the shower. That was only thirty minutes ago. It was astonishing, she never imagined the infection could take hold that fast. And yet it had spread through Sakima with incredible speed, hadn't it? The infection had brought the city to its knees in less than a day. Laura cursed under her breath. She was a doctor, she should have realized how quickly the spores were affecting people.

She sat Sofia down on the rolling chair in the forensics lab, then went to get the light summer jacket she knew Sofia kept in the closet. Laura brought it back and draped it around Sofia's shoulders. It didn't conceal much, but it would help keep her warm.

Sofia flinched like she saw something awful in the doorway, but there was nothing there. Her expression shifted to sadness and anger. "There's nothing you can do, Laura. Just go."

"I'm not leaving you here," she said. "We'll take you someplace where you can get help."

Sofia pulled the jacket tight around her shoulders. "And where would that be?" She laughed bitterly. It turned into a chuckle. "Where would that be?" she said again, and her chuckle turned into a throaty laugh. "Where would that be?"

"Sofia, look at me," Laura said.

She looked up at Laura. Her pupils were dilated.

"You're so beautiful, Laura," Sofia said. "Did you know that? Everyone is so beautiful. Everyone and everything." She sat up straight, as though coming to attention. "That sound is beautiful, too. Don't you hear it? It's calling me."

Damn. Sofia was slipping away, and Laura was helpless to stop it.

"Ignore it," Laura said. It terrified her that Sofia could hear the God of Dirt calling even this far from the park, but she kept the fear out of her voice and tried to sound calm and reassuring. "Please, try to concentrate, Sofia. Stay with me."

"I have to go to it." Sofia rose from the chair. She brushed the jacket off her shoulders and onto the floor. "It's like a song. I wish you could hear it, Laura. It's so beautiful. It's like God is singing just for me."

Laura moved to get between Sofia and lab door. "Wait."

The smile stayed on Sofia's face, but the look in her eyes changed to anger. She was furious that her path was blocked, but coupled with the unwavering smile it gave her normally attractive features a malevolent appearance. "Get out of my way."

"Sofia, please, just—"

"I said get out of my way!"

Sofia leapt at Laura and tackled her to the floor. Laura fell on her back, knocking the wind out of her. The attack had happened so quickly she was in a state of shock even as Sofia straddled her and smacked her across the face with one open palm. Laura's cheek stung, and the blow set her goggles askew.

"Sofia, stop!"

Sofia smacked her again with her other hand, then sprang to her feet and ran out of the lab.

"Sofia!" Laura scrambled to her feet, quickly adjusting her goggles and respirator, and then ran after her. She spotted Sofia in the hallway, jogging toward the door that led back to the police station, her feet slapping wetly on the linoleum floor. Laura chased after her. "Sofia, stop!"

Sofia laughed as she ran, like she was a child playing a game. "It's God! God is summoning me!"

Laura caught up to her, and grabbed Sofia by the arm. Sofia shoved her back forcefully, sending Laura crashing into the wall. Her hip flared with pain where it struck the hard cement.

"You don't understand," Sofia said. "But you will once you hear it, too. Come with me, Laura!"

Sofia grabbed her wrist and tried to drag her forward, but Laura pulled free.

"Sofia, please…"

With another throaty laugh, Sofia spun on her heel and hurled herself against the push bar that opened the Science Wing door from the inside. Laura chased her through the station and out into the lobby, but Sofia was too fast, unencumbered by the PPE and shoe coverings Laura wore.

"Summoning, summoning," Sofia sang, her drugged brain fixated on the word. "Sum-mon-ing!"

She jumped over the low dividing barrier into the public

waiting area, then burst out the front door. Laura followed only seconds behind her.

Outside, Booker, Victor, and Sean were standing beside the SUV, keeping an eye out for infected townspeople. With their faces hidden behind goggles and N95 respirators, they looked like they'd just stepped out of a spaceship. They turned with startled surprise to watch a naked Sofia run past them into the street.

"Holy shit," Victor said.

"It's calling me!" Sofia yelled. "Can't you hear it? God is calling all of us to worship!"

Laura ran after her. From the corner of her eye, she saw Sean raise the rifle to his shoulder. She skidded to a stop and shouted "No!" just as he pulled the trigger.

There was a deafening crack. Sofia was knocked forward as though someone had pushed her. Laura saw a red hole appear between her shoulder blades, saw a red mist explode out of her chest as the bullet passed through her. And then Sofia fell face first onto the blacktop.

22

Laura froze in the middle of the street, staring at Sofia's pale body. Her mind couldn't process what she was seeing. Sofia, her coworker, her friend, the woman whom she'd helped to move out of her abusive boyfriend Chuck's house just last weekend. (Chuck, who'd looked so much like Mr. Clean as he glared at Laura—how they'd laughed about that afterward!) And now she was...this. Lifeless meat lying in the middle of the road, destined sooner or later for Laura's autopsy table.

I hear you've got a new customer.

She choked back a sob. She couldn't do this anymore. She didn't want to be here. She wished she could curl up and hide until it was over.

Booker yanked the rifle out of Sean's grasp with one hand and punched him with the other. Sean fell onto his backside on the sidewalk.

"You're out of your damned mind, ni—" He cut himself off.

"What were you going to call me?" Booker demanded.

"Nothing," Sean said. He adjusted his goggles, which had been knocked askew, and made sure his N95 respirator wasn't damaged. Then he got back on his feet. "I couldn't just let her go and tell the others where we are!"

"She was our friend," Booker said, "and you shot her in the damned *back*."

"Just because the three of you are too chickenshit to do what has to be done doesn't mean I'm going to stand by and do nothing," Sean insisted.

Victor walked up to them. "I've had enough of this son of a bitch. We ought to tie him up and leave his sorry ass here."

"You wouldn't," Sean said.

"That's right, we wouldn't, because we're not assholes like you," Booker said. "When all this is over, you'll stand trial for what you did to her, and Melanie Elster, and anyone else you decide to play judge, jury, and executioner for."

"Stand trial?" Sean laughed disdainfully. "Buddy, when this is over, they're going to give me a fucking *medal* for what I did."

Laura couldn't listen to any more of this. She found the strength to walk to Sofia's body, then crouched over her. Sofia was lying face-down. The hole between her shoulder blades was red and angry, leaking blood across her back. More blood pooled out from beneath her, spilling from the exit wound in her chest. Laura put two gloved fingers on Sofia's neck over the carotid artery, hoping against reason that she was still alive, but the lack of a pulse confirmed what Laura already knew. The bullet had gone right through her heart. It was likely she was dead before she hit the blacktop.

Laura bit back tears. She refused to leave Sofia in the middle of the street, alone and exposed like this. She turned the body over. Sofia's eyes were still open, staring past Laura into nothingness, and the gaping exit wound in her chest was so grisly Laura had to look away to compose herself. Then she slipped her arms under Sofia's body and lifted her off the road.

Booker rushed over to help her, and together they carried Sofia into the police station. They couldn't bring her to the morgue now that it was contaminated with spores from Kat Bishop's corpse, so instead they laid her down on the floor of the forensics lab. Laura covered the body with a shock blanket from the station's supply closet. She took a piece of paper from the desk, wrote Sofia Hernandez on it, and placed it on top of the blanket, in case she was found by someone who didn't know who she was.

They didn't stay at the police station long after that. They got back into the SUV, but this time Victor insisted on sitting in back with Sean so he could keep an eye on him. Laura didn't argue and climbed into the front with Booker. As they pulled away from the curb, Sean didn't ask where they were going the way he usually did. Maybe it was finally sinking in that he was skating on thin ice. When Laura glanced at him in the rearview mirror, his mouth was set tight, his gaze focused out the window, deep in thought.

She didn't ask where they were going, either. Booker just drove. Leaving City Square, they found themselves in a thick bank of smoke drifting across the road from the fires. It seeped in through the SUV's broken windows, swirling like a haze through the cabin. Thankfully, their goggles and respirators kept the smoke from irritating their eyes and lungs. For a time, Laura couldn't see anything in front of the SUV but an airy, undulating grayness, and Booker was forced to slow their speed to avoid accidentally hitting anything.

"I don't like this," Victor said from the back seat.

"They're out there, watching us," Sean said. He clutched his rifle closer. "I'm sure of it."

"Everyone, keep your head," Booker said. He squinted behind his goggles. "I think the smoke clears up just ahead."

He was right. The smoke dissipated a few minutes later, allowing Laura to see the road and surrounding trees again. The sky remained a dark gray. It looked like a ceiling to her, a lid placed over Sakima to keep them trapped.

"What's that?" Booker said, focusing on something in the road.

Laura sat up straight in the passenger seat. A boy sat slumped by the side of the road, head down on his chest. He was small, not yet fully grown, maybe early teens. Booker slowed as they approached him. Laura couldn't tell if he was unconscious or dead.

"We should see if there's anything we can do for him," Laura said.

"Don't stop," Sean insisted from the back seat. "We should keep going."

"Why don't you shut yer trap?" Victor said.

Sean ignored him. "Keep driving! Don't stop!"

Booker stopped the SUV. Sean groaned and shook his head. "These bleeding-heart idiots," he mumbled.

"This will just take a moment," Laura said. "You can stay here if you want."

"You're damn right I'm staying here," Sean said.

"I'll hang back with Captain Charming," Victor said. "You two stay sharp, okay? For all we know, this could be a setup."

Laura got out of the SUV. Booker was right behind her, taking his shotgun with him and leaving the engine running in case they needed to make a quick escape. They hurried over to the boy, but as they drew closer Laura could already tell he was dead. She knelt beside him, pushed his head back to see his face, and recoiled from the gruesome sight.

It was Jeff Miller, the young violinist. His eyes had burst, leaving bloody sockets filled with dark mushrooms like the ones growing out of Kat's body. His mouth hung open like he was screaming, but it was only more mushrooms growing inside it, forcing his jaw open wide.

"Jesus," Booker said. "What happened to him?"

"The fungus killed him," Laura said. "The more it grew inside him, the more it digested his organs for nutrients until finally his body shut down."

"It's still alive. It's still eating him, and now it's fruiting on him," Booker said. "Is this what's going to happen to all of them?"

She nodded gravely. "Jeff was only infected two days ago. That means there's a good chance the others will die two days after their own infections began."

"Except that won't be the end of it," Booker said. "Once they die, their bodies will fruit just like this one, or Kat's in the morgue. That means more spores, and more people infected."

"And more of the fungus will spread out across the state, maybe even the country," Laura said. "If an infected person gets on an airplane and fruits like this in another country, we're talking about a global pandemic."

The sound of raised voices from the SUV drew their attention. The back door opened and Victor came tumbling out onto the blacktop. He howled in pain, rubbing the shoulder he'd landed on. As Booker and Laura ran toward him, the SUV's engine revved and the vehicle peeled away, tires screeching. Laura watched in shock as their only means of transportation flew down the street, turned a corner, and was gone.

Booker helped Victor to his feet. "You okay?"

"Yeah," Victor said, rubbing his shoulder again. "Just bruised, nothing broken."

"What happened?" Laura asked.

"I should have known that son of a bitch was planning something," Victor said. "He got my gun away from me and pushed me out the door."

"That motherfucker," Booker said. "Did he say anything?"

"Yeah," Victor replied. "He said we're on our own."

With no other option, they began walking along the road, Booker's shotgun, their only remaining weapon, slung over his shoulder by its strap. They kept to the side of the road, near the tree line where they were less likely to be seen. They walked for half a mile without seeing anyone, only the occasional burning house that pumped more dark smoke into the air. Soon it became hard to see very far in front of them. In every direction she looked, Laura only saw smoke. It made everything look otherworldly, like a dream. She wished this were a dream. Then at least she could wake up from it and put it behind her.

What would she do then? If she woke up to discover it was still the day of the town hall meeting and none of this had happened, if there were no mutant fungus infecting the town, if she were given a second chance, would she do anything differently? Yes, she decided, there was one thing she would change. She would be honest with Booker from the start. She would tell him how much she'd missed him. She would tell him she still loved him. As they walked through the smoke, Booker took her gloved hand in his, and she wondered if he knew those things already.

The smoke began to dissipate once more as they approaching a residential street. Only a few houses in the distance burned, all the others remained intact. A group of forty or fifty people moved down the street in a herd, with smaller groups breaking off to kick down doors and enter the houses. Laura's chest went tight. They were searching for people who hadn't been infected yet. People like her, Booker, and Victor.

"Into the woods!" Booker hissed.

They ducked into the thick forest. They didn't go too deep, only far enough to hide behind trees while still being able to see the road. Laura peeked out from behind the thick trunk of a sugar maple. The group was still several yards away. There was no way they could have spotted her and the others yet.

"Fuck!" Victor whispered.

She turned to see what was wrong. Victor stood a few feet away, between her and Booker, hiding behind a northern red oak. He glared at a cluster of toadstools that poked up from between the roots.

"Damned things!" he said, and kicked at them until they broke loose and were knocked away.

Booker shook his head. "I don't think that was our mutant fungus, Victor."

"I don't care," he said. "I saw what was in that boy's eye sockets, and in his mouth. It was just like those ants in the Amazon. I don't know about you, but I never want to see another mushroom again. Not on my pizza, not in my salad, not in my soup…"

"Shhhh." Laura nodded at the street.

The group of infected people moved past the woods. It was like a parade, albeit a parade of lunatics. They laughed and yelled and spun in circles. They pawed at the air in front of them, clutching at things no one else saw. Their clothes were torn and dirty. Some were naked or close to it, their bare skin smeared with dirt and handprints, but they didn't seem to care. It put Laura in mind of the bacchanalia she'd seen in the painting in Victor's basement. This wasn't just insanity. It was religious ecstasy. The God of Dirt was their Dionysus.

A few of the passing townspeople clutched handfuls of spores, ready to infect anyone they encountered. Laura watched them closely, praying they would just keep walking.

One man in the group stopped and turned to look into the woods. Laura's heart crammed into her throat. It was Chuck, Sofia's abusive ex-boyfriend. Mr. Clean. His bald head was beaded with sweat. He was shirtless, a patch of red, burnt skin marring one muscular arm as though he'd gotten too close to one of the fires. A flash of anger burned through Laura at the sight of him. Mixed with her grief over Sofia's death, it made her want to punch Chuck in the face or club him with a fallen tree branch, but it was too dangerous with the other infected people right there. Instead, she ducked back behind the sugar maple.

Her heart beat loudly in her ears, drumming with adrenaline from her anger, and from the fear that Chuck had seen her.

Dead leaves crunched under his feet as he stepped off the road and into the forest.

"Who's there?" Chuck called out.

23

Laura stayed hidden behind the sugar maple, her heart pounding. She heard more leaves crunch as Chuck took another step into the woods. Were the other infected townspeople joining him? Were they about the search the woods en masse? She didn't dare look around the tree to find out. If Chuck spotted her, if *any* of them spotted her, they wouldn't stand a chance against this many people.

Booker unstrapped the shotgun from his shoulder, moving slowly so as not to make a noise. He put the stock to his shoulder and aimed down the barrel. If Chuck got too close, Booker would be forced to fire, but the sound would draw the others' attention, and that would be even worse. Laura held her breath.

"Who's there?" Chuck shouted again. "Come out!"

She glanced at Booker and Victor. Both of them were silent, waiting to see what happened. Booker's finger hovered near the trigger.

"If you don't come out, I will fucking *crush* you!" Chuck yelled. More leaves crunched underfoot as he took another step into the forest.

Booker's finger curled around the trigger. Laura gritted her teeth, preparing herself for the deafening bang, and the inevitable aftermath. How fast could they run through the woods? How far would they make it before they were caught? And they *would* be caught, there was no doubt of that.

"Come on, Chuck," another male voice said. "There's no one there. No one got past us."

"But I saw something," Chuck said.

"That's one of its blessings to us, the gift it gives to our eyes," a third voice said, female this time. "But there's no one in the woods."

"There's no one left," the other male voice added.

Laura closed her eyes. *No one left.* That couldn't be true, could it?

There was a rustle of leaves as Chuck backed out of the woods and onto the road again. Laura squatted at the base of the sugar maple and peeked around the trunk. She saw Chuck walking away. With him were Heather and George Bishop, who escorted him back to the group. Booker lowered the shotgun, and Laura let out a silent sigh of relief.

A few minutes later, the last of the group had drifted down the road away from them. Laura, Booker, and Victor waited until they couldn't hear their shouts and laughter anymore, then ventured out of the woods and back onto the road.

"Stick close," Booker said. "There may be more of them."

Victor glanced behind them, in the direction of the group. "I hate to agree with the jackoff who stole our car, but I'm starting to think we should just get the fuck out of Sakima while we can."

"We'll never make it without a car," Laura said. "We're too slow on foot, and there must be dozens of groups like that all over the city. Our best bet is to find somewhere to hide and wait for help to arrive."

"Laura, it's time to face facts," Victor said. "There's no help coming. We're alone here. We can't rely on anyone but ourselves."

She shook her head, refusing to hear it. "They'll be here. They're coming."

"You've got a lot more faith in government institutions than I do," Victor said. "But even if by some miracle you're right, where exactly can we hide in this mess?" He swept his arm to show her every house on the street was burning now. Massive columns of dark smoke billowed into the air.

"Let's keep moving," Booker said. "We'll find someplace. We have to."

They walked down the street, sticking to the yellow line in the middle to stay as far from the fires as they could. The smoke was thick and disorienting, and when they turned corners onto other streets Laura couldn't be sure where they were anymore.

House after house raged with fire, flickering in windows and doors like huge jack-o'-lanterns. The air was superheated by all the fires, and Laura found herself sweating under her scrubs. In some places, the smoke was so thick she couldn't see more than a few inches in front of her. The goggles kept the smoke from blinding her, and the N95 respirator kept it from choking her, but that was little consolation. Was the whole city like this now? Was nothing left?

What if Victor was right and no help was coming? What if they really were alone?

A small shape lay spread out on the road. Laura went cold, thinking it was another dead person, but as they drew closer she saw it was a yellow Labrador. She crouched over the dog. It was dead, which was heartbreaking enough on its own, but the dog's hind legs and back were badly burned. It must have crawled out of one of the burning houses and only made it this far before succumbing to its wounds. Laura thought she didn't have any tears left after shedding them for Sofia, but her body heaved and shook as she knelt beside the dog, thinking about how confused and frightened it must have been.

Her tears were about more than just the dog, she knew. The dead dog in the middle of the street meant something she didn't have words for. A sign of the end of the everything.

Booker put his hand on her shoulder. "I'm sorry, Laura. We have to keep moving."

She nodded and stood, sniffling, and together the three of them walked deeper into the roiling smoke. It got so thick that even the glow of the flames looked muted and distant. She didn't know what street they were on, or what part of town they were in. She couldn't see any street signs. They might as well have been on another planet.

"You know what I think?" Victor said, breaking the silence that had stretched on for many long minutes. "I think we should just kill the fucker."

"Which fucker would that be?" Booker asked.

"The fungus," he said. "My grandma used to get fungi in her garden all the time. She would pour cornmeal on 'em and dry those bastards right up."

"Are you suggesting we swing by a supermarket, buy some cornmeal, and just sprinkle it around the park?" Laura asked.

Victor shrugged. "Buy it? Let's be real, at this point we could probably just take it."

She laughed. It felt good to laugh, if even for a moment.

"Killing the fungus in the park won't stop the infection from spreading," Booker said. "It's not just one fungus we have to worry about anymore. It's countless fungi in walking hosts, all of them ready to fruit in a matter in days."

"Always a ray of sunshine, aren't you, son?" Victor teased. "I don't suppose we could just sprinkle all the infected folks with cornmeal and hope for the best?"

"Maybe we can get them to eat some polenta," Laura said, laughing again. "You know, attack the infection from the inside."

Victor grinned. "I make a pretty mean cornbread—"

Booker stopped and raised a hand for the others to stop, too. "Hold up. What's that up ahead?"

A red light burned in the distance, hazy and diffuse in the smoke. She thought at first it was a stop light, but no, it was too low to the ground for that. It looked eerie, a blood-red glow in the roiling gray.

"Stay close," Booker said. He took his shotgun off his shoulder.

As they approached the red light, a dark, bulky shape began to manifest in the smoke, and soon they saw there were actually two red lights. They were looking at the back of a car, a big one. It sat motionless in the road, the engine still running. They hurried toward it, and when they were close enough they saw it was an SUV.

Booker's SUV.

The driver's-side door was open. Laura looked inside. The vehicle was empty. "Where the hell is Sean?"

Had the infected townspeople gotten him, or had he stopped for some reason and continued on foot? There was no way to know. The exterior of the car was already so banged up from the attack in the drug store parking lot that she couldn't tell if there were any new signs of violence.

"Good riddance to bad rubbish," Victor said. "And good timing, too. My feet are killing me. I don't think I've walked this much since I was in the Kuwaiti desert. Come to think of it, I felt a lot safer over there, too."

Booker climbed into the SUV and got behind the wheel, while Laura took the passenger seat once again. Victor crawled into the back seat and twisted around to inspect the weapons cache in the cargo area. Everything was there except for Sean's rifle. It made Laura wonder again what had happened to him. If he'd been infected, or worse, it was no less than what he deserved for killing Sofia. It was a harsh thought, but it was an honest one. On the other hand, if Sean had gotten away, she hoped their paths never crossed again. For his sake.

As they drove through the smoke-enshrouded streets, Laura's eyelids felt heavy. They drooped until she closed them, lulled by the purr of the engine, the relative safety of being back in the SUV, and her trust that Booker would bring them someplace safe. She hadn't realized how much she needed to rest. They'd been on the run since early this morning. However, her eyes only stayed closed for a minute before they opened again. As exhausted as she was, her nerves were too on edge to let her sleep.

They drove in silence through a dreamlike world of smoke and distant flames. The roads were empty, no people and no traffic, although there were plenty of abandoned cars they were forced to weave around. Finally, the smoke parted in front of them.

"Shit!" Booker shouted.

They'd gotten turned around in the smoke and somehow wound up in the heart of the city, right in front of Dradin Park. Here, the street wasn't devoid of people. Here, there were hundreds of them, and they all noticed the SUV at the same time.

24

Booker threw the SUV into reverse and stepped on the gas. As the infected townspeople ran after them, the vehicle roared backward up the street. Booker tried to turn the SUV around, but the mob swarmed them before he could complete the turn. In a frenzy, people crawled onto the engine hood and clambered onto the roof. Hands reached through the broken passenger-side window to grab Laura by the arm and the collar of her surgical gown. The hair cover was ripped off her head, and another hand grabbed a fistful of her hair. She tried to bat them away, but their grip was too strong. More hands yanked at her seatbelt, prying it loose. She could see the mania in their eyes as they pulled her to the window, their pupils dilated into bottomless black holes. Their mouths were agape with laughter and ecstatic hollering.

Booker yelled something, but she couldn't see him through the tangle of grabbing, groping arms. The butt of his shotgun came ramming through, trying to knock people back, trying to make them let go of her. It was no use. She was halfway out the window now, her back against the car door, and more hands grabbed her, pulling and prying. Victor let loose a stream of obscenities, and she knew he was being pulled out through the window in back.

She heard rather than saw Booker get out of the SUV. Through the grasping arms that had her almost all the way out of the window now, she saw his shotgun again, only this time it was the barrel end pointing at the mob.

And then, suddenly, they let go of her. Laura fell, landing hard on the blacktop, but she was only slightly bruised. The crowd paid no attention to Booker and his shotgun. They turned and walked back toward the park. Laura stood up, checking to make sure her goggles and N95 respirator hadn't been damaged, and that her makeshift protective suit wasn't torn. Her hair cover was on the ground, and she quickly put it back on. When she looked up again, the infected were filing into the park.

"What the hell?" Victor said. He had a scrape on his forehead but looked otherwise unharmed. "It's like they just stopped giving a shit about us."

Booker slung the shotgun over his shoulder. "Something called them away."

"The fungus," Laura said.

"It's *talking* to them? Fuck this," Victor said. "Let's get the hell out of here while we can."

But Laura didn't move. Neither did Booker. They looked at each other, and she knew he was thinking the same thing she was.

"Oh no, come on, you two," Victor said. "Let's not press our luck. Let's just go!"

"We won't get a chance like this again," Booker said.

"They're distracted," Laura said. "We can get close. We can see what's really going on in there."

"And maybe even destroy the fungus," Booker said. "It won't cure the people who are already infected, but it'll stop any more spores from spreading."

"It'll be dangerous," Laura said. "We don't know how much time we've got before they come after us again."

"Then we'd better be quick," Booker said.

"Christ, this is insane," Victor said. "You can't be serious. You really want to go *in* there?"

Booker nodded. "You can wait here if you'd rather."

"You think I'd let you two go it alone? Like hell." Victor went to the back of the SUV and opened the cargo door. "If we have to go in there, we're going in armed."

"Just remember, try not to kill any of them," Laura said. "If they come at you, go for the legs, or anything non-lethal, to slow them down or stop them."

"Sorry, Laura, but if they try to grab me like that again, I ain't makin' no promises." Victor pulled a shotgun from the pile, broke it open, and loaded two shells into it. He grabbed a handful of additional shells from the ammunition box and stuffed them into his pants pocket under his scrubs. Then he opened the black metal box and removed one of the grenades. He put it in his other pants pocket, where it bulged like a wineskin. "Just in case," he said.

Booker took a few more shells for his own shotgun. He picked up a sleek, nickel-plated handgun, loaded a magazine of .45-caliber bullets into it, and held it out to Laura. She shook her head.

"Please," he said. "Just to be safe."

With a heavy sigh, she took the gun from him. She didn't like the way it felt in her hand. It was a weapon designed for one purpose, to kill, and that went against everything she stood for as a doctor. She prayed she wouldn't have to use it.

Weapons in hand, they moved as quickly and quietly as they could toward the entrance to Dradin Park, sticking close to the buildings around it until they dashed across the street. The last of the infected filed into the park, not taking any notice of them. Laura and the others waited until there was a safe distance between them, then followed them inside. The infected didn't stay on the paved paths, she noticed. They trampled across the grass and weaved their way through the trees like drunkards, but always in the same direction. Always toward the community garden.

She moved from tree to tree, making sure never to lose sight of Booker and Victor. The infected were a slow-moving stampede, and though she stayed hidden she got the sense they wouldn't have cared if she didn't. Booker was right, it was like they were being summoned, and that summoning took priority over everything else. Laura slipped behind a sycamore tree for a closer look. Within the group of infected townspeople were many faces she recognized. Paul and Lisa Miller were there, still dirty and bruised from the tussle in the drug store parking lot. She wondered if they knew their son Jeff was dead. Or were they too far gone to care? Was she fooling herself thinking the infected could still be cured? Rithvik Panchal, who owned the parking lot near Heuler's Tavern on MacLeod, trudged along behind the Millers. Like Chuck, he was seriously burned on one arm. Rithvik had been busy setting fires.

Her foot hit something soft and yielding. She looked down, and put a hand over her mouth to keep from crying out. A dead body slumped against the base of the tree. She'd been so busy scanning the crowd she hadn't even noticed it. It was the body of a teenaged girl, stout with short hair and facial piercings. When Laura saw the men's bowling shirt with the name Norton on it, she recognized the girl as one of their attackers in the drug store parking lot. Now, like Jeff Miller, her eyes were gone, replaced by clusters of mushrooms. Her mouth was full of them too, and some more had broken through the rotting, discolored skin of her neck. Laura fought to keep her gorge from rising.

She left the body behind, dashing behind a nearby white oak. Peeking out, she spotted Dahlia Mintz, the police station's desk officer, walking with the others. She still wore her uniform, although her badge had been torn off and had taken a strip of her unform shirt with it, exposing part of a bra strap underneath. Dahlia grinned madly, her thick black hair tangled with leaves and twigs. She stopped to pull a handful of leaves off a tree. Laura watched as others did the same. Some collected leaves while others yanked plants out of the ground—weeds, flowers, fronds, whatever they could pull out of the dirt to carry with them.

Booker nodded to Laura and Victor from behind a tree, and the three of them moved forward, following the group to the community garden. They didn't enter the garden, instead skirting around it, and marched into a thick wood just beyond the garden wall. Laura, Booker, and Victor hung back and waited until the last of the infected had entered the woods, then followed. Moving through the trees, the forest seemed to grow darker with each step Laura took. She looked up and saw smoke from the fires had blotted out the sun.

Up ahead, the infected townspeople gathered in a clearing. They stood in a circle several bodies deep, surrounding something at the center that she couldn't see.

"This way," Booker whispered. He led her and Victor up a

hill and into the safety of the trees there.

Laura pushed the branches aside so she could see. The incline of the hill gave her a better view of what stood in the center of the circle. It was a tall, dark pillar that loomed more than twenty feet over everyone. It resembled a stone obelisk, like Cleopatra's Needle in Central Park, but it was clearly organic in nature, coated with a layer of tightly-packed dirt that hid what was underneath.

"What is that?" Laura whispered.

Victor's mouth hung open. "It's impossible. The size, the shape... If I didn't know better, I'd say it's *Prototaxites*."

"But you said those were from the Paleozoic Era," Laura said.

"I know," Victor said. "But that's exactly what it looks like. The first *Prototaxites* in three hundred and fifty million years."

"Booker, is that even possible?" Laura asked.

"All living things carry the genetic codes of their ancestors in their DNA, just like we do," he said. "The only explanation I can think of that the mutation must have awakened the genetic code of *Prototaxites* in the fungus somehow."

Below, the infected townspeople carried their bundles of leaves and plants to the *Prototaxites* and dropped them into a ditch at the base of its pillar-like form. Laura stood on her tiptoes, trying to get a better look. The ditch held a mass of white fibers, as thick as the stuffing in a plush toy. The fungus's hyphae. Just one small part of the mycelial network that would be spread out underground around it. By why was this mass of hyphae exposed?

The answer came immediately as the hyphae in the ditch moved, groping blindly forward with snake-like tendrils to engulf the leaves and plants, and digest them. Just then, as if in return for the food, the fungus released a shower of spores from the top of the pillar. They poured down upon the infected, who gathered them in handfuls or luxuriate in the deluge with an almost ecstatic reverence. It reminded Laura of a baptism, and the realization came over her that this massive pillar, this impossible *Prototaxites*, was the God of Dirt Kenneth Dalpe had mentioned.

And this was its congregation at worship.

The crowd parted, and Ralph Gorney stepped forward. Laura's throat became tight. Ralph was one of them now. Infected, part of the congregation. He carried his baby boy, Darius, and his wife Debra stood at his side. Dear God, his whole family was infected! The baby cooed and reached for the giant fungus with the same joyous smile as if reaching for a beloved toy. Ralph scratched away the thick layer of dirt and dug out a small piece of the fungus within, thick and stringy. Ralph pushed it into the baby's mouth. Little Darius happily gummed it and swallowed it down.

Laura thought she was going to be sick. It reminded her of the leafcutter ants Booker had told her about. That was what the infected had become, human leafcutter ants, feeding and protecting the fungus in this, their nest, and in return the fungus was allowing part of itself to be eaten by their young to keep the cycle going. The thought was so revolting she had to look away until the feeling of sickness passed.

The offerings to the God of Dirt continued. Plants and leaves were dumped into the ditch for the hyphae to break down and absorb. Laura put her hand over her mouth to silence a gasp of terror. One man stepped forward who wasn't carrying vegetation. He was carrying a woman's dead body, the young mother in the yellow sundress who'd shot herself this morning. The bullet wound in the side of her head was crusted with dried blood. The man dumped the body into the ditch, and Laura watched in horror as the hyphae crawled over it and began to digest it. Laura made a fist and bit her knuckle. It was the only way to stop herself from screaming.

She recognized so many of the infected townspeople, but they were different now, twisted by mania and madness. A large number of them were bleeding from their eyes, which made her think about Jeff Miller again. When they found his body, his eyes were gone, replaced with mushrooms growing from the sockets. It was the same with the dead teenaged girl she'd found by the tree. Was that what the bleeding indicated, that the fungi inside them were ready to fruit? It made a sickening kind of sense that the eyes were the first place they would come through. The orbital sockets were readily accessible from within, and the eyes were soft and easily displaced. Mushrooms had sprouted from Jeff's mouth too, another path of least resistance. It was only once a body began to decompose, like Kat's in the morgue, that mushrooms would break through the liquefying skin and emerge from other parts.

Below, Ralph addressed the others like a preacher addressing his flock.

"The time has come," Ralph said. "Step forward, chosen ones."

Eight people stepped out of the throng. Chuck was among them, as were Kenneth Dalpe and Dahlia Mintz. All of them were bleeding heavily from their eyes.

"You are our missionaries," Ralph said. "Leave this place and spread our divine blessing to the surrounding cities. Bring them all into the fold. Be fruitful and multiply, and fill the earth."

The group of eight turned and walked away from the others, back in the direction of the park entrance.

"We have to stop them," Laura whispered to Booker and Victor. "They're on the verge of fruiting. If they leave Sakima, they'll spread the infection."

"Christ," Victor said. "They're walking spore bombs!"

Booker ran down the hill, gripping his shotgun. Laura followed with Victor behind her, running as best he could but clearly winded by the exertion. Booker caught up to the group of eight first, grabbing the closest one from behind and turning him around. It was Walter Monahan, the green grocer. His eyes bulged, and blood ran down his face so heavily it looked like paint.

Booker tried to restrain him, but Walter squirmed out of his grasp and shoved him away. With single-minded determination, Walter continued following the others on their march out of the park.

There was a commotion behind Laura. She turned and saw a crowd of infected people running toward them from the nest.

"Shit, they saw us," Victor said. "Now what?"

Booker fired a shot over their heads. They didn't even flinch. Victor fired buckshot into the legs of two people at the front of the crowd. They stumbled and fell, but they were instantly replaced by dozens more. Laura raised her gun. She put her finger on the trigger. Could she do it? Even if she didn't shoot to kill, could she willingly hurt these people? She knew them. Many of them were her patients. Some, like Ralph and Debra, she considered close friends. Her hand trembled.

Booker grabbed her by the shoulder and pulled her back into the trees, where they ran up the hill again. "There's too many of them. We need a plan."

"We've got to stop them from leaving Sakima," Laura insisted. "If they reach another city, they'll infect hundreds more, thousands if it keeps spreading like it did here."

The infected swarmed up the hill toward them.

"We're out of time," Victor said. "I'll draw these pathetic hopheads away. You two stop the ones that are leaving town."

"No, it's too dangerous to split up," Booker protested.

"If we stay together, we'll get caught," Victor said, loading two more shells into his shotgun. "This way, at least we have a chance."

"Victor…"

"Don't argue with me, son," Victor said. "Just go."

Laura looked through the trees and saw the crowd closing in on them. "Booker, we have to go."

"Be careful," Booker said.

"I will, son, now go. Both of you!" he said. He caught Laura's eye and said, "Remember what I said."

She nodded, and then she and Booker ran. When she looked back, Victor had disappeared into the trees, and the crowd poured into the forest after him.

25

When Victor was in Kuwait during the Gulf War, he took a small amount of shrapnel in his right hip from an IED boobytrap in an abandoned Iraqi bunker. The scar was no longer visible thirty-plus years later. It didn't even hurt anymore, except on days when the temperature changed too quickly. Most of the time he forgot there were still tiny bits of metal inside him. Now, running as fast as he could through the trees in Dradin Park with an angry mob of doped-up townspeople chasing after him, he was all too aware of it. His hip stung worse with each loping stride he took, until finally it felt like he was being jabbed with a red-hot poker.

He couldn't go on like this. He was already limping and losing speed. He hoped he'd led his pursuers far enough in the wrong direction for Booker and Laura to get away. Running was quickly becoming not an option, so, breathing hard, he looked desperately for a place to hide. Behind him, the deranged laughter and whooping cries of the infected drew closer. He was running out of time.

Victor spotted a fallen tree deep in the woods. Its trunk was thick, and when it fell it had pulled up a massive tangle of roots and dirt. He limped over to it and dropped down behind it, hoping it would provide enough cover. He heard the crowd over the pounding of his heart in his ears. Twigs snapped and dead leaves crunched under their feet. They weren't trying to be quiet. They didn't need to be crafty or cunning. They had numbers on their side.

How many were there? Victor peeked over the fallen tree, but there were too many to count. They filled the whole forest. He supposed that was a good thing. It meant there were fewer of them to go after Booker and Laura. At least he hoped that's what it meant.

Victor ducked down again and put his back against the tree. He didn't like his odds. His hands shook as memories of the war came back to him, the gritty dust and sand, the smell of gasoline and grease, the heat from the burning oil fields. *Fuck! Keep it together, Cunnigham!* He reached under his scrubs and into his pants pocket. With trembling hands, he pulled out shotgun shells until he found what he was looking for—the small glass vial he'd taken out of the chest of drawers in his basement. Laura had almost caught him putting it in his pocket. He was glad she didn't see, because she never would have let him take it.

The vial was filled halfway with cocaine. Unscrewing the cap was no easy feat with the nitrile gloves he wore, but he was determined and got it open. A long silver rod was attached to the inside of the cap, ending in a small snuff spoon. He pulled his N95 respirator down, dug out a scoop of the snowy white powder, and snorted it. He snorted a second scoop up the other nostril for good measure, then capped the vial and put it back in his pocket. Returning the respirator to where it belonged over his nose and mouth, he felt better already. Just let those toad-stool lickers try to catch him!

Booker wouldn't approve of the coke any more than Laura, but neither of them were here to argue to point. Besides, humankind had been doing drugs since their earliest days. There was evidence that people had been chewing betel plant leaves as early as 2660 B.C. for their stimulant- and euphoria-inducing properties. As far as Victor was concerned, early man was really onto something. Worried about getting speared by some Mesopotamian douchebag or forced into shitty slavery in Pharaoh's Egypt? Chew a leaf, get fucked up, and you won't worry anymore!

He'd heard a theory once that the "manna from heaven" that sustained the Israelites while they were lost in the desert was actually a truffle that grew in the arid ground in much of the Middle East at the time. There was no proof of it, but Victor thought there must have been psilocybin in those truffles. How else could you explain why it took them *forty years* to travel the three hundred and eighty miles from Egypt to Israel?

So why should anyone not approve of Victor's drug use? He was just one in a long line of psychonauts stretching all the way back to the cavemen.

Someone hollered, loud and close, and Victor peeked over the fallen tree again. The infected ran toward him through the woods, a crashing surf of grasping, sweating flesh and psilocybin-induced madness. They'd found him, sniffed him out like a truffle.

Fine, come at me, you shiteaters! I'm ready for you!

Victor stood and aimed down the barrel of his shotgun. With a squeeze of the trigger, he blew a hole in the chest of the shirtless bearded man at the head of the pack. The bearded man was knocked backward, his chest an angry red mess, and he took down an older woman behind him, both of them toppling like bowling pins. Victor swung the shotgun and fired at the next one, a clean-shaven man in a plaid shirt. The buckshot tore through the flesh on the left side of the man's face and sent him spinning before he fell.

Victor dropped behind the tree again, broke the shotgun open, and quickly pulled out the two spent shells. He grabbed two new ones off the ground where he'd left them and shoved them into their chambers. He snapped the shotgun closed again, stood, and lifted it to his shoulder.

The horde had moved in while he was reloading, and before he could fire, his shotgun was knocked aside and snatched from his hands. More infected townspeople came around both sides of the fallen tree, cutting off his escape and grabbing him. A heavyset woman in a dirt-smeared Lynyrd Skynyrd t-shirt pinned Victor's arms behind his back. He struggled to break free, but she had him good.

A fat, mustached man in the tattered remains of a gray suit approached him. It was Mayor Harvey, Sakima's so-called leader, the one who'd sold the park out from under them so Bluecoal could turn it into condos. Victor laughed at the irony. The development deal was dead—as dead as the community garden Bluecoal had poisoned, setting off this whole damned chain of events—and now the park was home to Mayor Harvey and his new god, along with the rest of the infected townspeople. In a sick way, it was almost funny.

Mayor Harvey held a handful of spores in his palm like coffee grounds. He walked up to Victor, and with his free hand he tore of Victor's goggles and N95 respirator.

Victor spat at him. He spat at all of them, the whole goddamn ants' nest of them.

"Bring it on, you pig-fucking mushroom humpers!" he yelled, and Mayor Harvey blew the spores into Victor's face.

26

Laura and Booker didn't stop running until they reached the park entrance. Stepping around the fallen police barricades on the ground, Laura took a moment to catch her breath. Booker's gaze was locked on the street before them.

"Shit! There they are!" he said.

He pointed to an abandoned minivan in the street, into which the group of eight infected "missionaries" were climbing. The engine started, and the minivan peeled off with a squeal of burnt rubber. Booker fired two blasts from his shotgun, but the speeding minivan was too far away.

"Shit," he said again. He patted his pockets. "I'm out of shells. Come on, there are more in my car."

"Wait," Laura said. "We're going to need to split up. I'll take my car. It's still parked in front of your house."

"It's not safe," Booker insisted. "It's bad enough we left Victor behind."

"We have to," she said. "Think about it. They're heading north, right? If I'm right and they're leaving Sakima to infect another city, there are two ways they can go. Over the bridge to Kingston, or straight up to Rhinebeck. If we split up, we can cover both of them."

"I don't like it," he said. "If something happened to you…"

"Booker, we have to stop them," Laura said. "You know what will happen if we don't. I'll take the bridge, you take the road to Rhinebeck."

He nodded, accepting that splitting up was their only hope. "Okay. Be careful. Keep your gun on you. I don't think they're going to let you stop them without a fight."

"You be careful, too," she said.

She wished she could kiss him, but it wasn't a good idea to take off their N95 respirators. There were a thousand things she wanted to tell him, but there was no time. Booker sprinted to where he'd left the SUV, and Laura ran in the opposite direction, around the side of the park to Booker's street. She was relieved to find his block had been spared from the fire, at least for now. Her car was where she'd left it, parked at the curb next to Booker's driveway. She hurried to it.

On Booker's lawn, next to the car, Adam sat cross-legged like a guru in meditation. His face was covered in blood that oozed from his swollen eyes. His neck was swollen too, as though the mushrooms were already forming inside him, preparing to burst out of his throat. He held a chef's knife in one hand, turning it around and around like a toy, staring at the blade. He looked up at her. Laura stopped in the street and held her pistol in front of her.

"What are you doing here, Adam?" she said.

"I knew you would come back, so I waited." When he spoke, the bloated part of his neck moved in a way that reminded her of a frog. His voice was distorted by the blockage, making him sound like he was talking underwater. "You're missing out, Laura. You can't know what it's like. It's wonderful. The things you see. The things you feel."

"I'm going to need you to put the knife down, Adam."

He grinned like she'd said something funny. He lifted the blade and regarded it with a childlike fascination. "I feel sorry for you, Laura. You'll never understand what I've become. What *you* could have become, if we were together."

"Just stay where you are," she said. She took another step toward the car.

"It's inside me now, waiting to be born. But I don't want to wait anymore," Adam said. "I want to let it out. I can feel it growing, pushing. It wants to be free."

His hand moved quickly, jamming the tip of the chef's knife into his right eye. He twisted the handle, turning his eye into a red, gushing mush that dropped out of the socket. A torrent of blood streamed down his face.

"Come out, come out, wherever you are," he sang as he

pulled the knife free of the bloody socket and plunged it into his other eye.

Laura ran for the car door. She pulled it open, threw herself into the seat, and slammed it shut again, making sure to engage the autolock. Tossing the gun onto the passenger's seat, she dug out her key and started the car. In the rearview mirror, she saw Adam turn blindly toward the car, his attention drawn by the sound of the engine. His face was a mess of gore, with dark, bloody holes where his eyes used to be. Laura hit the gas, pulling away from the curb on screeching tires, and sped away.

She drove down empty streets, swerving to avoid abandoned cars that turned the roads into obstacle courses. She passed the spot where Booker's SUV had been and was relieved to see it was gone. Her encounter with Adam had slowed her down, giving Booker a head start. She just hoped one of them would be able to stop the minivan in time.

She drove until she reached the fork where the road continued north to Rhinebeck and turned westward toward the bridge over the Hudson. She took the turn and spotted the minivan ahead of her. She sped up, tailing it through the tree-lined street that led to the bridge. There were only two lanes, one for westbound traffic and one for east, but with no one else on the road, Laura crossed the double yellow lines and pressed the gas pedal to the floor. She pulled up beside the minivan. A glance through the window showed her Chuck was behind the wheel, blood on his cheeks like war paint. She sped up again and passed the minivan. They were almost at the foot of the bridge. The twinkling water of the Hudson River appeared just beyond the tree line. Once she was far enough ahead of the minivan, she yanked the steering wheel hard to the right and slammed on the brakes. Her car skidded across the road and came to a rest in the minivan's path.

The minivan didn't slow down. Through its oncoming windshield, she saw Chuck's face was a mask of frenzied determination. He was going to drive right through her! Laura opened the door and leapt out a split second before the minivan plowed into her car with a deafening crunch of metal and fiberglass. Laura rolled into the ditch on the side of the road, the world turning cartwheels around her as she tumbled, her ribs and shoulders spiking with pain. When she came to a stop, her head struck something hard, and for a moment she was too dazed to move. The minivan pushed her car to the edge of the road, where it collided with a sign that read Historic Jack M. Haringa Bridge, and then, finally, both vehicles came to a stop.

The side door of the minivan slid open, and she watched as eight figures dropped onto the blacktop. She realized she didn't have her gun with her. She'd left it in the car when she jumped out. The eight figures started toward her. She didn't have any other option now except to run, but getting to her feet was more difficult than she expected. How hard had she hit her head? Was that blood trickling through her hair?

Chuck loomed over her. He grabbed her roughly and dragged her from the ditch into the street. He pulled her up onto her feet and shoved her toward the other seven. They crowded around her in a tight circle. She kicked and swatted at them until Dahlia Mintz grabbed her from behind and pinned her arms back.

"Dahlia," Laura said, "Dahlia, please let me go."

"It's almost time," Dahlia said. "If you're lucky, you'll get to see it happen."

"See what happen?"

Kenneth Dalpe appeared before her. "See the children of the God of Dirt being born."

The old widower's voice was distorted like Adam's. The mushrooms were already growing in his throat. His face was slick with blood, and his eyes bulged in their sockets, so big they looked fake, like ping-pong balls in an old sci-fi movie's alien makeup.

He tore the goggles and N95 respirator off Laura's face.

"It's time you joined us, Laura," he said. "I don't know why you resisted for so long, holding on to the old world. For what? What were we before the God of Dirt found us? Lost, alone, yearning for meaning in our lives. But we're not alone anymore. Now we have a purpose. To serve it. To worship it."

"Kenneth, please," she said. She struggled in Dahlia's grasp, trying to break away. "You've got to fight this!"

"Fight it? Why would I do that?" Fresh rivulets of blood seeped from his eyes. He groaned, doubled over, and fell to his knees. "It's time. Finally."

Kenneth's body seized. He fell onto his back. The bulge in his neck bloated larger. His eyes swelled in their blood-lined sockets. His convulsions stopped suddenly, and he went limp. He was dead, Laura realized. Damaged and drained by the fungus's appetite, his organs had shut down. A moment later, Kenneth's eyes burst, their oozing remains forced from their cavities by a multitude of sprouting earth-colored mushrooms, their caps round and glistening with blood. They opened like umbrellas, revealing their gills underneath.

Walter crouched over Kenneth's body with his back to Laura. She couldn't see what he was doing until he stood again and turned to face her with a pile of new spores, straight from the gills, cupped in his hands.

"No!" Laura shouted. She struggled again, but Dahlia had a firm grip on her, the officer's training coming through even now. "Please, stop!"

Walter blew the spores at Laura. She felt them hit the bare skin of her face, felt them enter her nose and mouth. Like tiny hot coals, they burned through her skin and into her body.

27

Mayor Harvey dragged Victor like a prisoner back to the nest among the trees and threw him onto his knees in front of the tall pillar of the *Prototaxites*. It loomed over him like a cemetery monument. Mayor Harvey held him by the wrists, keeping his arms up over his head so he couldn't move. The rest of the infected townspeople crowded around him.

Everything hurt, his knees from being thrown to the ground, his hip from the decades-old shrapnel inside it. Sometimes he forgot how old he'd gotten. He'd been in his thirties when the Gulf War ended in '91, and back then he never could have imagined himself in his sixties like he was now. Sometimes he thought he was still that same young man who'd survived all of Saddam's bullets, missiles, and IUDs and came out the other side feeling invulnerable. The pain was there to remind him he wasn't. Three decades had passed, and this was what he was now. An old man. A drug addict. A captive.

Ralph Gorney knelt down before him. The police chief had an idiot grin on his face, and his dilated pupils looked like black saucers. His eyes were rimmed with red, not yet bleeding like some of the others. He grabbed Victor's face in both hands and turned it from side to side, inspecting him the way a slaughter-house butcher inspected a cow for imperfections in the meat.

"Brutalized by a cop while the mayor stands back and watches," Victor said. "Sounds about right."

Ralph let go of Victor's face and stood up again. "Why isn't he one of us yet? Didn't you bestow God's blessing upon him?"

"I did," Mayor Harvey said. "But this man has always been a troublemaker. Maybe he's been rejected. Maybe God doesn't want him in the fold."

Troublemaker. Victor took that as a compliment. He laughed, and Ralph looked down at him in consternation. That only made Victor laugh more.

"Why are you laughing?" Ralph demanded. He sounded angry, but the creepy, vapid smile never left his face.

"You addle-brained mushroom-junkies thought you could dope *me* up?" Victor said. "You don't know who you're dealing with!"

Ralph and Mayor Harvey exchanged looks of confusion.

"Don't you get it?" Victor said. "I've partaken of substances you didn't even know existed. Narcotics you've never even heard of. I've taken drugs that make your limp-dick mushroom spores look like the oregano your high school dealer told you was pot!"

"You're...*immune* to God's blessing?" Ralph cocked his head like a confused spaniel. The very idea seemed to confuse him.

"Heh," Victor chuckled. "Let's just say I've built up one hell of a tolerance."

Ralph squatted down in front of him again. The idiot grin never left his face. "I used to be like you. Filled with worries about every little thing. This city. My family. Did you know Debra and I lost a child before we had Darius? It devastated us. The rage, the depression. Even after Darius was born, the loss followed us like a shadow, eating away at our souls." He turned to look at the *Prototaxites*. "But after I heard its voice, I understood those feelings didn't matter. They never mattered. Only *it* matters. It can replace everything we lost. I'm no longer filled with worry. Now what I have inside me are *worlds*. Worlds of colors you've never seen, of sounds you've never heard. A connection so all-encompassing that I can't remember what it was like to feel alone. We are one, through these worlds and through its voice. Its glorious voice."

"Oh yeah?" Victor said. "What's that overgrown salad topper telling you now?"

"That it still has use for you."

Ralph stood and nodded at Mayor Harvey, who pulled Victor to his feet. Victor's arms ached at the shoulders. Another reminder of the old man he'd become.

Victor wasn't stupid, he knew they weren't going to let him go. But whatever came next, whatever they did to him, he was content in the knowledge that he'd spun them for a loop. It was a small victory, but it was still a victory. He'd learned in the deserts of Kuwait that you took them where you could find them.

They brought him to the edge of the gaping ditch at the base of the *Prototaxites*. The fungus towered over him, silhouetted by the dark, smoke-filled sky, and a primal, deep-rooted fear stirred inside Victor. The *Prototaxites* was something ancient and unknowable, utterly beyond his comprehension. It was nothing like his boys back home. It didn't need him. Truthfully, it didn't need any of the people it had infected with its spores. It *wanted* them, and that was what chilled him the most. It wanted to be served. It wanted to be worshipped as a god. And that kind of desire implied, at least on some level, consciousness. Awareness. Intelligence.

The offerings of leaves and plants that had been dropped into the ditch below were fully devoured now, but the writhing mass of hyphae still embraced the remains of the dead woman in the yellow sundress. She'd been transformed into a mass of exposed bone and raw meat, half-digested and clotted with dark blood. The white of her skull was partially revealed in the pulpy hamburger flesh of her face. One wide, round eye stared from its socket.

Victor nodded. "I see. It's dinner time, eh? Now that it's almost done with the appetizer."

Ralph shoved him forward. Victor's arms pinwheeled as he tumbled over the edge. With a dreadful understanding of what was happening to him, he let out a sound that was more moan than scream. He landed on top of the thick heap of hyphae, buoyant and springy enough to break his fall without injury. The woman's corpse lay beside him, glaring at him with her one open eye like he'd walked in on her taking a bath. Before he could move, the hyphae rose around him like hungry serpents. They twined around his legs and moved upward, coiling around his stomach. They released their acidic enzyme to burn through his scrubs and the clothes underneath. A moment later he felt their sting on his skin.

Victor laughed through the pain and horror of the moment. He laughed at the absurdity of it all. But mostly he laughed because he had a secret, something those devilish grinning fuckers staring down at him from the edge of the ditch didn't know about. If they did, they never would have thrown him into the arms of their mushroom god.

He reached into his pants pocket and pulled out the M67 fragmentation grenade. Gripping its round, apple-like body in one hand, he pulled the pin from its lever with the other, releasing the spring-loaded striker. From above, Ralph stared at the grenade and let out a low, desperate animal keening. Even with psilocybin warping his brain, he knew what it was.

"I hope your god chokes on it," Victor said.

When the grenade detonated and the fragments of metal blew outward in every direction, Victor died instantly, painlessly, and with only a single regret—that he wouldn't get to watch their God of Dirt come tumbling down.

28

The dull thud of a distant explosion came from the direction of Dradin Park. Kenneth Dalpe's dead, fruiting body remained motionless where it lay in the road, but Laura watched in surprise as the other infected people reacted strongly to the blast. They became confused, bewildered like children who'd lost sight of their parents in a crowd, and that gave Laura enough time to slip out of Dahlia Mintz's grasp. The confusion didn't last long. As soon as they saw Laura was free, they lunged for her. She ran, although deep down she wondered why she bothered. They'd already infected her. The spores were inside her even now, sprouting their hyphae to begin knitting together a mycelium across her muscles, organs, and bones. How much time did she have before the fungus released psilocybin into her system? It had taken Sofia less than half an hour to succumb to the drug. That wasn't much time at all. The clock was ticking.

She wondered how far she could run in half an hour.

She wondered if it mattered.

Chuck grabbed her from behind. With his muscular arms, he yanked her off her feet and into a crushing bearhug. "Where are you going, Laura? You're one of us now. You can feel it, can't you? You know it's true."

Booker's SUV turned the corner into view, racing down the street toward her. He blared his horn. Laura elbowed Chuck in the gut. He keeled over, releasing her, and she leapt out of the way as the SUV slammed into him at full speed. Chuck flew backward, his arms and legs limp like the tails of a kite. He struck the Historic Jack M. Haringa Bridge sign and bounced off it like a ricochet, leaving behind a red smudge. He landed on the road in a bloody, broken heap. Chuck was dead. Somehow,

Laura knew it. She felt it like an absence in her mind. A broken connection.

We're all connected, Laura, and it's beautiful, it's so beautiful. You can be one with us.

She shook her head violently, as if she could rattle Melanie Elster's words out of her skull. It couldn't be happening already. Not yet.

Please, not yet!

The SUV's brakes screeched, and it spun out of control. It skidded across the road, tires screaming on the blacktop. It clipped the minivan, tipped over precariously, then fell onto its side, scraping across the road in a shower of sparks. Laura ran to it. On the other side of the SUV, Walter, Dahlia, and the other infected missionaries slowly closed in.

Laura found Booker crawling out of the shattered windshield. His goggles and N95 respirator were gone. There was a smear of blood along one eyebrow and his right leg was a mess of gore and shredded pants. She helped him up and let him lean on her as she brought him limping around the side of the SUV. She kept the vehicle between them and the infected like a barricade, although not a very effective one. It would be easy enough for them to walk around the SUV. It didn't matter. Laura just wanted—needed—a moment alone with Booker before the others were upon them One last moment together before they both lost themselves to the God of Dirt. She sat Booker down with his back against the tipped-over SUV's roof. He winced with the effort. Sweat streamed down his face, drawing the blood from his eyebrow with it.

Laura examined his leg. It wasn't just a flesh wound. She could tell the patella and fibula were both broken.

"It looks bad," she said.

She didn't know what else to say. They weren't getting out of this. She could already feel the psilocybin starting to work. The wound in Booker's leg swelled and receded like a lung drawing breath. When his arm moved, she saw a trail of color stretch and blur in its wake. The disturbance of visual motion perception was a common effect of hallucinogens. It was in her brain. She was the cicada now, pleasantly doped up by its *Massospora* hijacker. She didn't have much time left.

"When I got up north and saw they weren't there, I—I figured they must have come to the bridge," he gasped through the pain. "I got...here as...soon as I could."

"It's okay," she said, stroking his face. "You're here now."

Around them, trees bent and twisted. Shapes moved in the forest without showing themselves. More infected townspeople, or more hallucinations? She couldn't tell. Maybe it didn't matter anymore.

Booker was holding the black metal box from the cabinet in Victor's basement. She hadn't noticed it when he came out of the SUV. Another effect of the drug, she figured.

The infected on the other side of the SUV drew closer. She could hear them. More than that, she could *sense* them, almost as though she were seeing through their eyes—slowly approaching the steaming exposed machinery of the SUV's underbelly, one wheel still spinning. She felt their thoughts, not as words or images but as a swell of emotion, a dark and raging religious ecstasy that would have put the cult of Dionysus to shame. It crashed over her in a tidal wave, her psilocybin-laced brain interpreting it as an endless tunnel of colors and sounds. The further she fell down that tunnel, the closer she approached something that remained just out of sight, massive and dominating. It called her name wordlessly, its voice a beam of warm sunlight after a rain, a cool spring on a hot day, the taste of her favorite ice cream. It was the caress of a lover and the command of a master. The God of Dirt. It was in pain. It had been grievously injured, but it still lived, still thrived in the comforting darkness underground.

Laura squeezed her eyes shut and shook her head until she was back in her own skin. "They're coming," she told Booker.

He nodded. "I can't let them get any farther. I can't let them leave Sakima."

Laura felt herself slipping again. It felt like tendrils were unfurling from within her, stretching outward invisibly, connecting her to the others, just like Kat Biship had drawn in her sketchbook. Laura hadn't understood the image then, but she did now. She could feel their breath in her own throat, their heartbeats in her chest. When she looked at her hand, she saw pieces of her skin flaking off and floating up into the sky like embers from a bonfire.

It's a hallucination. You have to stay focused!

Booker opened the metal box and pulled out an apple. His hands left an arcing trail behind them. Laura's mouth watered, and her stomach rumbled at the thought of a delicious apple. How long had it been since she'd eaten?

She closed her eyes, forcing herself to concentrate. It wasn't an apple. She knew that. When she opened her eyes, she willed them to see the object in Booker's hand for what it was. The second fragmentation grenade Victor had brought back with him from the Gulf War.

"No, Booker," she said. "You have to get away. Let me do it."

"I can't go anywhere with my leg like this," he said. "You run, Laura. I'll only slow you down. Get out of here before it's too late."

She laughed at the idea that it wasn't already too late. She didn't mean to, but it bubbled up inside her, beyond her control. Another effect of the psilocybin.

"Booker, they—they got me," she said. "Before you came. The spores. I can already feel it affecting my mind. It's too late for me, but it's not for you. I have to do this."

His body shook. At first, she thought it was from the pain, but then she realized they were sobs. Tears streamed down the sides of his nose.

From around one end of the SUV, Walter led two of the infected toward them. Dahlia led two around the other end, boxing them in. Booker gathered himself and put his arm around her.

"I won't leave you again," he said. "I've already spent too much time without you, and I won't do it again. I can't. If we do this, we do it together."

She nodded. He pulled her to him and kissed her.

"I love you, Laura," he said.

"I love you, too," she said. "I never stopped."

The infected drew closer, grinning madly, reaching for them. Booker put his finger through the grenade's pull pin. Laura felt a swell of fear inside her, and the strong impulse to run, to live by any means necessary. She wondered if her mother had felt the same way after she took all those sleeping pills, or if she'd simply accepted her fate and drifted peacefully into darkness.

Laura put her hand over Booker's. "Together," she said.

29

Laura didn't expect to open her eyes again, but here she was, opening them, still alive. Why wasn't she dead? She couldn't remember anything after agreeing to set off the grenade with Booker. Blinking her eyes against the harsh, bright light overhead, she saw she was lying in a narrow, unfamiliar bed. Smells came to her first—ammonia, industrial-strength cleanser—before her brain registered that she was in a hospital room. She was too weak to move much, but from what she could tell, her body was whole. Two arms, two legs, nothing lost to the grenade. How was that possible?

One of her arms was hooked up to an IV drip beside the bed. Her clothes were gone, replaced with a hospital gown. Noises came from the hallway outside her room. Shapes in white passed by her door. She heard people talking, call bells buzzing, telephones ringing. A woman's face appeared over her, fair-skinned and red-cheeked, leaning in from the side of the bed.

"Oh, good, you're awake, Dr. Powell." The woman wore a nurse's scrubs and wheeled a blood pressure monitor behind her. "I just need to check your pressure."

Laura tried to speak, but she still felt sluggish. All that came out was a groan.

"Give yourself a minute, you've been unconscious for quite a while." The woman took a corded blood pressure cuff off the monitor and fixed it around the bicep of Laura's other arm. "My name is Jacqueline Ristretto. I'm your on-duty nurse today. You can call me Jackie."

"Jackie, where am I?" Laura asked. Her voice was scratchy, her throat dry.

"Hudson Valley Medical Center, just outside Pleasant Plains," she said.

Pleasant Plains was just south of Sakima. She hadn't been taken far. Laura had heard of the Hudson Valley Medical Center, but she'd never been there. She never imagined her first visit would be as a patient instead of as a doctor.

Jackie finished securing the blood pressure cuff, which automatically tightened around Laura's arm. "You were part of the first group we took in. They're still bringing more down from Sakima."

Booker's voice came from the doorway. "Is she awake?"

Laura turned and saw Booker sitting in a wheelchair, his injured leg raised in a cast. There was a small bandage over one of his eyebrows.

"Booker!" she said. "You're okay!"

The relief was so strong she thought she was going to cry. He wheeled over to her and put his arms around her. She kissed his face over and over again, until Jackie said, "Okay, lovebirds, chill out. You're throwing off my readings."

"Sorry," Laura said, blushing. "Booker, what happened? I thought…"

"You passed out," he explained. "You didn't see it."

"See what?"

"They came over the bridge before I pulled the pin," he said. "The CDC Emergency Response Team, police cars, fire trucks…"

"They came?" This time the relief was so overwhelming she did break into tears. It hurt to cry. Her ribs were sore. She couldn't remember how she injured them, but it didn't matter. She let the tears come.

"Try not to get her worked up," Jackie told Booker.

"I don't think I can stop her," he replied.

Laura laughed and wiped her eyes. "I'd given up hope. I didn't think anyone was coming."

"They did. They mobilized out of Albany, Hartford, Springfield, even New York City, and it was all thanks to you."

She cried again, overwhelmed with relief and a knot of other, more selfish emotions. Booker put his hand on hers gently and waited until she was finished.

"You've been out for six hours. A lot has happened."

Six hours? Laura turned to the window and saw it was nighttime outside. Her view was of the hospital's parking lot, which was filled with overflow tents set up under the lamps.

"Are all those people from Sakima?" she asked.

"Yup," Jackie said. "With more coming every hour."

"They're still putting out the fires in town," Booker told her. "It's going to take years to rebuild. They're still rounding up everyone who was infected, too, and bringing them here."

"Including me," Laura said. "The fungus is still inside me, isn't it?"

Booker nodded grimly. "Yes."

"The doctors are doing everything they can," Jackie told her, undoing the cuff and hanging it on the monitor again. "We have CDC public health experts on site, and more doctors are coming in from all over to help out. There are a lot of you who need treatment."

"What are they giving me?" Laura asked.

Jackie wrote Laura's blood pressure on her chart, then flipped through it to see what she'd been prescribed. "Let's see. First, they've got you on Effexor. That's a Serotonin-Norepinephrine Reuptake Inhibitor."

"I know what it is," she said. "Why are they giving me an anti-depressant?"

"It's supposed to reduce the effects of the psilocybin," Jackie explained. "It boosts serotonin and norepinephrine levels in the brain to counteract the drug. It's only temporary, obviously. Once the fungal infection is cured, the drug will be out of your system once and for all."

"How are they treating the infection?" Laura asked.

"They've got you on an antifungal called Noxafil. It's strong stuff, so if you have any bad reactions, they'll switch you to Sporanox. That one might take longer, but it's gentler on the system. We've got you on a saline drip to keep you hydrated, and the doctors have added a combination of vitamin D, vitamin A, and selenium to rebuild your immune system, which was weakened by the fungus. A healthy immune system will help the Noxafil kill off any of the fungus that's left."

"Thank you," Laura said.

Jackie put the chart back and wheeled the blood pressure monitor to the door. "I'll leave you two alone now. Dr. Powell, I'll be back later with more medication."

"Thank you," she said. "And please, call me Laura."

Jackie nodded, then gave Booker a pointed look. "Remember, don't get her too worked up. I'm counting on you to let her rest."

"I'll do my best," Booker said. When Jackie was gone, he took Laura's hand again. "You saved us, Laura. If you hadn't made that call to the CDC, we'd both be dead right now. A lot of people would be. The whole town owes you their lives."

"It was just a phone call. People like Jackie, the doctors, the CDC, they're the ones saving lives." She sat up in bed, positioning the pillow behind her back. "How many of us are here?"

"I don't know. No one could give me a definitive count. A couple hundred so far, I think," Booker said. "The good news is that not everyone in Sakima was infected. It turns out a lot of people were hiding. I heard the police found a few dozen holed up in the high school."

"Is Ralph here yet?" she asked. "Have you seen him?"

Booker's face fell. His grip on her hand tightened gently. "I'm sorry, Laura. Ralph didn't make it. They found his body in the park, along with some others. There was—there was an explosion. But Debra and the baby are okay. They're here, and they're recovering."

Laura leaned back in her bed, heartbroken. Ralph, Sofia, Kenneth, Adam, so many people she knew were gone. Each death stung, even Adam's, but Ralph's loss hit the hardest. He'd been her closest friend, always standing by her, always ready to let her bend his ear at Heuler's Tavern when she needed to. It didn't feel possible, it didn't feel *right*, that she would never see him or talk to him again. She vowed that as soon as she was fully recovered, and if Heuler's was still standing, she would go there and raise a glass to his memory.

"Victor didn't make it either," Booker said, wiping his eyes. "The crazy old son of a bitch blew up the *Prototaxites*. Blew it right to hell."

"That was the explosion?"

He nodded. "He must have used the other grenade."

"I'm so sorry, Booker." She squeezed his hand. "He loved you, you know. He told me as much."

"He did? I'm surprised. He was never one for talking about his feelings." Booker wiped his eyes again. "He was my father in so many ways. It didn't matter that he wasn't my biological father, he was always there for me when I needed him. He complained about everything in the world, but never that. I hope the old bastard knew how much I loved him, too."

"Of course he did," she said. "You risked your life to make sure he was all right when it would have been easier and safer to just leave town instead. He knew. He asked me to look after you, you know. To make sure you're okay." She looked at the cast on his leg, the bandage on his forehead. "A fine job I did."

"We're both alive," he said. "I'd say you did just fine. In fact, I'm hoping you'll stick around and keep up the good work."

She smiled. "Are you asking me to go steady, Professor Coates?"

"Only if you'll have me, Dr. Powell," he replied.

She leaned over and kissed him. "You better heal up. We have a lot of lost time to make up for."

She lay back on her pillow, exhausted. Her eyelids drooped as drowsiness overtook her. The distant tug of the anti-depressant turned her mind into something soft and fuzzy. But there was something else there, deep down, lurking under her thoughts. A muffled call from far away. All the way from Dradin Park. It was much duller than before, but it was still there, like an echo. She opened her eyes again. Booker was still in his wheelchair next to the bed, watching her.

"It's not dead," she said. "It's still out there."

"I know," he said. "Victor destroyed the fungus on the surface, but its mycelial network is still alive underground. I've been consulting with the CDC on what to do."

"Let me guess," she said. "Cornmeal?"

"Not this time," he said with a laugh. The memory of Victor made them both smile. "Tomorrow morning, they're going to dig up as much of it as they can, and then fill the ground with salt. They're bringing salt trucks down from Albany tonight."

"They're literally salting the earth?" Laura shook her head. "I guess Sean got what he wanted after all. That'll be the end of the park."

Thinking about Sean Hilton, the asshole vice president of Bluecoal, made her wonder again what had happened to him. Was he here at the hospital with the others? Or had he died along with Ralph and Victor? Maybe she would never know. She was okay with that.

"They don't have a choice. They can't risk the fungus coming back," Booker said. "If there's even one strand of hypha left, one spore, it'll come right back. Salting the ground is the only way to make sure nothing is left. I just wish I could be there when they kill it."

"Me too," she said. Her eyelids drooped again, and this time she couldn't fight the oncoming wave of exhaustion pulling her down into unconsciousness.

"I'll let you rest," Booker said. "I'll come back in the morning."

He rolled the wheelchair out of her room. Once she was alone, she let her eyes close all the way. She heard the distant call of the God of Dirt again. It was weak but insistent. It wanted her to come back. It wanted all of them to come back. What was a god without worshippers?

Laura dozed in and out, alternately listening to the sounds from the hospital hallway and sinking into a thick, inky blackness. At some point, Jackie came in and gave her some pills and water, but Laura fell right back to sleep afterward. Finally, as the sun rose outside her window, she had a dream, or maybe it was one final, last-gasp hallucination of the psilocybin. She was buried underground in cool, comfortable soil. The sound of shovels piercing the dirt came to her, and the mechanical roar of a backhoe as it tore open the earth. (Or were they just more noises from the hospital hallway, shoes squeaking on waxed tile, announcements blaring over a speaker system?) Laura's body was a long, immense web of fibers that stretched for hundreds of feet in every direction, but she found herself suddenly and violently exposed to the battering wind and the searing light of the morning sun. Shapes loomed over her in yellow CDC hazmat suits and gas masks. They used their machinery and tools to wrench pieces of her out of the earth and toss them into a large metal tub, where hungry flames burned them to ash. Next came a fleet of dump trucks, their beds tipping toward the ground and releasing wave after wave of coarse white salt, turning the earth barren and destroying what was left of her.

Laura woke up with a scream. An alarm blared in the hospital, and over it she heard other patients were screaming too, just like her, screaming with a pain that wasn't theirs. The screams came from nearby rooms and from the overflow tents in the parking lot. Finally, Laura's scream faded away along with the others, and she collapsed back onto the bed.

Booker rolled into the room in his wheelchair, alarmed and concerned. "Laura? Laura, are you all right?"

She put her hands over her eyes, making the morning-bright room dark again. She turned her attention inward and listened. There was nothing. The God of Dirt had grown silent.

"I heard you scream," Booker said. "I heard *everyone* scream."

"It's over," she said, taking her hands from her face and looking at him. "It's dead. The God of Dirt is dead."

He gave her a funny look. "How did you know? I only just got a text from the team at the park saying they finished."

She knew Booker would never understand what it was like to be connected on such a deep level to something like the God of Dirt, or to the others it had infected. She had a hard time grasping it herself. Was it a form of telepathy? Some kind of mass hysteria? Like the ants Victor had seen in the rainforest hijacked by the *cordyceps*, or the cicadas enslaved by the *Massospora*, she would probably never fully understand what happened to her. She didn't try to explain it to Booker. Instead, she put her arms around his neck, held him tight, and kissed him.

"It's okay," she whispered in his ear. "I just know."

30

The morning sun hung high over the forest, and far below, through the curtain of smoke from the few houses that still burned, Sean Hilton stumbled through the trees. He'd been moving through the woods for hours, but he'd lost track of time and was surprised to see the sunrise. He must have wandered the woods all night. It was hard to tell. Time kept warping and bending, just like the tree branches all around him.

Sakima was under quarantine. Some time ago, he passed one of the various police roadblocks that had been set up around the edges of the city. He stayed in the woods and walked right past it. The police officers didn't even notice him. It took all his strength not to laugh out loud at how inept they were. He'd been fighting off the laughter ever since.

Now, he stopped to look out of the woods again. Not a hundred feet away was the foot of the bridge that crossed the Hudson River to Kingston. The sign that read Historic Jack M. Haringa Bridge was dented and adorned with an ugly red splotch. There was debris in the road that made him think there'd been an accident, but the vehicles involved had been removed. In their place was another police roadblock preventing any traffic in or out of the city. He kept walking, moving ever northward.

Sean's right ankle felt weak. It didn't hurt, exactly. Nothing hurt anymore, but it slowed his pace. He'd injured his ankle when the crowd of infected people came out of nowhere and surrounded the SUV he'd taken from Booker, Laura, and Victor. When they yanked open the door and dragged him out, he fell hard on the asphalt, twisting his ankle, or maybe breaking it. He had a dim memory of the pain, sharp and insistent, but it went away not long after the tiny, gritty spores were blown into his face.

His baptism. Sean Hilton, born again.

For a time, he felt a deep and inexplicable connection to the others of his strange new congregation—even, to his surprise, Laura. He felt her and wondered if she felt him. Could she hear his thoughts? Did she know how much he hated her, how much he despised her constant nagging not to kill anybody, how much he wanted to turn his rifle on her and make the bitch shut up for good?

Could she see his memories of dumping the MCA 8564 herbicide into the community garden under cover of night?

His connection to the rest of them was severed when the God of Dirt died. He felt it die like a blast of searing white heat. Did the others feel it too, he wondered, or was he special, favored by God to share its final moments in private? Now he felt lost and empty without it, but that didn't matter. A new God of Dirt was growing inside him. He could already feel its threads tickling the back of his throat, the back of his eyes, eager to be born.

The God of Dirt resurrected. The second coming.

Staying hidden in the woods, he passed another roadblock in the street, undetected. His right ankle felt even weaker now. He paused to roll up his muddy pants and inspect it. The ankle had turned an array of colors—purple, blue, and green. The colors were so beautiful. He rolled his pants down again, his fingers leaving smeared trails in the air behind them. He walked until his whole leg felt numb, and then he walked some more. He walked because he knew that was what the God of Dirt had wanted him to do.

Finally, he emerged from the woods on an empty stretch of road where a sign declared, WELCOME TO RHINEBECK, POP. 7,700.

A short time later, he came to a parking lot next to a small restaurant with a turtle-shaped sign that read TORTOISESHELL DINER. A few cars were parked in the lot, restaurant workers and the weekday breakfast crowd. Sean's leg gave out halfway through the parking lot. He fell between two cars and lay on the pavement, laughing.

A balding man in his forties with round glasses and a blue

dress shirt appeared over him. "Oh my word, are you okay?"

Sean smiled up at him. "Never better, brother."

"Can you stand?" The man held out his arm, a trail of dress-shirt blue smearing behind it.

Sean took his hand and got to his feet. He put all his weight on his good ankle and hopped on one leg. The man put his arm around Sean and helped him limp toward the diner.

"Let's get you a place to sit down," the man said. "How about I buy you a cup of a coffee?"

"Thank you," Sean said. "You're very kind."

"You know the story of the Good Samaritan?" the man asked. "It's in the Gospel of Luke."

"You're a man of God?" Sean asked.

"I am. Are you?"

"Oh, yes," he said. "I have a very personal relationship with God."

Sean smiled at the man, his Good Samaritan, but all he truly felt for him was pity. Pity for his stunted, limited existence, unconnected to anyone or anything. He couldn't wait to bring him into the new God of Dirt's congregation. He wanted this man to feel what he felt and know what he knew.

Because Sean knew something this poor fool and everyone like him didn't. Not yet, at least, but soon. They'd know it soon.

The future was fungus.

AFTERWORD

While I was writing this novel, it was important to me to keep the mycology as true to life as I could. I didn't want my mutant fungus to do anything that was outside the realm of possibility for real-world fungi. Of course, I took a few liberties in the name of storytelling—it's highly unlikely, for instance, that a honey fungus mutated by an experimental herbicide would revert back to the primeval form of *Prototaxites*—but a lot of what you read in this novel *can* happen and *does* happen. As frightening as it sounds, fungal spores really can invade and control the bodies of other living things.

The *Massospora* fungus that Booker tells Laura about is quite real, as is its frightening ability to hijack a cicada's body in order to spread its spores. And certainly by now many of us are familiar with the real-life *Ophiocordyceps* fungus—the same "zombie ant" fungus Victor saw in action in the Amazon rainforest—thanks to the popular video game *The Last of Us*, as well as M.R. Carey's exceptional novel *The Girl with All the Gifts* and its subsequent film adaptation. There are over 600 species of *cordyceps* worldwide, and they're a danger to all manner of insects, and sometimes other creatures like spiders. The *cordyceps* has been zombifying its insect and arachnid victims for at least forty-eight million years. Considering *Homo sapiens* only appeared about three hundred thousand years ago, that means when it comes to farming animals, fungi have a massive head start on us. (By the way, if you're interested in more fiction based on *cordyceps*, my good friend Karen Heuler's science-fiction novel *Glorious Plague* offers an interesting riff on it.)

Insects aren't the only creatures fungi can manipulate. Animals that some might consider higher life forms, such as mammals, hardly have immunity. Consider for a moment the delicious and highly prized truffle. The fruiting body of a subterranean *Ascomycete* fungus, the truffle's irresistible scent causes animals to dig it up and eat it, which results in the dispersal of the fungus's spores throughout the forest in the animals' fecal matter. This may strike you as a simple circle of life situation, no different from when an animal eats fruit that falls from a tree, but there's one major difference. The truffle is deep underground, completely buried and invisible to animals on the surface. If truffles didn't release an enticing scent, animals wouldn't eat them. They wouldn't even know the truffles were there. That scent is the fungus's way of summoning forest animals to do its bidding.

The concept of bodily invasion and manipulation by fungal spores was something I was eager to explore in this novel. During my research I was most fascinated by the leafcutter ants and their relationship to the *Lepiotaceae* fungus, which was my biggest inspiration for the story. Here we have a fungus controlling ants' behavior again, but without the deadly results of the *cordyceps* or the *Massospora*. Scientists call it ant-fungus mutualism, a beneficial relationship that both the fungus and the ants get something out of it, but to me it seemed more like the relationship between a god and its worshippers. The worshippers bring their god offerings in the form of leaves to eat, and in return their god allows a small portion of itself to be given to its congregation's children as sustenance, a communion of sorts, ensuring these young ones grow up to continue the ritual. The idea frightened me and got under my skin. What if a fungus could take control of people, not only to spread its spores but to be worshipped in this same way?

Could fungi really make the jump from manipulating insects and animals to manipulating human beings? It's hard to say for sure, but it's worth pointing out that our lives have become just as intertwined with fungi as insects' lives have. Everything Victor tells Booker, Laura, and Sean about the developing scientific and manufacturing uses for fungi is true. From penicillin to immunosuppressant drugs for organ transplants to the incredible, experimental idea of growing temporary, decomposable emergency dwellings, we're using fungi more and more to improve our lives. Even the citric acid in the Diet Coke my family and I are addicted to is produced by fungi! Of course, in order for us to utilize fungi for the creation of all these wonderful things, we first have to farm them. That means growing them in the most beneficial soil, feeding them their favorite foods, and allowing them to reproduce as they please in an environment safe from threats. In other words, in exchange for unlocking the beneficial potential of fungi in human life, all we have to do is give them everything they could ever want in return. Hmm, are we sure they aren't manipulating us already?

I'll leave you with one last extremely creepy bit of information. Even though fungi could not be less humanlike, what with being a limitless, essentially immortal network of subterranean filaments with no brain or central nervous system, the genetic composition of fungi is more similar to humans than to plants. We share certain proteins that plants don't. Additionally, fungi breathe in oxygen and breathe out carbon dioxide, which is the opposite of what plants do, but the same as what animals like us do. Some think this is because fungi and animals shared a common ancestor once, back in the misty reaches of time, and although we belong to separate kingdoms, fungi and humans are actually close relatives. Is it really such a stretch that someday they might turn their attention to us, their distant cousins? Just something to think about the next time you throw some mushrooms into your sauté pan.

I owe a great deal of thanks to Dr. Merlin Sheldrake and his remarkable, eye-opening book on the fungal-human relationship *Entangled Life: How Fungi Make Our Worlds, Change Our Minds & Shape Our Futures,* as well as to my agent, Richard Curtis, for recommending the book to me. The concept of fungal intelligence that Sheldrake puts forth in his book blew my mind. Each page held enough fascinating information for a dozen novels. If you want to know more about fungi and what they're capable of—and why wouldn't you?—I highly recommend *Entangled Life.* My thanks also to the invaluable research resources Ask A Biologist, Deep Look, McGill University's Office for Science and Society, Merck Manual, Microdelics, National Geographic, PBS

Evolution, Seeker, Wikipedia, and WVU Today.

Thank you to David Dodd and David Niall Wilson at Crossroad Press for believing in this book. Thank you to my aforementioned agent, Richard Curtis, for his enthusiasm and patience. And special thanks, as always, to my wife Alexa, whose love and support mean the world to me, and who puts up with all the grousing and heavy sighing that are an unfortunate part of my creative process.

About the Author

NICHOLAS KAUFMANN is a critically acclaimed author of horror and dark fantasy whose works have been nominated for the Bram Stoker Award, the Shirley Jackson Award, the Thriller Award, and the Dragon Award. He lives in Brooklyn, NY, with his wife and a loudly snoring cat.

Visit his website at nicholaskaufmann.com

Bibliography

100 Fathoms Below (with Steven L. Kent)

Chasing the Dragon

Die and Stay Dead

Dying Is My Business

General Slocum's Gold

Hunt at World's End

Jack Haringa Must Die! Twenty-Eight Original Tales of Madness, Terror, and Strictly Grammatical Murder (editor)

In the Shadow of the Axe

Still Life: Nine Stories

Walk in Shadows

Curious about other Crossroad Press books?
Stop by our site:
http://store.crossroadpress.com
We offer quality writing
in digital, audio, and print formats.